A

Preparatory Exercises for the Religious Profession

SALZWASSER VERLAG

Anonymous

Preparatory Exercises for the Religious Profession

Reprint of the original, first published in 1863.

1st Edition 2022 | ISBN: 978-3-37500-162-9

Verlag (Publisher): Salzwasser Verlag GmbH, Zeilweg 44, 60439 Frankfurt, Deutschland
Vertretungsberechtigt (Authorized to represent): E. Roepke, Zeilweg 44, 60439 Frankfurt, Deutschland
Druck (Print): Books on Demand GmbH, In de Tarpen 42, 22848 Norderstedt, Deutschland

PREPARATORY EXERCISES

FOR THE

RELIGIOUS PROFESSION;

A Series of Meditations

ON

THE VOWS OF RELIGION,

AND

THE SACRED PASSION OF OUR LORD.

TRANSLATED FROM THE FRENCH

BY A MEMBER OF THE URSULINE COMMUNITY

"I will pay my vows to the Lord before all His people."—Ps. cxv. 5.

DUBLIN

[illegible]

[illegible] ROW.

1863.

CONTENTS.

SECOND PART OF THE EXERCISES PREPARATORY TO PROFESSION.

PREPARATORY EXERCISES

FOR

THE RELIGIOUS PROFESSION.

OF THE DESIGN AND ORDER OF THE FOLLOWING EXERCISES.

THE irrevocable consecration of the Religious soul may justly be deemed an action of extreme importance, whether it be considered in its connection with the Almighty Being to whom the spiritual sacrifice is offered, or viewed in its reference to the soul on whom the Vows entail a weighty obligation of leading a life totally opposed to the inclinations of corrupt nature, and practically embracing the perfection of the Evangelical counsels. An action of so much consequence evidently demands due preparation, to ensure which the Constitutions of the Ursulines (Part 2, chap. 6), besides appointing a Noviciate of two years, which should be a continual preparation for the great act destined as its termination, further require, that for the two months immediately preceding Profession, the Novice should lay aside all other occupations, devoting that time exclusively to more particular preparation, according to the plan laid down in the following Exercises, which have been in use since the establishment of the Ursuline Order. They are divided into Three Parts, in imitation of the three days which the Israelites employed by God's command in preparing themselves to offer Sacrifice in the Desert. (Exod. iii.) The First Part is sub-divided into four weeks, the three first of which are devoted to meditating on the obligations imposed by the Vows of Poverty, Chastity and Obedience. The fourth is called the Week of Charity, because destined for the study of that virtue, which should be the characteristic of the daughters of Saint Augustine, as it is the leading principle of his Rule, which commences by these words—*Before all things love God, and then your Neighbour.* This is the end, and principal Institute of Ursulines, who make a vow to instruct young girls in the only really necessary science, that of religion, including a practical knowledge of the virtues which lead to eternal happiness.

The Passion of our Lord forms the subject of meditation for the twelve or fifteen days to which the Second Part of the Exercises extends. The object of these Meditations is, first, to purify the soul by sincere contrition, which nothing so effectually excites as the consideration of Christ's sufferings; and secondly, to animate the Religious to the imitation of her Redeemer's virtues, the Religious life, properly understood, being in fact a lively representation of Jesus Christ crucified. The Third Part of the Exercises consists of a Retreat of eight days immediately before Profession, during which, total separation from all creatures, and the observance of strict silence, facilitate the efforts of the soul to dispose herself by holy meditations, and fervent affections, for her approaching sacrifice to God, and the glorious union she is about to contract with Jesus Christ her Divine Spouse.

The object of the Meditations proposed in the first four weeks, is to impress the soul with the excellence of Religious Vows, the obligations they entail, and the perfection to which they will infallibly lead when perfectly observed. Filled with esteem for these sacred Vows, and inflamed with a holy ambition to conform to her Lord and model, she should excite herself to an ardent desire, first to pronounce them worthily, and then to observe them with courageous perseverance to the end of life.

The following is the order observed in the Meditations. The Preparatory Meditation of each week demonstrates that the Vow treated of has been taught by the lessons, and enforced by the example of the Son of God. The succeeding Meditations point out its excellencies and advantages, and the method of reducing it to practice—as regards, first the strict obligation of the Vow, and then its perfection. The Meditation of each Thursday, though relating to the subject of the week, is peculiarly directed to the most Blessed Sacrament, to serve as a preparation for the holy Communion, whence the soul derives strength to advance courageously in the career of perfection, like Elias, who was, according to God's command, enabled to continue his journey even to the mountain of God, after he had eaten bread. (3 Kings, xix. 8.) In this history we have an express figure of the Blessed Sacrament and its effects. The attention of the soul is next directed to the example of the virtue in question left her by her Divine Model, Jesus Christ, in the two great mysteries of the most holy Sacrament, and the Passion, which should be the two principal objects of the devotion of all Religious souls, whence they may derive not only the knowledge of their obligations, but strength and grace to practise them. The Blessed Virgin being the patroness of all Religious Orders, but particularly of that of St. Ursula, every Saturday is destined to honour her, by meditating on the perfect example she has left us, of the practice of the Evangelical counsels, that animated by the example of the glorious Queen of Heaven, as well as that of her Divine Son, we may embrace them with courage and fervour. These Meditations may not only serve as a preparation for Profession, but will be found a useful means of renewing the fervour of those already Professed, and may for this end be profitably used at the renovation, or the anniversary of Profession, or at any other period of the year. On this account some matters are treated of in a manner more suited to the comprehension of persons advanced in virtue, than that of Novices—yet, both may derive much benefit from the exercises. The consideration of the exalted sanctity of the Religious state, far from being useless, may, on the contrary, prove very serviceable to Novices. If early and deeply impressed with the extent of the perfection to which they aspire, they will, doubtless, be animated to proportionate efforts, and will thus advance far in a short time. In order to throw more light on the Meditations, the subject of each day's Lecture is made to correspond with that of the Meditation, the affections and aspirations are on the same subject, and should be repeated frequently during the day.

In fine, an exterior practice of devotion, connected with the Vow under consideration, is prescribed for nearly every day, that combining the actual practice with the meditation of her obligations, the Novice may be better disposed to assume them at Profession.

THE PREPARATORY MEDITATION.

1st Prelude.—Represent to yourself that our Lord invites you into solitude, saying to you, as he did to his Apostles, "Come apart into a desert place and rest a little." (St. Mark, vi. 31.)

2nd Prelude.—Implore perfect disengagement of thoughts and affections from all creatures, that you may fully comply with his invitation.

First Point.—The period of your Probation has now come to a conclusion. During your Noviciate, the Almighty continued to lavish on you graces as powerful as that which first attracted you into Religion, and to crown His mercies, He has granted your earnest petition to remain in His house all the days of your life. (Ps. xxvi.) Excite yourself to lively gratitude for such a favour. 2nd. Acknowledge your total unworthiness of this pure gift of God's mercy. 3rd. Reanimate the fervour with which you gave yourself to God on the day of your entrance into Religion, and renew the solemn agreement you then entered into with Him, when in the words of Deuteronomy, "You chose the Lord to be your God, and to walk in His ways, and keep His ceremonies, and precepts, and judgments, and obey His commands.—And the Lord chose thee to be His peculiar people, and to make thee higher than all nations which He hath created,—that thou mayest be a holy people of the Lord thy God." (Deuteronomy, xxiv. 17, 18, 19.) These words are deserving of attentive consideration, because they point out the end to which the soul aspires, on entering Religion; the perfection to which she should afterwards tend, and the designs of God in giving her so exalted a vocation, by which He intends to raise her to a degree of sanctity, happiness, and glory far elevated above that of the generality of Christians.

Second Point.—Consider that it is to little purpose to enter Religion, if our lives do not correspond with the sanctity of the state we have adopted. "To embrace the Religious life," says St. Eucherius, "is to enter on the road to sovereign perfection, but, to live imperfectly therein, is to walk in the path which leads to perdition." Consider this well, before you contract any further obligations. Three descriptions of persons are often to be found in Monasteries. The first embrace the state without a decided vocation for it, or, if they have at one time possessed this treasure, they afterwards lose it through their own fault. Such persons can only be called Religious in name, for under the habit of Religion they retain the spirit of the world; they follow the bent of their own will; they dispense as far as possible with the observance of Rule, gratifying their senses without restraint, and make no account of venial transgressions, avoiding mortal sin only, because it involves eternal damnation. The second class consists of those who love their state, respect their Rules, and even endeavour to avoid gross imperfections; but whose hearts are still attached to creatures; who have not courage to aspire to high perfection; who will not sacrifice some favourite passion; in fine, who do not belong entirely to God, but wish to unite perfection with imperfection, and combine the service of the Lord with the love of self. The third class includes those who have generously broken every tie to the earth, and devoted their whole hearts to God, to accomplish His will, and to aim with all their energies at the perfection to which He calls them.

To the first, Religion must be a hell; they have renounced the pleasures of the world, and at the same time forfeited the consolations of Heaven; they are oppressed by remorse of conscience, they are objects of scandal to others, and in great danger of perdition. To the second it is a Purgatory; they do not entirely belong to God, therefore cannot enjoy perfect happiness —the trifles to which they cling are to them an insuperable bar to peace. "When I shall be totally united to Thee, O Lord," said St. Augustine, "I shall experience no pain—no sorrow; I shall begin to live, but not being yet replenished with Thee, I am burthensome to myself."—10 Confes. The third class of persons find a Paradise in Religion, because being intent only on pleasing their Creator and advancing daily in virtue, they enjoy unalloyed content, in the possession of God, their end, their beatitude, who, even in this life rewards their fervour by favours which sweeten all their pains. In one day they experience more bliss, even amidst their sufferings, than the tepid can feel in their whole lives.

Examine among which of these three classes you rank, and consider what place you mean to occupy in future. If your ambition do not extend beyond the first, contract no further obligation; it would be far more your advantage to return to the world, because to embrace the Religious state in such dispositions, is to run a great risk of losing your soul. If your views be limited to the second, as is more probably the case, consider the danger of this tepid state, and if you do not feel courage to aim higher, earnestly beg of God to give you strength to aspire to a place among those who are totally devoted to Him. The following Exercises will dispose you for this, if performed in their true spirit.

Third Point.—Consider now the dispositions in which these Exercises should be commenced and continued, in order to produce in your soul the fruit you hope to derive from them. The Prophet Jeremiah alludes to these dispositions in his Lamentations, when he says—"It is good for a man when he has borne the yoke from his youth;" and adds, "he shall sit solitary, and hold his peace; because he hath taken it upon himself. He shall put his mouth in the dust, if so be there may be hope." (Lam. iii. 27, 28, 29.) Consider each of these expressions with serious attention.

"He shall sit."—These words inculcate the necessity of interior peace, which enables the soul tranquilly to devote her attention to the duty of each day without anticipating that of the next. "He shall sit solitary and hold his peace." Here, you learn the obligation of observing interior and exterior silence as far as possible, that your mind be not distracted by exterior objects. The soul must be elevated above herself, by the constant exercise of the sublime virtues of faith, hope, and charity. The light of faith, superior to that of reason, should be your guide in meditating on the truths presented to your consideration; hope will encourage you to aspire to perfection far above the reach of your natural strength; charity will detach you from self and creatures, to unite you to God of whom you should never lose sight, endeavouring to make His presence and His conversation a substitute for those of creatures.

In fine, the last disposition required is humility, understood by these words—" He shall put his mouth in the dust." The more profoundly you humble yourself before God and man, the more capable will you be of receiving the graces of Heaven, and rising above yourself: add to this, perfect submission to those placed over you, and readiness to receive the reprehensions, humiliations, and contradictions which may await you—to which you are exhorted by these words of the Prophet —" He shall give his cheek to him that striketh him, he shall be filled with reproaches." (Lam. iii. 30.) These are the dispositions in which you should commence your Exercises; endeavour to acquire them, at least in desire, and renounce all that may be an obstacle thereto. Ask them of God, through the intercession of the Blessed Virgin, our holy Father St. Augustine, St. Ursula, and the other Saints to whom you are particularly devoted.

The 20th and 25th chapters of the first book of the Imitation of Jesus Christ, and the 10th chapter of the third book, to be read for the Lecture of this day.

The Aspirations are—" Show, O Lord, Thy ways to me, and teach me Thy paths; direct me in Thy truth and teach me, for Thou art God, my Saviour; and on Thee have I waited all the day long." (Ps. xxiv. 4, 5.)

OF THE ORDER TO BE OBSERVED BY THE NOVICE DURING THE EXERCISES OF THE FOUR WEEKS.

She will remain in her cell, unless differently directed, and will observe silence, except at recreation.

Each Friday she will spend in absolute retreat.

She will assist at the general Lectures and other

Exercises of the Noviciate, except the Point of Meditation, during which she will read that appointed for herself.

She will make a quarter of an hour's lecture every morning about nine o'clock, and another in the afternoon, immediately after Vespers.

She will make a daily visit to the Blessed Sacrament, to implore grace and light to profit of the Exercises; and she may then read a chapter of the Imitation of Jesus Christ, or some portion of the Constitutions treating of the Vow on which she is meditating.

Every evening, before or after Matins, she will read the Meditation and Practice for the next day.

EXERCISES FOR THE WEEK OF POVERTY.

To acquire the true spirit of poverty, you should aim at perfect disengagement from all earthly things:—humility and poverty of spirit should animate you in your intercourse with God in prayer, and accompany all your exterior actions, teaching you to consider yourself as the last and most unworthy member of your community. You should make frequent interior acts of disengagement from the conveniences you possess, resolving to bear the want even of necessaries, considering yourself unworthy of those you have, and receiving them in the spirit of gratitude. You should also embrace the exterior practice of poverty, when God provides the opportunity of doing so,—depriving yourself occasionally of an article which may not be absolutely necessary, selecting the worst of what may be left to your choice, and voluntarily embracing humiliation and suffering as your portion.

The chapters of the Constitutions on Humility and Poverty should be read this week.

SUNDAY.

FIRST MEDITATION.

On the Descent of Jesus from Heaven, to teach the Practice of Evangelical Perfection.

First Point.—The world being plunged in sin, and men in general under the dominion of the concupiscence of the flesh, and the concupiscence of the eyes, and the pride of life" (1 Ep. St. John, ii. 16), the Eternal Word, moved by His own infinite goodness, came down from Heaven to regenerate the human race, and to reconcile man with the Divine Author of his being, from whom he had unhappily estranged himself by yielding to the influence of these three incentives to sin. "Jesus Christ came from Heaven," says St. Gregory, "as a new man, to teach a doctrine yet unknown, and to substitute His sanctity, and newness of life, for long prevalent habits of vice; and He came also as a heavenly Physician to apply a suitable remedy to our diseases; opposing poverty to avarice, or the concupiscence of the eyes;—chastity to the concupiscence of the flesh;—and humble obedience to the pride of life." Return our Divine Lord most ardent thanks, for having descended from His throne of glory to become your instructor; venerate the sacred lessons taught by the Increated Wisdom, and if the maxims of the world still retain any empire in your heart, renounce them totally, and for ever, that you may be enabled to understand and to embrace those of Jesus Christ.

Second Point.—Our Divine Redeemer, having come into the world to destroy its pernicious maxims, declared voluntary poverty to be the foundation of the system of Evangelical perfection He designed to substitute for them. It is the first step of the mysterious ladder, by which we are to ascend to Heaven; Jesus Christ, our Divine teacher, has ranked it as the first of the Beatitudes—. "Blessed are the poor in spirit, for theirs is the kingdom of Heaven." (St. Mat. v. 3.) By declaring that whoever "doth not renounce," at least in desire, "all that he possesseth cannot be His disciple" (St. Luke, xiv. 33), he at once cuts off "the root of all evils," which, according to St. Paul, is "the desire of money" (1 Tim. vi. 10), and restores our forfeited claims to Heaven, of which he tells us poverty is the key. God created man in a state of happy indigence, in which, having nothing of his own, he possessed all things in God;—but the devil having persuaded him to appropriate the fruit which belonged to his Creator, it became necessary that the second Adam should commence the regeneration of the world, by establishing Evangelical poverty, which eradicates the love of earthly things. Esteem the spirit of poverty, which is the foundation of the Religious perfection to which you aspire. Beg of God to impress indelibly on your heart this fundamental maxim of the Gospel, that you may deserve to rank among those who, renouncing all things for His love, become His disciples.

Third Point.—Consider, on the one hand, the transgression by which Adam entailed misery on his posterity, and contemplate, on the other, all our Lord endured to repair that misery, and raise man from his fallen state. Adam, by desiring the forbidden fruit, coveted what he could not lawfully appropriate;—Jesus Christ, on the contrary, though the Creator of the Universe, and Lord of all things, reduced Himself to extreme poverty, and renounced even the necessaries of life. Adam aspired to be equal to God; but Jesus Christ, though in the form of God, debased Himself, taking the form of a servant (Phil. ii. 6, 7), that He might live poor, humble, and despised. Adam, by ambitioning what he had no lawful claim to possess, deprived himself and his posterity of the blessings God had bestowed upon him:—Jesus Christ, by despoiling Himself of the splendour of His glory, has purchased Heaven and the rich treasures of grace for men.

How great should be your gratitude to your Redeemer, for having willingly clothed Himself with your miseries and infirmities, in order to render you a participator in His own happiness and riches! "Jesus Christ," says St. Paul, "being rich, became poor for your sakes, that through His poverty you might be rich." (2 Cor. viii. 1.) Renounce the love and desire of the perishable things of this earth, and ambition no higher honour than a share in the poverty of Jesus Christ.

Aspirations.—"I count all things to be but loss, for the excellent knowledge of Jesus Christ my Lord; for whom I have suffered the loss of all things, and count them but as dung, that I may gain Christ." (Phil. iii. 8.)

"Now I begin to be a disciple, desiring nothing visible, or invisible, that I may attain Jesus Christ." (Saint Ignatius.)

Receive our Lord to-day in the holy Communion as your Divine Master, who comes to instruct you in the maxims of His Gospel, particularly in that of poverty.

The Lecture.—The first and fourth chapters of the Treatise on Poverty in Rodriguez.

SECOND MEDITATION.

On the Excellence of Poverty, proved by our Divine Lord's Esteem for it.

First Point.—In his first Sermon on the Nativity, St. Bernard says, " that as poverty could not exist in Heaven, where all riches abound, and could dwell only on earth, where its merits were unknown, the Son of God descended from His Eternal throne, to teach us by His example the value of this virtue. The excellence of poverty is clearly manifested from the estimation in which it was held by our Lord Jesus Christ, the Increated Wisdom, who, in selecting it as His inseparable companion through life, exalted, ennobled, and rendered it almost divine, recommending it to us by His example as most profitable. Consider with confusion how opposed your ideas have hitherto been to those of Jesus Christ, since you have even esteemed riches and despised poverty; endeavour to reform these erroneous impressions, regulating your opinions in future according to those of the Son of God.

Second Point.—Reflect on the various proofs which our Divine Model gave of His love and esteem for poverty. Consider His birth in a stable, whereby, at His very entrance into the world, He chose this virtue for His spouse, together with its three inseparable companions, *want, contempt,* and *privation of all comfort.* The mysteries of His holy infancy, His hidden and public life, His death and burial, all display striking examples of poverty. How deplorable are the blindness and folly of man in despising a virtue, which Infinite Wisdom so highly prized! It remains for you to decide which of the two opinions you will adopt as your rule of conduct.

Third Point.—Consider the multitude of souls whom the example of Jesus Christ has influenced to despise riches, and embrace poverty. "Moses," says St. Paul, "esteemed the reproach of Christ greater riches than the treasures of the Egyptians" (Heb. xi. 26), valuing the poverty of the Son of God more than the crown of Pharaoh, because he knew that "it is great glory to follow the Lord." (Eccles. xxiii. 38.) Such was also the disposition of the Apostles and Saints of the New Law, who voluntarily embraced and cordially revered poverty, rendered glorious in their eyes, because Deified in the person of Christ. "The world contemns my poverty, says St. Gregory Nazianzen, "but I glory in it, because it renders me conformable to Him, who being rich, became poor for our sakes." Desire ardently to follow this example in its utmost perfection, and thank our Lord for having inspired you with a wish to do so.

MONDAY.

FIRST MEDITATION.

On the Excellence of Poverty as a means of elevating the Soul to high Perfection.

First Point.—"If thou wilt be perfect," said Christ, "go sell what thou hast, and give it to the poor, and come follow me." (St. Matt. xix. 21.) Perfection may be embraced in three different ways, that is, by the practice of the exercises appertaining to the Purgative, the Illuminative, or the Unitive life. In the first, the soul is occupied in weeping over past sins, and resolving against future relapses; both which objects are included in the practice of poverty. The Almighty speaking to the sinful soul by His Prophet, says, "Thy silver is turned into dross" (Isaiah, l. 22); thou hast lost the innocence in which I first created thee; thou hast stained the purity which I restored to thee by Baptism; thou hast defiled thy heart by fixing it on creatures, as silver is tarnished by mixing it with a base metal; but because I design thee for a vessel of honour, "I will turn my hand to thee, and I will clean and purge away thy dross, and I will take away all thy tin." (Ibid., 25.) Poverty is the crucible in which the soul is thus purified, as God declares by the same Prophet—"Behold I have refined thee, but not as silver, I have chosen thee in the furnace of poverty" (Isaiah, xi., viii. 10); I have so purified thee in the crucible of privation and suffering, that I consider thee worthy of my love—and select thee now to be my spouse. If compulsory poverty, borne with patience and resignation, be capable of producing this effect, that which is embraced voluntarily and by vow must be, of course, far more efficacious; it is therefore the opinion of theologians, that the deliberate renunciation of wealth by Religious Profession, has the efficacy of second Baptism in purifying the soul from sin. Poverty is likewise a safeguard against relapses, for it banishes the spirit of covetousness, which, as St. Paul assures us, "is the root of all evils." (1 Tim. vi. 10.) As the root of the tree imbibes the earth's moisture, which it diffuses through the branches for their nourishment, so the love and possession of riches maintain the vice of pride and the love of pleasure, which are the two chief sources whence all sins flow. Conceive a high esteem of poverty, which secures you in a great measure against sin, the only real evil. Rejoice when God sends you an opportunity of bearing privation or inconvenience, this being the fire destined to purify you from all that is disagreeable to His divine eyes.

Second Point.—Poverty carries the soul forward with no less rapidity in the second road to perfection, which is the Illuminative life, wherein she studies to increase in virtue. "Riches," says St. Ambrose, "being the source of every vice, poverty must be, on the contrary, the mother of every virtue." Observe the close connection between this virtue and the four called cardinal or principal virtues. To exchange temporal for eternal possessions, is eminently to exercise the virtue of Christian *prudence.* 2nd. To renounce lawful rights, is a sure guarantee for the exercise of *justice*, which commands us to respect the property of others. 3rd. To sacrifice the desire of riches, and with it, the natural inclinations which riches satisfy, embracing in exchange the painful attendants of poverty, is certainly a noble act of *fortitude.* 4th. To renounce superfluities, and to be disposed even to want necessaries, includes the perfect practice of *temperance.* Poverty places its votaries among the disciples of the Son of God, obliging them to walk in His footsteps, by the imitation of His virtues, especially of humility, which was His distinguishing characteristic. Renew the affections excited by the first point, saying of poverty as Solomon said of wisdom, "that all good things came to you together with her." (Wisdom, vii. 11.)

Third Point.—Poverty of spirit leads the soul to a high degree of perfection in the Unitive life. It elevates her above transitory things, which she esteems unworthy of her affection, and contemns with a generosity that God alone can inspire. It unites her intimately with the Almighty, by means of Faith, Hope, and Charity; having sacrificed all earthly things, through faith in the maxims of the Gospel, she is influenced in her conduct by the truths of that sacred faith alone,—"looking not at the things which are seen, but at the things which are not seen. For the things which are seen, are temporal: but the things which are not seen, are eternal." (2 Cor. iv. 18.) From this disposition springs a lively hope of eternal happiness, grounded on the promise of Jesus Christ; "Blessed are the poor in spirit, for theirs is the kingdom of heaven." (St. Matt. v. 3.) The more destitute she is of exterior resource in creatures, the more confidently she expects from God all the succours she stands in need of, both spiritually and corporally, saying with David, "I am a beggar and poor, the Lord is careful for me." (Ps. xxxix. 18.) St. Augustine says, "that the decrease of concupiscence is the increase of charity;" because, the more perfectly the affections are detached from earthly things, the more freely they can soar to God; consequently, the soul which has totally renounced temporal things, and thereby removed the great obstacle which intervened between her and God, becomes capable of uniting herself to Him by the most ardent love, and may say with the Prophet, "what have I in heaven? and beside thee, what do I desire upon earth? thou art the God of my heart, and the God that is my portion for ever." (Ps. lxxii. 25, 26.)

The Lecture.—The fifth, sixth, and seventh chapters of the Treatise of Poverty.

In this, and the following Meditation, after having considered the advantages of poverty, direct your particular attention to the word *Omnia, all things,* which our Lord makes use of whenever He speaks of the renunciation of earthly goods. If we mean to share in the blessings promised to the poor, that renunciation must be absolute.

How great, then, is the folly of those, who, after sacrificing worldly possessions, attach their hearts in religion to trifles, which deprive them of the precious favours promised to the poor in spirit! Reflect attentively on this subject, and resolve to keep your heart disengaged from all created things, that so it may be worthy to possess its Creator. "Too avaricious," said St. Augustine, "is he to whom God does not suffice."

For the Practice, see the "Supplement."

SECOND MEDITATION.

On the Advantages of Poverty, as contrasted with the Sufferings inseparable from Riches.

First Point.—The first misfortune attendant on riches is the loss of internal peace. They cannot be acquired without labour; their possession involves uneasiness and fear; their loss, which must be endured at death, if not before, is attended with pain and regret. A soul engrossed by the love of earthly things is like a stormy ocean;—its insatiable desires constantly clashing, as the angry waves dash against each other. The possession of God, for whom we were created, can alone satisfy the human heart, and while it seeks anything beside him, agitation and disquietude must be its portion. This truth is applicable not alone to worldlings, whose whole being is centred in earthly things, but even to religious persons, who suffer their hearts to be attached to trifles; it is not always the object we love, so much as the inordinate affection by which we cling to it, which impedes our spiritual interests. How unalloyed, on the contrary, is the peace of the truly poor in spirit, who are totally detached from things created! "Their poverty," says St. John Climacus, "frees them from the anxieties of the worldling; it leads directly to God; it expels sadness; it establishes peace; it purifies the soul,—and is a security against the cares of this fleeting life." What advantages can be preferable to these?

Second Point.—Riches degrade the natural dignity of man, who, as St. Augustine observes, "becomes earthly in loving the earth." They entail a disgraceful slavery,—for, in order to acquire and preserve them, it is necessary to pay servile homage to the great, as also to submit to much painful self-renunciation. The Scripture calls the wealthy, "men of riches" (Ps. lxxv. 6), because they are enslaved to their earthly possessions. The poor in spirit, on the contrary, enjoy a glorious freedom; by despising the treasures of the world, as St. John Climacus observes, "they are elevated above them," and in the words of the Apostle, "having nothing, they possess all things." (2 Cor. vi. 10.)

Form a generous resolution to elevate yourself, by poverty of spirit, above all earthly things, and since your origin is from Heaven, do not permit that terrestrial objects should hold your heart in bondage.

Third Point.—The third, and most awful danger of riches is, that they frequently create an obstacle to salvation. Our Lord has expressly declared, that "it is easier for a camel to pass through the eye of a needle, than for a rich man to enter into the kingdom of heaven." (St. Matt. xix. 24.) This is easily accounted for. 1st. Because, as St. Paul assures us, "they that will become rich, fall into temptation, and the snare of the devil, and into many unprofitable and hurtful desires, which drive men to destruction and perdition." (1 Tim. vi. 9.) 2nd. They are so engrossed by worldly cares, that they have not leisure to attend to their spiritual concerns. Riches are "the thorns which choke the word of God" (Luke, viii. 14), and prevent it from producing fruit. The succession of pleasures, amidst which the wealthy live, completely banishes the remembrance of death and eternity; and they are surprised by the approach of their last hour, like the rich man in the Gospel, whose prosperity and enjoyment were interrupted by the fatal sentence, "thou fool, this night do they require thy soul of thee" (St. Luke, xii. 20); or like his unfortunate companion in prosperity, who when he least expected so dire a misfortune, was "buried in hell." (Ibid. xvi. 22.) In both were verified the words of Job, "they spend their days in wealth, and in a moment they go down to hell." (Job, xxi. 13.) "Woe to you that are rich," said our Divine Redeemer: "for you have your consolation. Woe to you that are filled: for you shall hunger. Woe to you that now laugh: for you shall mourn and weep." (St. Luke, vi. 24, 25.) What facilities, on the contrary, does not poverty afford, for gaining heaven? 1st. Having renounced temporal things, which render the soul an easy prey to her mortal enemy, the poor can with little difficulty escape his snares and temptations. 2nd. Free from the solicitude attendant on the acquisition and preservation of riches, they have leisure to attend to God, and their eternal interests. 3rd. The prospect of death and eternity, far from intimidating, cheers and delights them. Having no expectations from this world, their thoughts are all directed to the next, and they say with St. Paul, "we have not here an everlasting city, but we seek one, that is to come" (Heb. xiii. 14), dwelling by anticipation in the eternal kingdom already secured to them, by the promise of the Son of God. Return thanks to God, for having inspired you with a desire to enter on the road of poverty, which is so sure a path to heaven, and resolve in future to live as a pilgrim on earth, totally detached from its passing joys.

TUESDAY.

FIRST MEDITATION.

On the Rewards promised to Voluntary Poverty.

First Point.—"Every one that hath left house or brethren, or sisters, or father, or mother, or wife, or children, or lands for my name's sake, shall receive a hundred-fold; and shall possess life everlasting." (St. Matt. xix. 29.) These are the promises of Jesus Christ, to all who have renounced everything for Him. The hundred-fold, promised in this life, is understood by St. Gregory to mean the perfection of spiritual gifts and graces, which God communicates abundantly to the soul, in exchange for the temporalities she has abandoned; loading her, as St. Bernard says, with His caresses and consolations; and enriching her with the gifts of His Holy Spirit, which are a superabundant compensation for all she has quitted, and far exceed her desires. The Providence of God provides her likewise with the necessaries of life, according to the promises of Jesus Christ. "Seek first the kingdom of God and His justice, and all these things shall be added unto you." (St. Matt. vi. 33.) Admire the goodness of God, who so liberally rewards our trifling services, and accepts our offerings, though we can give Him nothing, which is not already His. Thank Him from your heart,—and desire to render yourself more pleasing to Him, by vowing the practice of poverty.

Second Point.—To complete the promised hundred-fold, God gives Himself to us, becoming our inheritance, instead of that we have renounced.

"They shall have no inheritance; neither shall you give them any possession in Israel, for I am their possession." (Ezech. xliv. 28.) He is the Father and Protector of the poor, and seems to be occupied only in providing for their wants. "The Lord hath heard the desire of the poor, thy ear hath heard the preparation of their heart." (Ps. x. 17.) He provides for their corporal wants; He is their comforter in affliction, "their strength in distress, a refuge from the whirlwind, a shadow from the heat." (Isaiah, xxv. 4.)

It would be too long to enumerate many other passages of Scripture on this subject—but these will suffice to animate your confidence, since, if you feel that God takes care of you, you surely cannot apprehend ever wanting anything. Excite in your heart the most lively esteem for your holy state, and say with David, "my inheritance is goodly to me" (Ps. xv. 6); or with St. Francis, "my God and my All!" in Thee I find all my heart can desire.

Third Point.—Elevate your thoughts to Heaven, and contemplate the rewards bestowed there on the poor. Nothing less awaits them, than the possession of a kingdom; for the Lord having "raised the needy from the earth," will elevate them to a throne of glory, "that He may place them with princes, with the princes of His people" (Ps. cxii. 7, 8), to reign for ever in the mansions of bliss. Admire the infinite liberality of the Almighty, who, in exchange for the perishable wealth abandoned for His love, gives us the rich reward of Heaven, and recompenses the poverty endured for a short time, by the abundance of eternal joys. Cherish poverty, to which is annexed so great a recompense, and remember the words of St. Francis ;—" in vowing poverty, we promise a great deal, considering the frailty of human nature ; but much more is, on the other hand, promised to us. Let us deeply ponder our obligations, but let us at the same time contemplate and sigh for the rewards which await us."

Aspirations.—" The Lord is the portion of my inheritance and of my cup." (Ps. xv. 5.)

The Lecture.—Second and third chapters of the Treatise on Poverty.

For the Practice, see the " Supplement."

SECOND MEDITATION.

On the Privilege of judging Men at the last Day, promised to those who have embraced Voluntary Poverty.

First Point.—" You who have followed me, in the regeneration, when the Son of Man shall sit on the seat of His Majesty, you also shall sit on twelve seats, judging the twelve tribes of Israel." (St. Matt. xix. 28.) This was the promise which our Lord made to His Apostles, and in their persons, to all who, like them, have embraced voluntary poverty. What a happiness, to be not only exempt from fear, but to have the glorious privilege of judging the world, on that dreadful day, when the assembled universe shall tremble before the Sovereign Judge of the living and the dead ! Then it is that, having raised the needy from the earth, and lifted up the poor out of the dunghill, the Lord will place him with the princes of His people." (Ps. cxii. 7, 8.) The impious, who considered voluntary poverty a folly, will then exclaim, in bitterness of soul, "These are they whom we had some time in derision, and for a parable of reproach: we fools esteemed their life madness, and their end without honour. Behold, how they are numbered among the children of God, and their lot is among the saints." (Wisdom, v. 3, 4, 5.) Rejoice at having been called to a state, which, provided you comply with its obligations, will secure you peace and confidence, on the day of universal terror. Compassionate the blindness of worldlings, who, absorbed in the enjoyment of present comforts, live in the forgetfulness of their future fate, the horrors of which will burst on their terrified vision, only when it is too late to avert them. Return thanks to God, for having enlightened you to know the vanity of the world, and the value of poverty.

Second Point.—The first reason, why so great a triumph is promised to those who have embraced voluntary poverty, is, that honour and glory are the rewards promised by God to humiliation. As poverty entails contempt, and excludes its votaries from dignities, authority, and exaltation, God delights in rewarding it munificently. Secondly, poverty, being the first of the Evangelical counsels, and the road to perfection, our Lord has ranked it as the first of the Beatitudes; therefore, the poor in spirit, who, by the practice of this virtue, have attained the perfection not only of the commandments, but even of the Evangelical counsels, shall be, as it were, a living and animated law, to confound and condemn the wicked, who imagined the observance of its precepts impossible.

Embrace from your heart, poverty and humility, which

lead to so great glory, and rejoice at being poor and contemned, since God has promised hereafter to exalt you.

Third Point.—Consider that these encouraging promises were first made to the Apostles, who possessed only a boat, and a few nets, which they gave up to follow Jesus Christ. Whence we learn, that God looks not so much to the value of the sacrifice, as to the love and generosity with which it is offered.

Examine your dispositions, and see what your intentions are, in embracing a life of poverty. Are you sincerely determined to renounce, and detach your affections from all created things? If so, you may be sure of that munificent reward, the prospect alone of which should fill your heart with joy, sweetening the bitterness, and alleviating the pains of this short life.

WEDNESDAY.

FIRST MEDITATION.

On the Practice of the Vow of Poverty.

First Point.—"Blessed are the poor in spirit; for theirs is the kingdom of Heaven." (St. Matt. v. 3.)

Poverty of spirit is of two kinds; it is practised by those who possess the temporal things which God has given them, with a heart perfectly detached from them; it is also practised by those, who are not only detached in heart from the things of the earth, but who actually renounce them for the love of God, saying with St. Paul, "I count all things but as dung, that I may gain Christ." (Phil. iii. 8.) Poverty, confirmed by vow, is the basis of the Religious profession; it is the most excellent and perfect description of poverty, being more meritorious and more pleasing to God, than that practised without a vow, the obligation of which solemn act seals the soul's decided and irrevocable resolution to persevere to the end of life in the observance of poverty. By thus abandoning, and totally subjecting herself to God, she offers Him, says St. Bonaventure, "a most pleasing sacrifice." Return thanks to God, for having called you to this state, and desire ardently to embrace it. Implore the graces necessary for making and fulfilling your vow of poverty with the greatest perfection.

Second Point.—Consider the obligations imposed by the vow of poverty. They are, not to possess, or receive anything, either for your own use, or to dispose of to others, without leave from the Superioress, whether the article belong to the monastery, or be given you by your relations, friends, or others. This is the strict obligation of the vow of poverty, by violating which, the guilt of mortal or venial sin is incurred, according to the value of the thing taken, received, or given. Reflect seriously on this obligation, that you may understand clearly the nature of your engagement. The perfection of this vow, moreover, obliges you to have nothing superfluous, valuable, or rare; to limit yourself to what is necessary, in food, clothing, furniture, &c., to rejoice at receiving the worst of everything. Secondly, to be satisfied and even desirous to want necessaries, both in health and sickness, in imitation of the Son of God, who suffered the want of all things, as we see in His birth in a stable, and during His sojourn in Egypt and Nazareth, &c. These examples should prompt you to embrace the perfection of poverty for the love of our Lord Jesus Christ. See what your resolutions are on this head.

Third Point.—The vow of poverty, practised in the manner you have now considered it, will lead you to perfect disengagement from, and even contempt for, all the world values, and to an ardent desire of being despoiled of earthly things, that so you may be united to Jesus Christ crucified. Being thus totally detached from temporal conveniences, you will use them reluctantly and through necessity, and soon will you experience the truth of God's promises,—"behold I will allure her," by the sweetness of spiritual consolations, "and will lead her into the wilderness:" withdrawing her affections from earthly objects; "and will speak to her heart" (Osee, ii. 14), encouraging her with my cheering promises. God promises to the disengaged heart, "that kingdom, which is justice, and peace, and joy in the Holy Ghost." (Romans, xiv. 17.) Justice, with the abundance of good works; unalloyed peace, spiritual joy, and solid consolation, unmingled with sadness or disquietude. Consider at leisure the profound peace of a heart detached from all things, and the abundance of the spiritual treasures with which it overflows. As nature cannot admit of a vacuum, neither will God, the Author of grace, permit a void in the soul which has renounced all things for Him; that faithful soul He replenishes with the profusion of His graces. Examine if your heart retains any attachment, which could be an obstacle to these great blessings. Resolve to renounce that attachment, and ask grace to do so.

Aspirations.—"To Thee is the poor man left; Thou wilt be a helper to the orphan." (Ps. x. 14.)

"Look thou upon me, and have mercy on me; for I am alone and poor." (Ps. xxiv. 16.)

Lecture.—The tenth, eleventh, and twelfth chapters of the Treatise on Poverty.

For the Practice, see the "Supplement."

SECOND MEDITATION.

On the Virtues which should accompany Poverty.

First Point.—The first virtue which should accompany poverty is humility, without which, poverty cannot be pleasing to God, or entitled to the appellation of poverty of spirit. These two virtues are so inseparably allied, that St. Augustine understands the poverty of spirit, to which our Lord attached a blessing, to mean humility. Those are indeed truly poor in spirit, who attribute no good to themselves, but refer all to God; who deem themselves unworthy of the favours they receive, and the blessings they enjoy; who believe that their sins entitle them to be overlooked, and if not absolutely deprived of every convenience, at least furnished only with the worst of every thing; who look on themselves as beneath all creatures, and desire to be despised and neglected; who even rejoice at having resigned the power of making presents, which might entitle them to the gratitude of creatures, desiring nothing but God. Weigh attentively these different effects of humility, and be persuaded that whoever possesses this virtue must practise poverty perfectly, whereas it will be exercised with reluctance, and exist only superficially in those who are not humble. Resolve to embrace humility, with the poverty you are about to profess, and never to separate in your conduct the two virtues which Jesus Christ combined throughout His life. Impress deeply on your heart the words you pronounced when receiving the habit,—"I have chosen to be an abject in the house of our Lord Jesus Christ;" endeavour to imbibe the sentiment they express, and let it ever influence your words and conduct.

Second Point.—Patience is the second virtue, which

should accompany poverty; since the practice of the latter virtue necessarily includes the tranquil endurance of all the inconveniences attendant on its exercise. Consider those which may await you, in health or sickness, as to your dwelling, clothing, diet, &c.,—determine to accept them at your Profession, and ever to bear them patiently, "looking on Jesus, the author and finisher of faith, who having joy set before Him, endured the cross, despising the shame, and now sitteth on the right hand of the throne of God." (Heb. xii. 2.) Considering the great rewards promised to the poor and suffering, say, with the Apostle, "I reckon that the sufferings of this time are not worthy to be compared with the glory to come that shall be revealed in us." (Rom. viii. 18.) Animate yourself to embrace courageously all the trials which may await you, and to follow our Lord in the road of poverty and the Cross.

Third Point.—The third virtue allied to poverty is labour,—"Man is born to labour." (Job, v. 7.)

Adam was commanded "to eat bread in the sweat of his brow." (Gen. iii. 19.) From this precept, the rich easily dispense themselves, but their very condition renders its observance incumbent on the poor. Our Lord, though the Creator of the universe, and the great fountain of all riches, embraced not only poverty, but labour, gaining His subsistence by His own exertions. Contemplate Him working as a carpenter, until the age of thirty; consider Him in the midst of His Apostles, condescending to serve them, stooping so low, as even to wash their feet, and declaring "that He was in the midst of them," as He that serveth." (St. Luke, xxii. 27.) If you desire to imitate Him, you must embrace labour, and say, after His example, I have not come into religion to be served, as the great ones of the world; I have come to serve others, as the poor. In this spirit, value the lowest functions, such as sweeping, serving, &c.—and never dispense yourself from such general duties, while your health permits. Labour embraced in imitation of Jesus Christ, and in the spirit of poverty, is most meritorious; and as a practice of your Vow, it is a constant and acceptable sacrifice to God. Ask the grace to fulfil your good resolutions on this head.

THURSDAY.

FIRST MEDITATION.

Jesus Christ in the Blessed Sacrament, is the Treasure of Religious Souls, and the abundant Reward of their Poverty.

First Point.—Consider the boundless riches of Jesus Christ, in whom are the infinite treasures of the wisdom and knowledge of God. He himself tells us, that with Him are riches and glory, glorious riches and justice. For His fruit is better than gold and the precious stone, and His blossoms than choice silver. (Prov. viii. 18, 19.) "I walk," he says, "in the way of justice, in the midst of the paths of judgment, that I may enrich them that love me, and may fill their treasures." (Prov. viii. 18, 19, 20, 21.) "In Jesus Christ," says St. Ambrose, "we have all things," and He is in Himself all things to us. If you desire to be healed of your wounds, He is the physician; if you are overwhelmed with iniquity, He is sovereign sanctity; if you are weak, He is strength; if you fear death, He is life; if you desire Heaven, He is the way; if you wish to avoid darkness, He is the light; in fine, if you seek food, He is the divine and celestial bread, which alone can fully satiate, and replenish your desires. He dwells in the sacrament of His love, that you may find a constant resource in Him, in all your wants and miseries. Love our Lord Jesus Christ, hope in Him, and choose Him for your only treasure.

Second Point.—All Christians have, no doubt, a right to participate in this divine treasure; yet Religious persons, who have embraced voluntary poverty, for the love of God, have a special claim thereto; for if this adorable sacrament be the covenant which secures to us our inheritance, it is peculiarly so for those who have no other. "They shall have no inheritance, said the Lord, I am their inheritance." (Ezech. xi. iv. 28). It is a heavenly manna, given to those who have renounced the bread of Egypt: "These, after suffering want for a short time, tasted a new meat." (Wis. xvi. 3.) It is a strengthening milk, a wine, which inebriates, offered to those "that have no money." (Isaiah, lv. 1.) It is a torrent of grace, a fountain of living water which flows for the use of the poor. "The needy and the poor seek for waters," said the Lord by the same Prophet, "and there are none: their tongue hath been dry with thirst. I, the Lord, will hear them, I, the God of Israel, will not forsake them. I will open rivers in the high hills, and fountains in the midst of the plains; I will turn the desert," in which they live separated from all creatures, "into pools of water." (Ibid. xli. 17, 18.) It is a royal banquet, a magnificent entertainment, to which the poor are principally invited. This august Sacrament, under whatever point of view it be considered, is particularly the possession of Religious souls. For this reason, Jesus Christ dwells in their houses, as belonging more to them than to the rest of Christians, that they may at all times have recourse to Him. Renew the affections of the first point, and conceive a high esteem of poverty, which puts you in possession of so great a treasure.

Third Point.—Consider the reasons, why God communicates His riches more abundantly to those who have become voluntarily poor, than to others. The first is His infinite liberality, which prompts Him to repay a hundred-fold every gift received. So magnificent is His generosity in rewarding the sacrifices of Religious souls, that not finding in the range of creation treasures adequate to His liberality, He makes himself their reward exceeding great, according to His promise to Abraham. (Gen. xv. 1.) 2nd. The poor are better disposed to receive the graces of God, being detached from all things else. The treasures of the Lord cannot be mingled with those of the world. "He will not be the inheritance," says St. Jerom, "of him who desires to possess anything temporal with Him." Weigh this deeply, and after having exteriorly despoiled yourself of all things, beware of retaining any interior affection, which may be an obstacle to the perfect possession of Jesus Christ. Remember, that whoever claims the Lord for her inheritance must be reciprocally His possession. She cannot perfectly possess Him, unless she be possessed by Him. Reflect seriously on this important truth, and never approach the Holy Communion, without having detached your heart from exterior things, that you may present it to Christ, void of all but Himself, and therefore worthy to be replenished by Him.

Aspirations.—"The Lord is my portion, said my soul: therefore will I wait for Him." (Lam. iii. 24.) "The Lord ruleth me; and I shall want nothing. He hath set me in a place of pasture." (Ps. xxii. 1, 2.) "In

Thy sweetness, O God! Thou hast provided for the poor." (lxvii. 2.)

The Lecture.—First chapter in the 7th Treatise of the second Part of Rodriguez. On the great advantages and treasures we possess in Jesus Christ.

Give yourself entirely to our Lord, to-day, in the Holy Communion, with all you possess, and receive Him in exchange as your sovereign good, your only treasure, and all your happiness. You may say to Him with St. Augustine, "there is no happiness out of Thee, who art the sovereign good; I must be miserable without Thee, for all treasures, which are not Thee, my God, are but indigence!"

For the Practice see the "Supplement."

SECOND MEDITATION.

On the Example of Poverty our Divine Lord gives us in the most Blessed Sacrament.

First Point.—"The Lord will give you spare bread and short water:" said the prophet Isaiah; "and thy eyes shall be thy teacher, and thy ears shall hear the voice of one admonishing thee behind thy back: This is the way; walk in it." (Isaiah, xxx. 20, 21.) Adore Jesus Christ in the Holy Sacrament as your Divine Master, who remains on the Altar to instruct and enlighten you. Consider the importance he attached to our being deeply grounded in the maxims of the Gospel, particularly those regarding poverty, which are the foundation of the rest. This he proved, not only by embracing indigence in his Incarnation, selecting poor parents, choosing a stable for His birth-place,—living in want, and enduring the privation even of necessaries,—but further to show His love for this virtue, and to impress it more deeply on our hearts, He determined to practise poverty to the end of time on the Altar, thus effecting, by an invention of His wisdom, a miracle of love, which seems incompatible with His glorified state. Admire the virtue which Jesus so highly prizes, and practise it through esteem for the example given us in this august mystery by our hidden God and Saviour.

Second Point.—In the adorable Eucharist our Lord gives us an example of practical poverty. There He seems to possess nothing of His own;—He remains wherever He is placed, in a wooden or brass ciborium, as well as in one of gold or silver; in a village, as in a city; in the most abject dwelling, as in a sumptuous temple. He is clothed in the accidents of an inanimate substance, more despicable than the swaddling-clothes, which enveloped Him in the manger. He is usually left alone, day and night, and as little attended as the poorest of His creatures. Thank your Redeemer for His example, and endeavour to form yourself on this high model.

Third Point.—The motive of Christ's humiliations on the Altar is no other than love. In Him are perfectly verified the words of the Canticles, "If a man should give all the substance of his house for love, he shall despise it as nothing." (Cant. viii. 7.) He is not satisfied with having divested Himself of the riches of His glory, in the Incarnation, nor with having shed His blood for us on the cross; but He has discovered a means of despoiling Himself a second time of His treasures, and even of Himself, to transfer both to us in the sacrament of charity. Stimulated by this example, resolve generously to renounce all temporal things, not in consideration of the rewards and advantages attendant on poverty, but solely for the love of the Lord Jesus. Is it not reasonable that love, which has impoverished the Son of God, should likewise impoverish you?

If Jesus Christ has sold all things, like the rich merchant in the Gospel, to purchase your soul, which he values as a precious pearl, should you not give up all to attain the possession of Him? "You suffice to God," said St. Cyprian, "let God then suffice to you."

FRIDAY.

FIRST MEDITATION.

On the extreme Poverty our Lord displayed on the Cross.

First Point.—The cross is the sacred school, to which Religious souls should repair to learn the high and difficult lesson of detachment from exterior things. Our crucified model teaches us, first, the renunciation of temporal conveniences.—His bed is the hard wood of the cross; His pillow is a crown of thorns; His drink, vinegar and gall;—He is refused even a drop of water, in His extreme anguish. With what confusion should not this example overwhelm us, who so cautiously avoid inconvenience, and so perpetually seek for comfort! How powerfully should it animate you to embrace poverty, which Christ has almost deified in his own person! Examine in detail the sacrifices God requires of you on this head, and resolve to refuse none.

Second Point.—The poverty of Jesus Christ on the cross does not extend to His body alone, but He is likewise destitute of the comforts sweet to the mind of a rational being; deprived of friends, credit, fame. "I looked for one that would grieve together with me," said He by His Prophet, "but there was none; and for one that would comfort me, and I found none." (Ps. lxiii. 21.) "Thou hast put away my acquaintance far from me: they have set me an abomination to themselves." (Ibid. lxxxvii. 9.) He endured the loss of reputation, dying between two malefactors, as the most infamous of the three. His dignity, as King and Messiah, was so absolutely degraded, that He declares of Himself by the Psalmist, "I am a worm and no man, the reproach of men, and the outcast of the people." (Ps. xxi. 7.) Meditate with deep attention on this extremity of poverty, and resolve, in imitation of our Lord, to bear patiently the loss of those who assist you in your spiritual and temporal necessities, if God should deprive you of their aid, and determine also, to endure neglect and contempt courageously for His love.

Third Point.—To complete the measure of His destitution, our Divine Lord submitted to the deprivation of interior consolation, enduring excessive torments without sensible joy or comfort, as He proved by exclaiming in His dereliction, "My God, my God, why hast Thou forsaken me?" (St. Matt. xxvii. 46.) Job, speaking in the person of Christ, says, "I cry to thee, and thou hearest me not, I stand up, and thou dost not regard me; thou art changed in my regard to be cruel." (Job, xxx. 20, 21.)

Learn, from this example, patiently to bear interior poverty, and the privation of sensible consolation, when God is pleased to try you by this means; and seek no happiness on earth, but the perfect accomplishment of God's will.

Aspirations.—"I am poor and sorrowful; Thy salvation, O God, hath set me up." (Ps. lxxxviii. 30.)

The Lecture.—The 8th and 9th chapters of the Treatise on Poverty.

For the Practice, see "Supplement."

SECOND MEDITATION.

On the actual Renunciation of all Things, by interior Acts of Religious Poverty.

First Point.—Place yourself at the feet of Jesus Christ crucified, poor and abandoned, as you considered Him this morning, and there renounce, for His love—1st. the possession of all created things, and whatever right you may have thereto; 2nd. the desire of temporal goods, and all worldly hopes and expectations; 3rd. all affection to exterior things, transferring your undivided love to Him, who is your sovereign and only treasure. 4th. Renounce the use of temporal conveniences, except with perfect dependence on your superiors; desire none except at the time, in the name, and in the quantity they regulate. 5th. Sacrifice the power of giving, which accompanies the possession of riches, and renounce the authority they procure, and the honour they confer, embracing instead, indigence, contempt, and dependence, which are inseparable attendants on poverty. Accept from your heart the trials God may destine for you on these heads. 6th. Renounce pride and interior presumption, which usually accompany riches; embrace, on the contrary, humility and self-abjection. 7th. Renounce luxuries, idleness, pleasures, and the comforts which result from riches—accepting frugality, labour, and pain, which are the companions of poverty. Unite these acts to the poverty of Christ, particularly that He exhibited on the cross; offer yourself to Him with the most ardent love of which you are capable, and conclude by saying with the devout Thomas à Kempis,—"My Lord Jesus Christ, my hope and my refuge, having renounced all earthly things for Thy love, I choose Thee this day for my protector, my resource in my wants, my guide through life, and my consoler in all pains, temptations, and afflictions. Thou art my refuge; Thy heart is my home; Thou art my meat and my drink; my repose and my resting-place. Thou art my Friend by excellence, my good Father, my most dear Brother. Thou art the protector of my life, to whom I confide myself and all my concerns, because Thou art the only source of life, and the only hope of my salvation. Grant me Thy mercy, and may Thy grace ever accompany me; may thine eyes be ever on me, and Thy right hand open to protect me, that Thou mayest conduct me securely to the Kingdom of Thy glory.—Amen."

SATURDAY.

FIRST MEDITATION.

On the Example of Poverty, left us by the Blessed Virgin.

Having considered the examples of poverty left us by the Son of God, you will meditate to-day on those which the life of the ever-glorious Virgin displays. She is the second model proposed for the imitation of Religious persons, and you are specially obliged to follow her glorious example, because, on entering this Order, you chose her peculiarly for your Mother and Protectress.

First Point.—The Blessed Virgin first raised the standard of perfection, beneath which so many Religious persons have since pursued the road to sanctity; for although, as St. Thomas observes, the glory of having preached perfection to man was reserved for the Son of God, the Blessed Virgin had previously established its foundation in her own heart, and therefore possessed the plenitude of grace in a secondary degree, even before she had conceived Jesus Christ, its original source. The Blessed Virgin revealed to St. Bridget, that she had by vow renounced all things on earth, and that, in consequence of this obligation, she had retained only the absolute necessaries of life, whence it appears that Mary's poverty was not the result of inevitable circumstances, but a voluntary renunciation of superfluities, since St. Joachim and St. Anne must have left her some wealth, as to their only heiress. Observe the reasons for which God inspired her to make this vow. 1st. Because the Eternal Word designed to select a poor person for His mother, that from His birth He might experience the effects of poverty. 2nd. Because it was consistent that the Mother should resemble the Son. 3rd. Because poverty disposes the soul for the reception of spiritual treasures, which God designed to lavish on the Blessed Virgin, above all creatures, replenishing her even with Himself, in a peculiar manner. The desire of being associated with Jesus Christ and His Blessed Mother should inspire you with a great desire to imitate both in the practice of perfect poverty.

Second Point.—The Mother of God, having generously embraced poverty, practised it with fidelity throughout her life. Consider the privations she endured in her journeys to Bethlehem and to Egypt, as well as during her sojourn at Nazareth, where she had to depend for subsistence on the labour of a poor tradesman to whom she was espoused. After the death of her Divine Son, she lived on alms, like other widows, limiting herself to absolute necessaries in clothing, &c.,—endeavouring to imitate the extreme poverty of Christ on the Cross, which was ever present to her memory. With poverty, she united its inseparable companion, humility, rejoicing at the slights offered her as the wife of a poor carpenter. She aimed at the meanest offices and always sought the last place, though deserving of the first. Examine how far you imitate the Blessed Virgin in her poverty and humility, and regret to find yourself so remote from the perfection to which she carried them. Beg of her to implore from her Son, the grace to practise them perfectly in future.

Third Point.—Reflect on the interior spirit whence sprang the exterior poverty of the Blessed Virgin. She was ever annihilated before the majesty of God, referring to Him the graces she received, without attributing them to herself; always contemptible in her own eyes, and absorbed in the contemplation of her nothingness. This is evident from her answer to the angel, "Behold the handmaid of the Lord" (St. Luke, i. 38), which words she uttered in the most profound humility, and poverty of spirit, of which any creature was capable. She is really poor, who has nothing of her own, who does not labour for her own advantage—who can gain nothing for her own interest. The Blessed Virgin considered herself as belonging not to herself, but to God alone. In resolving to imitate the poverty and humility of the Mother of God, observe that as these virtues were the foundation of all her greatness, according to her own declaration, so they must be also the foundation of the perfection to which you aspire, for profound humility, and a deep conviction of her own nothingness, can alone prepare the soul to receive the graces of God, and render her capable of rising to a high degree of sanctity. "The poor and needy shall praise Thy name, O Lord" (Ps. lxxiii. 21); because attributing nothing to themselves, they refer all glory to Thee, and bless Thee without ceasing. Implore poverty of spirit through the intercession of the Blessed Virgin.

Aspirations.—"I have chosen to be an abject in the house of my God, rather than to dwell in the tabernacles of sinners." (Ps. lxxxiii. 11.) "My soul doth magnify the Lord. Because He hath regarded the humility of His handmaid." (St. Luke, i. 46, 48.)

The Lecture.—The 23rd and 24th chapters of the Treatise on Humility in Rodriguez.

For the Practice see "Supplement."

SECOND MEDITATION.

As your evening Meditation, read attentively the chapter of the Constitutions on Poverty, and endeavour to comprehend the high perfection it recommends. Take a brief view of the faults you may have committed against poverty; examining, 1st. If you have experienced pain or regret at being deprived of any article. 2nd. If by importunity or any other means you have procured its restoration. 3rd. If you have received, retained, or disposed of anything without permission. 4th. If you have kept anything superfluous, or too rare. 5th. If you have patiently borne the want even of necessaries, both in health and sickness. 6th. If you have preferred the worst and poorest of everything. 7th. If your heart has been detached from earthly things. After having observed your most ordinary failings and implored pardon for them, recall to mind the resolutions you made during the past week, and the reflections which struck you most forcibly in your meditations, and study to imprint both on your heart. Present them to God, through the hands of the Blessed Virgin, that He may render them efficacious; then at your leisure commit them to paper.

DIRECTIONS FOR THE SECOND WEEK OF EXERCISES, PREPARATORY TO THE VOW OF CHASTITY.

The great end of the Exercises of this week is, the acquisition of perfect purity of body and soul, which cannot be better attained than by disengagement from creatures and mortification of the senses.

Endeavour, then, to maintain a strict guard over the affections of your heart, and to keep your senses in subjection, that, like a spotless mirror, your soul may be prepared to receive the undimmed reflection of the lights and graces which it may please God to communicate to you in prayer. Produce frequent acts of disengagement from created objects, that Christ, your heavenly Spouse, may alone engage your affections. 2nd. Of renunciation of all pleasures but those found in Him. 3rd. Of lively contrition for having sullied the purity of your soul by sin, particularly by the gratification of sense, and the inordinate love of creatures. As regards the exterior practice of the virtue, mortify your senses when an opportunity of doing so occurs;—be more than usually exact in the observance of silence, and attend faithfully to the rules "on modesty." It may be useful, with permission, to perform some austerity in atonement for your faults on this point. The chapters of the Constitutions to be read this week are those on Chastity, Penance, Abstinence, Silence, and Modesty.

SUNDAY.

FIRST MEDITATION.

On Chastity.

First Point.—To embrace the practice of this counsel, is to advance a second step in the road leading to Religious perfection. You have already taken the first by renouncing all temporal and external things; by the vow of Chastity you proceed still further, renouncing your own body, and sacrificing even lawful pleasures. This is the angelic virtue, which the Son of God Himself taught, when, descending from Heaven to renovate our vitiated nature, He not only restored man to his primitive innocence by the grace of Baptism, and imparted to him strength to subject his natural inclinations to the control of reason, but moreover imparted to innumerable persons that superior help which enabled them to lead angelic lives in a mortal body, by the profession of perfect chastity. "No sooner was Jesus Christ born of a Virgin," says St. Gregory Nazianzen, "than the Divine virtue of Chastity began to effect a division of society, separating its members into two portions; some to remain in the world and people it; others to renounce earthly things, and belong more to heaven than earth; to merit the title rather of angels than of men." This is the interpretation of our Divine Lord's declaration, that "He did not come to send peace upon earth but a sword." "That He came to set a man at variance against his father, and the daughter against her mother, and the daughter-in-law against her mother-in-law." (St. Matt. xix. 34, 35.) "That there are eunuchs, who have made themselves eunuchs for the kingdom of Heaven's sake;" adding, he that can receive it, let him receive it" (St. Matt. xix. 12); thereby shewing that this state of perfection is not destined indiscriminately for all persons, but only for the privileged individuals whom God particularly calls to it.

You should thank God for having enabled you to comprehend this counsel, and for having inspired you with resolution to embrace it. Esteem the Religious state, which elevates you so far above the weakness of your nature. Implore perseverance, pray also for perfect purity of soul and body.

Second Point.—The state of virginity, almost unknown before the coming of Jesus Christ, became common after His birth. 1st. Because the Eternal Word, having dignified our corrupt nature by elevating it to a personal union with His Divinity, it was just that some privileged mortals should, by their purity, worthily honour the Immaculate flesh of the Son of God. "A Virgin conceived," said St. Ambrose, "and the Word was made flesh, that many might be induced to embrace a life of perfect purity." 2nd. Because as our first parent peopled the world with a posterity terrestrial like himself, Jesus Christ, the repairer of Adam's crime, resolved to fill it with regenerated beings, whom the practice of Chastity should assimilate here below to the Angels of Heaven. 3rd. Having come on earth to contract a Divine union with His Church, a pure and Immaculate Virgin free from spot or wrinkle, it was fitting that He should present Virgins to that holy spouse, according to the words of the Psalmist, "After her shall Virgins be brought to the King, they shall be brought into the Temple." (Ps. xliv. 15, 16.) These three considerations should inspire you with a great esteem for this heavenly virtue, and a firm resolution, to avoid all that could sully its purity. Respect your body as a temple sanctified by the Son of God. "Remember," as St. Leo recommends, "of what head you are a member, and having been made a participator in the Divine nature, beware of sensual pleasures which degrade the soul."

Third Point.—Jesus Christ having, from the moment of His Incarnation, embraced a life of mortification, and constant renunciation of the pleasures of sense, persevered therein until His death on the Cross, to show us with what caution we should guard this precious virtue. He chose a Virgin for His mother, from which we learn as St. Bernard observes, "that virginity must be something Divine, since a God could only receive birth from a Virgin, as, on the other hand, a Virgin could conceive only an incarnate God." Our Divine Lord selected Saint Joseph for His foster-father, because that great Saint was specially endowed with the angelic virtue of chastity, and thereby peculiarly fitted to watch over the immaculate Lamb who feeds among the lilies. When Jesus called the Apostles to be His followers and friends, He impressed them so strongly with the love of this virtue, that those among them who were married separated from their wives. The virginity of St. John attracted the peculiar tenderness of his adorable Master, procured him access to the Divine Sanctuary of his Redeemer's heart, and entitled him to receive the Queen of Virgins for his Mother, our Lord recommending His

Virgin Mother to His Virgin disciple, as St. Jerom remarks.

Desire perfect purity, which will introduce you into the heart of Christ, and render you dear to the glorious Virgin. Ask it of God through the intercession of the Blessed Virgin, of St. Joseph, and of Saint John. Let sincere contrition efface the sins by which you may have sullied this Divine virtue, and say with David "The sins of my youth, and my ignorances do not re member" (Ps. xxiv. 7); "Turn away Thy face from my sins, and blot out all my iniquities." (Ps. l. 11.)

Aspirations.—"Lord, who shall dwell in thy Tabernacles? Or who shall rest in Thy holy Hill? He that walketh without blemish, and worketh justice." (Ps. xiv. 1, 2.)

"Create a clean heart in me, O God, and renew a right spirit within my bowels." (Ps. l. 12.)

The Lecture.—from Platus, 4th chapter, Second Part, and 18th chapter of First Part.

Receive our Lord in the holy Communion as the Lamb of God, who comes to wash away the stains of your soul in His most precious blood, and in the course of the day repeat the Seven Penitential Psalms, in presence of the Blessed Sacrament, deploring the sins of your past life, and offering the merits of Jesus Christ in atonement for them.

SECOND MEDITATION.

On the first Excellence of Chastity, which is, to render Man like the Angels.

First Point.—Our divine Lord, in speaking of the happy condition which awaits men after the Resurrection, says, that "they shall neither marry nor be given in marriage; but shall be as the angels of God in Heaven" (St. Matt. xxii. 30), which words prove that virginity is an angelic state of being. "This virtue," says St. Ambrose, "derives its source from Heaven, and has been thence presented to us, for our imitation on earth." And in the words of St. Cyprian, "Virginity not only transcends all terrestrial things in excellence, not only reaches the dignity of the Angels, but soars yet higher, combating against, and gloriously triumphing over nature, in a manner not possible to incorporeal spirits." Virgins, and especially those consecrated to God in Religion, resemble the Angels in their purity and in their occupations, and in some sense may be said even to share the dwelling of those inhabitants of Heaven. Angels are pure spirits, totally free from the slightest blemish; and Virgins, by the renunciation of sensual gratifications, are secured, as far as can be, against sin. "Virginal purity, says St. Austin, "is an angelic condition, and the commencement of incorruption in a corruptible body." Admire the excellence of this virtue, which enables man to subdue himself, and by generous courage to render himself participator in a privilege conferred on the Angels by their very nature. Humble yourself before God, and distrust your own weakness, since many of the Angels, notwithstanding their spiritual nature, fell by pride from the height of glory.

Resolve to aim seriously at acquiring humility, which is the guardian of all virtues, but peculiarly of Chastity. Ask both these virtues of God through the intercession of the angelic spirits.

Second Point.—Virgins likewise imitate the Angels, in their employment, which, according to St. Augustine, "consists in seeing, loving, and praising God." The same exalted occupation is, in a great measure, that of souls who have chosen the Lord for their inheritance, for, as we learn from St. Paul, one of the great advantages of continency is that "the unmarried woman thinketh on the things of the Lord; that she may be holy both in body and in spirit." (1 Cor. vii. 34.) Virgins see God in contemplation, to which purity disposes the soul; they are consumed with His love and employed in praising His name. This office belongs so equally to the Angels, and to Religious souls, that the Prophet exhorts both to unite in one Choir, as they have but one common end in view—*Behold, now bless ye the Lord, all ye servants of the Lord;* not only ye glorious spirits, who minister before His Throne, but you who stand "in the house of the Lord, in the courts of the house of our God" (Ps. cxxxiii. 1), that is, the Sanctuary of Religion. From this reflection, infer the esteem you should have for purity of soul and body. Remember that mortification is essential to the attainment and preservation of this great virtue; without it we can have no facility for approaching God in prayer; unsubdued passions, and attachment to sensual pleasures, being like a thick cloud, which obstructs the view of the Divine Sun of Justice, and impedes the action of its vivifying heat. Remember also the necessity of cultivating the spirit of prayer, for as purity is a necessary predisposition for conversing with God, so is prayer a sovereign preservative of purity; "they that go far from God shall perish." (Ps. lxxii. 27.) This is to be understood not only of those who abandon Him by sin, but also of such as forget His presence, and are negligent at prayer; from this spiritual indifference, the transition to the commission of great sins, though gradual, is certain. The soul that has forfeited the heavenly consolation found in prayer, will be sure at last to seek her comfort in sensual gratifications. "The Angels themselves," says St. Augustine, "could not preserve the purity and sanctity bestowed on them by their Creator, unless perpetually united to God by vision and love; were they even for a short interval distracted from His presence, they would quickly lose their light and ardour."

Third Point.—The third point of similarity between the Angels and Religious persons, is in their dwelling. The habitation of the Angels is Heaven, where, separated from creatures, they possess God without impediment. When they descend on earth, in obedience to His Divine will, their watchful care of the souls confided to them neither deprives them of the vision of God, nor interrupts their bliss. Religious persons are also separated from the world, and dwell in a terrestrial Paradise, as the cloister is termed by the holy Fathers. St. Bernard observes, that there is a close resemblance between Heaven and the cell of a Religious; the exercises of contemplation performed in both are equally hidden from the eyes of mortals, and the inhabitants of each pursue the same occupation, the uninterrupted contemplation and love of God. The Angels make no distinction between these two abodes, but dwell with equal delight in each, and when the soul is summoned to appear before God, it is from the solitude of her cell that she ascends to Him, because this solitude is a holy sanctuary, where seclusion facilitates the union of the creature with the Creator. Prize your retreat, which gives you the anticipated possession of God and His Angels, in which consists the bliss of Heaven. When you are obliged to leave it, to converse with creatures, imitate the blessed Spirits who come on earth only by the express command of God, and from the charitable motive of ministering to the spiritual wants of men, and who, though they quit Heaven, never lose the vision of God. In like manner, leave your cell only in obedience; edify those with whom you converse, and carefully mantain yourself in the presence of God. Implore these graces through the intercession of the holy Angels, particularly of your Angel Guardian.

MONDAY.

FIRST MEDITATION.

On the second Prerogative of Chastity, which is to elevate Man to the Dignity of Resemblance with his Creator.

First Point.—When we consider God himself to be the first and principal model of the virtue of Chastity, its dignity is elevated far beyond the power of human language to express. The most holy Trinity is the first of Virgins, says St. Gregory Nazianzen. In it we discover an admirable fecundity without corruption, and so perfect an original purity, that compared with it, all other purity is unworthy the name. The Holy Ghost assures us that by Chastity man participates in His divine purity;—"incorruption bringing near to God." (Wisdom, vi. 20.) First, Chastity renders the soul a participator in the sanctity of God. That sanctity, according to St. Denis, is nothing more than perfect purity, free from spot, exempt from every blemish that demands expiation; and, in the words of St. Cyprian, "Chastity is an incorruptible work of praise and glory, and a lively image of God, partaking in His spotless sanctity." "The unmarried woman, and the Virgin," says St. Paul, "thinketh on the things of the Lord; that she may be holy both in body and in spirit." (1 Cor. vii. 34.) Conceive a high esteem of this angelic virtue, and a sovereign horror of every stain that could even slightly dim its lustre. By the vow of Chastity your body and soul are to become the temple of the Holy Ghost; beware, then, of profaning them by sin, and of admitting into your heart anything unworthy the sanctity of your Profession.

Second Point.—The second quality of Chastity, which imparts to the soul a resemblance with God, is its unity. "God," says St. Denis, "is all things in one;" it follows that we ourselves being converted from a multitude of objects to a single object, by the power and virtue of the Divine Unity, should worthily honour the one single essence of the Divinity. This is done by persons who profess Chastity. "The married woman," says St. Paul, "is solicitous for the things of the world, how she may please her husband, and take care of her children, and she is divided; but the Virgin is solicitous for the things that belong to the Lord, how she may please God, and attach herself to him alone" (1 Cor. vii. 32, 33); and as the same Apostle adds, "being joined to the Lord, she becomes one spirit with him." (Ibid. vi. 17.) Aspire to this high perfection, through the medium of purity of body and soul. Thank God for having called you to a state wherein, by His grace, you can easily practise it. Impress your mind deeply with the conviction, that in order to belong to God alone, and to participate in His unity, it is not sufficient that you be separated from the cares and perplexities of the world; you must, moreover, so completely disengage yourself from created things, that God may possess your undivided affections, for, what will it avail you, to have renounced those objects you might lawfully have loved, if in Religion you allow your heart to cling to any person, or thing, suffering your thoughts to be occupied and engaged to a perhaps greater extent than would have been the case in the world. Make a firm resolution to give your whole heart without reserve to God, saying, with a Saint, "Let one soul be consecrated to the unity of one God." I have but one affection, one desire, one ambition, which is to belong to God. Direct all your exertions to this end, alone worthy of them, and say with St. Augustine—"Permit not, O Lord, that I should be any longer divided between the multitude of creatures, and the one Object who alone should attract me. Separate me from exterior things, teach me to retire into my own interior, and thence into Thee; that I may say in truth—'Thy face, O Lord, have I sought.'"

Third Point.—From participation in the unity and sanctity of God, results participation likewise in His sovereign happiness. The soul which is perfectly pure and wholly consecrated to God, is enabled to taste the ineffable joy promised to the clean of heart, which joy is an anticipation of eternal bliss, as St. Cyprian declares. "Even during life," he says, "virgins enter on that blessed state to which all aspire after death; they already enjoy the glory destined to follow the Resurrection, and they quit the world without having acquired an experimental acquaintance with its deceits and dangers." Beatitude consists in possessing God by knowledge and love:—purity prepares the soul for both. "Blessed are the clean of heart, for they shall see God" (St. Matt. v. 8), not only in Heaven, but even here below; they shall behold Him in contemplation, as far as is consistent with the weakness of our mortal state. This vision of God produces a pure and inflamed love, which in its ardour and constancy resembles that of the Saints in Heaven. Souls most remarkable for their purity are also those usually honoured by this privilege, as we see in St. John the Evangelist, to whom were revealed the secrets of Heaven; in Saint Gertrude, Saint Teresa, and many other holy virgins, on whom our Lord lavished an abundance of heavenly light and ardent love, which imparted to them a foretaste of the joys of Paradise. Despise all sensual pleasures, which, compared with these Divine joys, are but despicable dross. Sensual gratifications are fleeting, and insufficient to satisfy the heart; they are unworthy the dignity of man, whom they degrade to a level with the brute creation; whereas, the pure and ineffable delights of Chastity elevate the soul to a participation in the happiness of the Godhead. Sigh ardently for purity of heart, that precious treasure, which the vow of Chastity you are about to make will materially assist you in acquiring. Remember that your soul is like a mirror, which a breath suffices to tarnish, and that the least inordinate affection will incapacitate it from perfectly receiving the impression of God's image. Ask for the great virtue of purity, saying with David, "Create a clean heart in me, O God, and renew a right spirit within my bowels." (Ps. l. 12.)

Aspirations.—"O how beautiful is the chaste generation with glory, for the memory thereof is immortal, because it is known both with God and with man." (Wis. iv. 1.) "Infuse into my heart, O Lord, the abundance of Thy sweetness, that I may no longer desire any earthly pleasure; that I may love Thee alone, who art the only object of my heart's affections." St. Austin.

The Lecture.—First and second chapters of the Third Part of Platus.

Spend an additional quarter of an hour in prayer before your morning examination of conscience; employ it in elevating yourself in spirit to Heaven, under the guidance of your good Angel, that you may there contemplate the angelic choirs, and implore those happy spirits, who participate more than any other creatures in the sovereign purity of the Divinity, to obtain for you this great gift from His Divine Majesty.

SECOND MEDITATION.

On the third Excellence of Chastity, which is to assimilate us peculiarly to the Incarnate Word.

First Point.—In the Meditation of this morning you saw that chastity renders us, in some degree, like God; you are now to consider how you may attain that resemblance. The imitation of Jesus Christ is the great means to be adopted for this end, since he is most like to God, who most perfectly imitates, and most closely follows our adorable Model, and in this consists the third excellency of chastity, as pointed out by St. John in the Apocalypse. "I beheld," says St. John, "and lo! a Lamb stood upon Mount Sion, and with Him a hundred and forty-four thousand, having His name, and the name of His Father, written on their foreheads.

And I heard a voice from Heaven, and a noise of many waters, and as the voice of great thunders, and the voice which I heard was as the voice of harpers, harping on their harps." . . . (Apoc. xiv. 1, 2.) From these words, we may infer the close connection virgins have with Jesus Christ, as well as the high privileges He bestows on them. These privileges are six in number. First, they are permitted to ascend Mount Sion in His company; for by the observance of chastity, they practise a sublime and heroic virtue; moreover, in consequence of their exemption from the corruption of the flesh, and worldly impediments, they are enabled to devote themselves more exclusively to the study of perfection which they are taught by the Divine Lamb, who leads them to the highest contemplation, figured by Mount Sion. Secondly, they have the name of the Lamb and that of His Eternal Father written on their foreheads, as a mark that they no longer belong to themselves, nor to any creature, but to Jesus Christ alone. "He has placed a sign on my forehead, to show that I am His possession." These words are used at the ceremony of Profession, and their import is, that the soul which has vowed eternal fidelity to Christ has been marked for His property, as with a royal signet, so that no one beside Him can again lay claim to her. When admitted among the number of His spouses, she assumes the name of Jesus, and of His Eternal Father, as the change of state in the world is marked by the change of name. How highly should you prize virginity, which so closely connects you with Jesus Christ! Desire to unite yourself intimately to this Divine Lamb by the bond of love and imitation, that you may be among those who follow Him faithfully. Offer yourself entirely to Him, praying to become so unreservedly His, that all your words and actions may proclaim you as His possession.

Second Point.—The third privilege of virgins is, that their voice is loud as the pealing thunder, their victories over nature having rendered them formidable to the demons; while it is at the same time sweet as the softest music, the harmony of their virtues delighting the angels, and the example of their mortification diffusing edification among men. Their fourth privilege is to sing a new canticle, to burn with an ever-increasing love, to rejoice with a happiness always new. Singing, as St. Augustine observes, usually marks love and jubilation. The canticle sung by virgins is new, because they are peculiarly exempt from the corruption of the old man, and faithfully walk in the new life of Jesus Christ. They alone can sing it, because they only can enjoy the privileges reserved to virgins. Renew the affections excited by the first point, and ardently beg of our Divine Lord to destroy in you all remnants of corrupt nature, that you may sing to Him a new canticle, by beginning now to love Him with renewed ardour.

Third Point.—Their fifth prerogative is, that they have been "purchased from the earth," by a peculiar application of their Redeemer's merits, so that being separated from the world, they may not be defiled among creatures. (Apoc. xiv. 3.) Sixthly, they follow the Lamb *whithersoever He goeth*" . . . (Ibid. 4); 1st, because they have the privileges of virginity, to which dignity all cannot attain; 2ndly, because, as spouses of Jesus Christ, they cannot be separated from Him, but must everywhere accompany Him by holy thoughts and affections; in return for which, this liberal King will bring them into the " store rooms " of His ineffable bliss. (Cant. i. 3.) To the affections of the preceding Point, add an act of fervent thanksgiving to God, for having called you to the Religious state, and an earnest inquiry whether you are really determined to follow Christ wherever He may lead you. It is necessary for this end, that you be disengaged from every object which could impede your progress; and 2ndly, that you be animated with courage to correspond with God's designs on you, not abandoning the practice of virtue, when it is accompanied with difficulty. The love of Jesus Christ will secure you these two dispositions,—for if you closely cling to Him, He will detach you from all things else, and the reflection, that you follow so great a Leader, must give you strength to walk in His company even through rugged ways. " Where love exists," says St. Bernard, " there can be no pain, but only peace and joy." Ask of God to give you His love, and resolve with His grace to labour in acquiring, and continually increasing it.

TUESDAY.

FIRST MEDITATION.

On the fourth Excellence of Chastity, which is, to render the Soul, in a peculiar manner, the Spouse of Christ.

First Point.—Virgins are peculiarly the spouses of Jesus Christ; this, their sixth and last privilege, eminently includes all the others. " The virgin," says St. Ambrose, " ascending above the heavens, and even above the angels, rests not until she has soared even to the bosom of God, where, beholding His Eternal Word, she unites herself to

Him by the most ardent love." It is not extraordinary that her life is angelic, since her Spouse is heavenly, nor that she is compared to the blessed spirits, since, by a Divine alliance, she has been united to the Lord of angels. Consider the advantages resulting from this Divine union. "They shall be two in one flesh" (Gen. ii. 24), said God to Adam, in speaking of his union with Eve: the same words may be applied, in a spiritual sense, to the union of the soul with her adorable Spouse, in virtue of which union, two spirits are blended in one; for, as St. Paul tells us, "He who is joined to the Lord is one Spirit." (1 Cor. vi. 17.) Thank God for having chosen you for His spouse, notwithstanding the infinite disproportion between His perfection and your nothingness. Do not limit your ambition merely to that union with God which sanctifying grace has already effected, and which you share in common with all the just, nor even to the union which Religious persons contract by their Vows, although they may lead an imperfect life; but aspire to the highest and most perfect degree of union which can be attained on earth; since this is the end God had in view in calling you to religion. "The generality of Christians," says St. Bernard, "are permitted to occupy the rank of servants in the house of God, but for you is reserved the incomparable honour of uniting yourself to Him, as your Spouse!" Purity of body and soul, and assiduity in prayer, are the means to attain this happiness. The former detaches the soul from every object which could intervene between her and God; the latter elevates, and unites her to Him. Resolve to adopt these means, and beg grace to do so.

Second Point.—The second advantage resulting from this Divine Union is the mutual interchange of possessions between the soul and her heavenly Spouse. Christ communicates to her His power, His wisdom, and His other perfections; He gives her His virtues, His merits, in fine, Himself—while the spouse offers Him in return her will, her affections, her body, her soul, and whole being; so that she no longer belongs to herself, but has become the possession of Christ, and may say with the spouse in the Canticles: "My beloved to me and I to him." (Cant. ii. 16.) How noble is this privilege! How advantageous this exchange! To deserve it, you must renounce all things, in imitation of your Divine Spouse—"I have forsaken my house, I have left my inheritance, I have given my dear soul into the hands of her enemies." (Jer. xii. 7.) He requires the same sacrifice from you, saying by the psalmist, "Hearken, O daughter, and see; incline thine ear, and forget thy people, and thy father's house; and the king shall greatly desire thy beauty." (Psalm, xliv. 11, 12.) Renounce earthly desires; sacrifice the vicious inclinations you inherit from your first parent;—in a word, quit all, if you will find all. If there be any inordinate affection, which you have not resolved to sacrifice, or any object which you have not determined to renounce, our Divine Lord will not communicate Himself to you with all His treasures. But if you give Him all, He will say to you, as He said to St. Teresa, His faithful spouse, "My daughter, thou art now my undivided possession; thy interests shall in future be mine, and mine shall be thine." Examine what your dispositions are on this head.

Third Point.—The soul thus united to Jesus Christ becomes happily fruitful in the production of virtues and good works; and by her words and example brings forth many souls to Christ, whose Divine image she forms within them, saying to them, as St. Paul said to the Galatians, "My little children of whom I am in labour again, until Christ be formed in you." (Gal. iv. 19.) This dignity is peculiarly that of Ursulines, who by their Institute are devoted to the salvation of souls. How truly may you then exclaim with the wise man, "O how beautiful is the chaste generation with glory, for the memory thereof is immortal, because it is known both to God and man." (Wis. iv. 1.) After having returned thanks to God for calling you to so high a dignity, desire to rank yourself among the most perfect of the spouses of Christ, by adopting the means presented to your consideration in the preceding points, and implore grace to this effect.

Aspirations.—"I love Jesus Christ who has chosen my soul for His spouse. In the possession of His Divine love I find the treasure of virgin purity."

"They that go from Thee, O Lord, shall perish; Thou hast destroyed all them that are disloyal to Thee. But it is good for me to stick close to Thee, my God." (Psalm, lxxii. 27, 28.)

The Lecture.—13th and 14th chapters of the Second Part of Platus.

For the Practice, see "Supplement."

SECOND MEDITATION.

On the Vow of Chastity.

First Point.—Your past meditations have tended, by laying before you the excellence of the virtue of Chastity, to animate you to practise it in its utmost perfection; it now remains to consider, in what that perfection consists, and what are the obligations, contracted by the Vow of Chastity. This virtue, which tends to weaken and repress man's natural inclination to sensual pleasures, has three degrees. The first is that embraced by married persons, who refrain from unlawful gratifications; the second by the continent, who abstain from even those which are lawful; and the third by Virgins whose purity has never been sullied. Chastity, as professed by Religious persons, is included under the two last heads, and being confirmed by Vow, it far exceeds in merit and excellence that practised without the same obligations; 1st, because the Vow removes the possibility of seeking any, but spiritual pleasures, gratifications otherwise legitimate being prohibited; 2nd, because the soul, by contracting so strict an obligation, evinces greater generosity, not only depriving herself of worldly pleasures, but even of the power of aspiring to them; thus, presenting to God the fruit, as well as the tree; 3rd, the Vow strengthens the human will, which embraces as strictly obligatory for salvation, what was before merely optional; 4th, it is the indissoluble bond of union between the soul and her Divine Spouse, Jesus Christ; and so completely consecrates her to Him, that she becomes a sacred object, which it would be sacrilege to profane.

Admire the high dignity to which you aspire, and resolve to observe the Vow of Chastity in its greatest perfection, that you may be pure and holy in thoughts, words, and actions. The delicacy of this virtue corresponds with its excellence; "We have this treasure," said St. Paul, "in earthen vessels" (2 Cor. iv. 7), which may easily be broken, and must therefore be guarded most cautiously. Ask of God to give you the perfection of Chastity, and in order to attain it, fly from the very shadow of sin, since God *hath chosen you*, that you *should be holy and unspotted in His sight in charity.* (Eph. l. 4.)

Second Point.—To bodily purity must be joined purity of soul, which banishes the love of created things, substituting for the pleasure naturally found in human attachments, the happiness of clinging to God alone. This degree of purity is only attained perfectly in Heaven ; yet we should aspire to it on earth, and aim at a daily progress therein. To this end tended all the mortifications practised by the Saints, and it is this end likewise, which the Almighty designs to promote, when mingling bitterness and disappointment with all earthly affections, He compels us to sacrifice these objects, and to direct our love to Him alone. Examine if your heart seeks its repose in anything which is not God; in inordinate attachment to creatures, in the esteem of the world, or the gratification of the senses. To indulge such attachments, is to recall the donation made of your heart to Jesus Christ ;and to restore it to creatures. Detach yourself from all earthly things, that you may present your being without reserve to your Divine Spouse, and say to Him in truth, "My beloved to me, and I to Him, who feedeth among the lilies." (Cant. ii. 16.)

Third Point.—Consider the advantages of these two branches of Chastity, as they are described in the Book of Wisdom; "Happy is the barren and the undefiled; happy the eunuch that hath not wrought iniquity with his hands, nor thought wicked things against God; for the precious gift of faith shall be given to him, and a most acceptable lot in the Temple of God." (Wisdom, iii. 13, 14.) By the "*barren*," and the "*eunuch*," is meant the soul, which has voluntarily renounced earthly pleasures, to attach herself to God alone. On this soul

He bestows the gift of faith or fidelity, which attaches her inviolably to Him, and which produces three special results. 1st. Ever to tend to Christ, by an upright intention, seeking only His glory in every action. 2nd. To place her happiness in Him alone, and to aim at no higher bliss than that of pleasing Him. 3rd. To be so engrossed by this desire to please Him as to lose sight of the very existence of all beside. St. Agnes eminently possessed the virtues of purity and fidelity, as she proved by her generous declaration, that it was an insult to her Heavenly Spouse to suppose her capable of desiring to please any one besides Him, to whom she had vowed fidelity, and consecrated her affections. Our Divine Lord will extend this favour to you likewise, if you study to acquire purity of body and soul, through the medium of mortification: He promises a glorious reward for these virtues, declaring that He will place you at His right hand in His kingdom. "The Queen stood on Thy right hand, in gilded clothing, surrounded with the variety of every virtue." (Ps. xliv. 11.) Prepare your soul, by detachment from all creatures, to become a partaker in these advantages, and beg grace to fulfil your resolutions to this effect.

WEDNESDAY.

FIRST MEDITATION.

On the Spirit of Retirement and Mortification of the Senses necessary for preserving Purity of Body and Soul.

First Point.—"My Spouse is a garden enclosed, a fountain sealed up." (Cant. iv. 12.) The first disposition required in a soul, who, by a Vow of Chastity, has consecrated herself to God, is the love of retirement and solitude. The holy Fathers and Councils have rigorously imposed perpetual cloister on Religious Communities, as a preservative against those dangerous occasions which expose the precious virtue of Chastity to a diminution of its lustre; desiring that the consecrated Spouses of Christ should live even in the midst of cities, as in a desert, conversing no longer with men but with angels. Esteem the voluntary seclusion from creatures which enables you to enjoy so uninterruptedly the company of your Divine Spouse, who, as St. Ambrose says, "is not to be found in the streets, or public places, but flying the tumult of worldly assemblies, retires, in the words of the Canticles, to the solitude of the mountains." Resolve to separate absolutely from creatures, and having left all for your Heavenly Spouse, mortify the natural inclination you may feel for the visits of even your nearest relations, lest a too frequent communication with the world may revive the love of its transitory joys.

Second Point.—If you desire that our Divine Lord should say to you with the Spouse in the Canticles, "My sister, my spouse, is a garden enclosed, a fountain sealed up," you must add to the exterior cloister which separates you from the world, another species of cloister which will separate you also from external things, and concentrate you within your own soul; this two-fold cloister is signified by the repetition of the words, "a garden enclosed," which, in the text, are expressed twice. External objects are admitted into the heart through the senses of vision and hearing, while the soul's attention is diverted from herself to earthly trifles through the medium of speech. These, then, are the avenues which must be cautiously guarded, that the heart may retain its purity, and present a worthy temple to its Divine inhabitant. Guard against curious, vain, or idle glances; this practice of mortification will become easy, if you habituate yourself to look constantly on Jesus Christ; you will thus soon instinctively join in the prayer of the holy Father in the desert, "Close Thou my eyes, O Lord, to all things on earth, for nothing beside Thee can now fix my attention." Secondly, mortify your hearing by never listening to worldly news, or such useless information as tends to distract the mind from God; let the ears of your heart be always open to the voice of Jesus Christ, and the soft whisperings of His grace, saying with the prophet, "I will hear what the Lord God will speak in me; for He will speak peace unto the people." (Psalm, xxxiv. 9.) Thirdly, watch with peculiar care over your words, which, if not restrained, must lead infallibly to dissipation of mind, the extinction of devotion, and an infinity of imperfections. Consider your tongue in future as the gate by which Jesus Christ enters your heart at Communion, and say of it in the words of Scripture, "This gate shall be shut, and no man shall pass through it:" no sinful words resulting from the corruption of the old man shall proceed from it, "because the Lord hath entered in by it." (Ezechiel, xliv. 2.) Let your words be regulated by the following advice of St. Gregory, "Speak, when words can be more profitable to your soul than silence, but except in this case, observe uninterrupted silence." Examine the faults you have committed through immortification of the senses, implore pardon for them, and determine seriously to embrace the practice of this species of mortification. Descend to particulars and pray for grace to observe your good resolutions. Say with David, "Turn away my eyes that they may not behold vanity." (Ps. cxviii. 3.) "Set a watch, O Lord, before my mouth; and a door round about my lips." (Ibid. cxl. 3.)

Third Point.—The advantages derived from the spirit of solitude, and the mortification of the senses, are thus enumerated by the Prophet Isaiah, "the Lord will comfort Sion," or the soul devoted to God in solitude, "and will comfort all the ruins thereof;" by amply indemnifying her for the sacrifices she has made to His love. He will bestow on her three signal favours; He will make "her desert as a place of pleasure," bestowing on her the abundance of spiritual consolations. 2nd. He will render her "as the garden of the Lord," a garden producing the rich fruits of virtue; she will no longer rank among those whose dissipated hearts are compared to the high way on which the seed of holy thoughts cannot spring up, because it is trodden by men. 3rd. "Joy and gladness shall be found in her; thanksgiving and the voice of praise" (Isaiah, li. 3), the natural result of gratitude for the special favours of God, whom she will uninterruptedly glorify in solitude, being undisturbed by exterior objects. Compare these spiritual delights with sensual gratifications, and see from which of the two results the most pure and substantial happiness; you must acknowledge that the deceitfulness and insufficiency of the latter are sufficiently proved by the remorse of conscience and anxiety which follow their possession; embrace, then, the solid and lasting joys which spring from the mortification of the senses, and interior solitude.

Aspirations.—"Who will give me the wings" of perfect purity of soul and body, and I will fly "to my God, and be at rest in His bosom." To attain this happiness, "I have gone far off, flying away;" "and I abode in the wilderness." (Psalm, liv. 7, 8.)

The Lecture.—The second, third, and fourth chapters of the Treatise on Modesty in Rodriguez.

For the Practice see "Supplement."

SECOND MEDITATION.

On Corporal Mortification.

First Point.—To retirement from the world, and the subjection of the senses, must be added the mortification of the flesh, so necessary for the preservation of purity, that the holy Fathers strenuously advise virgins to treat their bodies with a rational degree of severity. This virtue has two branches,—first, the renunciation of corporal gratifications; second, the practice of voluntary austerities. The first should extend to all that gratifies the sensual appetite, retrenching superfluity in eating, drinking, sleeping, &c., &c., and substituting a purer motive for the natural satisfaction, which may result from the use even of necessaries. We should be able to say with one of the ancient Fathers,—"I desire to find pleasure in God alone." Inquire into your dispositions on this subject; examining whether you are inordinately attached to your ease and convenience, or whether you are faithful in repressing the importunate demands of natural inclination. Implore light to discover your faults, and the strength and courage necessary for observing the resolutions of amendment which God's grace may suggest to you.

Second Point.—The second branch of the mortification of the body is the use of corporal austerities, which have been always highly esteemed and constantly practised by the Saints. "St. Paul assures us that he "chastised his body and brought it into subjection" (1 Cor. ix. 27); and David declares, that when "his enemies *were troublesome to him, he was clothed with haircloth.*" (Psalm, xxxiv. 13.) Such was, likewise, the practice of all the Saints, whose example you should resolve to imitate. Set a due value on the austerities prescribed by your Rule, and never seek a dispensation from them without a just and sufficient cause; occasionally add to those of obligation, with the permission of your superiors, when God inspires you with the desire to do so, and gives you strength to execute your design. St. Paul, in the 12th chapter of his Epistle to the Romans, enumerates the conditions necessary for rendering the mortification of the body a virtue pleasing to God:—It must first be a *living* sacrifice, that is, animated by the interior mortification of the passions, which may be called its soul: "Fasting will avail but little," says St. Leo, "unless, at the same time, the heart abstain from sin, and the tongue from detraction." Second, it must be *holy*, free from imperfection, particularly from any degree of self-will, or opposition to superiors. Third, it must be *pleasing to God*, inspired by the motive of giving Him glory, and totally exempt from the vain desire of surpassing others. Fourth, it must be *reasonable*, accompanied with prudence, which forbids the use of such austerities as might prove injurious, and so weaken the body as to incapacitate it from the discharge of duty. But as no one is a judge in his own cause, the most certain rule is, to be guided by the opinion of superiors. Examine what reformation your conduct may require on this head, and produce the same affections as at the first Point.

Third Point.—The consideration of the advantages

which result from this practice of the virtue will strengthen you to resist the natural propensity which all have to consult their ease and gratification. The Church, in the Preface of Lent, particularises four advantages which accrue to the soul from fasting, and which may be considered as extending likewise to the practice of every other species of austerity. 1st. *It subdues the passions* by weakening the body, whose irregular desires are a constant source of sin. 2nd. *It elevates the mind*, rendering it superior to the low and grovelling propensities of nature, which chain it to the earth, and impede its free ascent to Heaven. 3rd. *It strengthens virtue*, because, as the Apostle says, "Power is made perfect in infirmity" (2 Cor. xii. 9), and it moreover renders us like to Jesus Christ crucified, the perfect and finished model of consummate sanctity. 4th. It secures a glorious reward, "for, if we suffer with Christ, we shall be also glorified with Him." (Rom. viii. 17.) The body, which, for the love of its crucified Saviour, has voluntarily embraced the rigours of penance in this life, shall be rewarded by never-ending bliss in Heaven. "Our present tribulation, which is momentary and light, worketh for us above measure exceedingly an eternal weight of glory." (2 Cor. iv. 17.) How highly should you esteem, and how fervently should you embrace the salutary passing pains of mortification, which are productive of so many advantages!

THURSDAY.

FIRST MEDITATION.

The Holy Communion is a sovereign Preservative of the Virtue of Chastity.

First Point.—"What is the good thing of Him," said the Prophet Zacharias, "and what is his beautiful thing, but the corn of the Elect, and wine springing forth virgins." (Zacharias, ix. 17.)

The most amiable, the most attractive of the attributes of God, are displayed in the Blessed Sacrament of our Altars, which is truly the Wheat of the Elect, and the Vine-bearing Virgins. The peculiar effect of a good Communion is, an increase of purity in body and soul; because this Sacrament confers sanctifying grace more abundantly than any other, uniting the soul to the Eternal Source and Origin of all grace and sanctity. Now, the first effect of sanctifying grace is to banish sin, which it does, before the Author of purity can be admitted into His Temple; its second effect is, to preserve from future sin, which it accomplishes with peculiar efficacy when conveyed through the channel of the holy Eucharist, subduing concupiscence, and strengthening us against temptation. "Thou hast prepared a table before me," said David, "against them that afflict me." (Psalm, xxii. 5). "The bread of the strong, when received worthily," says St. Chrysostom, "imparts a strength, a courage, an ardent charity, by which we are enabled to face our enemies, and triumph over them."

Return thanks to God for having provided you with so powerful a preservative against sin, and recur to it with confidence, that you may experience its efficacy.

Second Point.—The Sacrament of the Eucharist confers purity of body and soul on those who receive it worthily, by an effect peculiar to itself, for, as corporal food communicates its qualities to those who partake of it, this Divine bread, incorporated with those who participate therein, transforms them into itself. Such was the promise made to St. Augustine—"Grow up, and eat—thou shalt not change me into thee as ordinary food, but I shall change thee into myself."

The bread which we receive from Heaven is the pure and immaculate flesh of the Son of God, which was never defiled by the slightest shadow of sin, and which, if received with suitable dispositions, communicates to the soul a share in its own spotless purity. It is given to us, glorious and immortal, as a pledge of the future bliss to which, through its merits, we aspire after the resurrection. The powerful efficacy of this most holy Sacrament so completely subdues the revolts of the flesh, that to those who approach it with suitable dispositions, the body not only ceases to be a source of sin, but becomes a faithful co-operator with the soul in her good works.

Third Point.—The spiritual delight and consolations which our Divine Lord lavishes in the holy Communion on fervent souls, are a third source of the angelic virtue of Chastity. The Blessed Eucharist is that "bread, which yields dainties to kings" (Gen. xlix. 20), that is, to generous souls, who have acquired an absolute dominion over the passions. In this Sacrament of love, Jesus Christ proves Himself truly the Spouse of the soul,—speaking to her heart in the excess of His goodness; conducting her, as St. Bernard observes, "first to the garden where bloom the flowers of holy desires, and the roses of ardent charity; then to the desert, where, forgetful of all creatures, and mindful of Him alone, she is prepared to receive the torrents of His grace, to enjoy the inebriating sweets of His love; to inhale the fragrance of His virtues—and finally disposed for an entrance into the secret sanctuary of His own Divine heart, there to taste the blessings of intimate union with the adorable object of all her affections." Can a soul thus united to Christ, thus honoured with His love, permit that an impure stain should sully the temple of her Divine Spouse?—or can she who has tasted the heavenly gift, still relish sensual enjoyments? Does she not rather declare with St. Gregory, that having been once inebriated at the fountain of spiritual delights, the streams of earthly joys have become bitter and insipid? She exclaims with the devout Blosius, "that being interiorly united to Him, who is the source, the exhaustless ocean of bliss, she can find no comfort among creatures." Prepare for Communion by endeavouring to acquire great purity of heart, that you may attain an intimate union with Christ, and thereby receive an increase of purity, which may dispose your soul for the most abundant communication of His graces. Respect your body and soul, which have been sanctified by the presence of your Divine Redeemer. Despise all earthly enjoyments, valuing only the pure delights which spring from union with Him, who is the joy of the angels.

Aspirations.—"My beloved to me, and I to Him who feedeth among the lilies" (Cant. ii. 16); "I consecrate my affections, and promise fidelity to Jesus Christ, my Divine Spouse, whose precious body is closely united to mine, whose sacred blood inebriates my soul."

The Lecture.—From the first part of "The Knowledge and Love of Jesus Christ," by Pere St. Jure, Book 3rd, Chapter 10th, 3rd and 8th Sections.

Receive our Lord to-day in the holy Communion as your heavenly Spouse, and the only object of your love; say to Him with the spouse in the Canticles—"Let Him kiss me with the kiss of His mouth—for thy breasts," that is thy consolations, "are better than the wine" of earthly joys—smelling sweeter "than the most fragrant of perfumes." (Cant. i. 2, 3.) Consecrate yourself without reserve to His love, and implore perfect purity of body and soul.

Spend a quarter of an hour during the recreation in prayer before the Blessed Sacrament, to atone for the vain gratification you have derived from intercourse with creatures.

SECOND MEDITATION.

On the perfect Example of Mortification of the Senses, which our Lord gives us on the Altar.

First Point.—Our Divine Lord, not content with giving us His sacred flesh at Communion as a preservative against sin, and as a sovereign means of attaining a high degree of purity, presents us likewise in the Sacrament of His love with the most perfect example of that mortification so indispensably necessary for acquiring the virtue of Chastity. Though Jesus Christ is corporally present in the Holy Eucharist, His operations therein are all spiritual; He does not see, hear, or feel through the agency of the corporal senses; He preserves an eternal silence; He seems divested even of life, hidden as He is under the accidents of an inanimate substance. Can you desire a more perfect model of absolute mortification of the senses? or can you seek more convincing arguments to induce you to embrace its practice with fervour? Will not love stronger than death compel you to study a virtue which assimilates the soul to her annihilated God and Saviour? Shall it be said you refused to sacrifice anything for Him who has sacrificed so much for you?

Second Point.—Jesus Christ is present on our Altars as an immaculate Victim constantly immolated to the glory of His eternal Father. In like manner, by the Vow of Chastity, you sacrifice to God your sensual life, and assume the quality of a victim, which is to be daily consumed, and never totally destroyed until the end of existence. Do not dread the mystical immolation of your being, which renders you like the Son of God, and consumes your life and energies for the greater glory of their Creator. Constantly bear in mind your glorious title of a victim of Jesus Christ; renounce, for His sake, the gratification of your senses, and all the vain pleasures of this earth, which you cannot lawfully seek, now that having sacrificed your life and your faculties to God, you have thereby centred the capability of enjoyment in Him alone.

Third Point.—Jesus Christ appears lifeless under the inanimate form which veils His glories on our Altars; yet in reality He is animated by a Divine principle of existence, and possesses the four qualities of a glorified body—brightness, impassibility, agility, and subtility; so it is with the perfectly mortified, or, more correctly speaking, the spiritually dead, whose life, as the Apostle tells us, "is hidden with Christ in God," and who, having shared here below in the humiliations of their Divine model, *shall* hereafter *appear with Him in glory.* (Col. iii. 3, 4.) They too are invested with the four qualities, peculiar to a glorified body,—brightness shall not only encompass their mortal envelope in Heaven, but darting its piercing rays into their understanding, it enables them even on earth to dive into the ocean of God's infinite perfections. "Whom shall He teach knowledge?" said the Prophet Isaiah, "and whom shall He make to understand the hearing? Them that are weaned from the milk of earthly pleasures." (Isaiah, xxviii. 9.) The example of their exterior modesty and reserve is as a light shining on all who behold it. 2nd. They are impassible, secure against the revolt of passions which they have so perfectly subdued; and quite insensible to many little annoyances and inconveniences which disturb the peace of the immortified. 3rd. They may be said to possess the quality of subtility, which planes their way through the innumerable difficulties attendant on the practise of virtue, difficulties more than sufficient to deter such as are ignorant of the necessary doctrine of self-denial. 4th. In fine, they are agile and fervent in the service of God; their body, subdued by constant mortification, no longer weighs down the soul, but seems, as St. Paulinus observes, "*to have been itself spiritualized.*" The prospect of so desirable a life should animate you to proceed courageously in the path leading to death to self, the path of mortification. Make a visit to the Blessed Sacrament to implore grace to do so; since Jesus Christ presents Himself to you on the Altar not only as the model on which you must form yourself, but likewise as the source of that strength, without which you cannot execute the good desires he has inspired.

FRIDAY.

FIRST MEDITATION.

On the perfect Examplo of Chastity and Mortification which our Divine Lord presents us on the Cross.

First Point.—Arguments are not requisite to prove the perfect mortification exhibited by Jesus Christ on the Cross—a single glance at the Victim for our sins shows Him to have been indeed *the man of sorrows.* (Isaiah, liii. 3.) Consider His sacred body, extended on the hard bed of the cross, bleeding in every pore, agonizing in every limb. Contemplate His eyes nearly glazed in death, resting only on His merciless enemies or on His sorrowing mother and disciple, whose anguish adds a new wound to His breaking heart. His ears are assailed by insults and blasphemies; His tongue is moistened only with vinegar and gall; in fine, His whole body is a prey to unmitigated torture. Even His soul is inaccessible to consolation, either from God his Father or from creatures. Kneeling in spirit at the foot of the cross, contemplate the suffering Victim who hangs on it, for the darkness which should conceal all creatures from you cannot shroud *Him* from the eyes of faith. Behold Him, then, with respect and love, and, for His sake, refrain from the indulgence of your senses, and treat your body with prudent severity, that you may be entitled to say with the Apostle, "I bear the marks of the Lord Jesus in my body." (Gal. xi. 17.)

Second Point.—Jesus Christ endured the torments of the cross only to crucify with Himself the old man, of whom the Apostle speaks, that is, to destroy the perverse inclinations of corrupt nature, and to subdue the revolts of the flesh against the spirit. This He has effected by His death, delivering us by Baptism from the captivity of sin, restoring us to the glorious freedom of the children of God; and teaching us, by His example, how to mortify and crucify those vicious inclinations which the grace of Baptism does not destroy, but which ever urge man to gratify his sensual appetites. "They that are Christ's have crucified their flesh, with the vices and concupiscences" (Gal. v. 24), "always bearing about in their body the mortification of Jesus, that the life also of Jesus may be made manifest in them." (2 Cor. iv. 10.) If you desire to belong to Jesus Christ, and to resemble Him, embrace the fervent, constant practice of mortification. By the Cross you must ascend to Heaven, and by mortification alone can you attain perfect purity, and the high rewards promised thereto.

Third Point.—The preceding points must have convinced you, that the consideration of the passion of Christ is a sovereign means of resisting our natural inclination to gratify the senses, and a preservative against impure temptations. "There is no more powerful remedy against concupiscence," says St. Augustine, "than the death of Jesus Christ and the contemplation of His wounds." The sight of our crucified Redeemer must inspire the love of mortification, for how can we behold Him in anguish, and not declare with St. Bernard, "that it is shameful to be a delicate member under a head crowned with thorns." Meditate frequently on the passion of Christ, "that the memory of Him who suffered for you may be indelibly engraven on your heart," according to the advice of St. Augustine, and that in the words of St. Ambrose, "the Cross of your Redeemer may be present to you, even when your corporal faculties are absorbed in sleep."

Aspirations.—"A bloody Spouse art thou to me." (Exodus, iv. 25.) "When I behold Thee, O Lord, covered with wounds for my sake, I desire never to be free from suffering."

The Lecture.—Twenty-second and twenty-third chapters of the Treatise on Mortification in Rodriguez.

For the Practice, see "Supplement."

SECOND MEDITATION.

On the Renunciation of Sensual Pleasures, by the Vow of Chastity.

Place yourself at the foot of the Cross, and considering our Divine Redeemer plunged in an ocean of anguish, offer Him the sacrifice of your whole being. Renounce for His love the power of exchanging your present state for a worldly condition. Offer Him the sacrifice of your freedom, choosing Him for your only spouse, your master, your support, your consolation, and the sole object of your love. Secondly, renounce the esteem you may feel for the pleasures and honours the world values, declaring that, even though these vain joys were really worthy your ambition, you would willingly forego them to place all happiness in God alone. Thirdly, offer to Christ the sacrifice of your senses, resolving to mortify your eyes, ears, tongue, &c., and embracing the mortification, austerity, and constant subjection, so necessary for the preservation of purity. Fourthly, present to your Divine Spouse the tribute of your undivided heart and affections, laying at His feet all inordinate attachment to creatures. Fifthly, renounce for your future life all excessive anxiety about your concerns; cast your solicitude on the Lord, since having chosen Him for your spouse, your interests must in future be His. Perform this exercise with great fervour, and an ardent desire to give up all created things, that you may be united to Jesus Christ. Say to Him with St. Augustine, "O Lord, who art a consuming fire, inflame me with the ardours of Thy burning charity, replenish me with Thy heavenly sweetness, teach me to sigh for the possession of Thee, who art spotless purity and immaculate sanctity, that being inflamed with Thy love, I may perfectly devote my heart to Thee, and admit no creature into the sanctuary Thou hast chosen for Thyself alone.

SATURDAY.

FIRST MEDITATION.

On the perfect Example of Chastity, which the Life of the Blessed Virgin affords us.

First Point.—The blessed Mother of God is the second model of purity proposed to your consideration. She, the glory of your sex, first raised the standard of Virginity, and is therefore peculiarly entitled to your respect and imitation. From her words to the Angel, recorded in St. Luke, it may be inferred that she had made a Vow of Chastity. "How shall this be done," she inquired—"because I know not man?" (St. Luke, i. 34.) So highly did she prize the angelic virtue of purity, that she preferred its preservation, to the dignity of Mother of God; knowing, as Saint Anselm observes, "that her union with the eternal source of all purity, would be proportioned to the degree in which that virtue should be found to exist in her heart." Learn from this example the high esteem in which you should hold it, and the watchful solicitude with which you should guard it. Beg of the Mother of God to obtain it for you in an eminent degree, and remember that one of the most efficacious preservatives against the contrary vice, is devotion to the Queen of Virgins.

Second Point.—From the immaculate purity of the Blessed Virgin, resulted that perfect exterior modesty, which regulates the senses and whole deportment. This virtue was conspicuous in the Blessed Virgin, "whose countenance," says St. Ambrose, "was meek; whose words were ever under control; whose whole conduct was reserved; whose voice was gentle; whose exterior modesty was a perfect emblem of her interior sanctity." So greatly did she excel in this virtue, that St. Denis, who had seen her, says, had he not been instructed in the Faith, the beauty of her countenance and the modesty of her deportment would have led him to suppose her a Divinity, instead of a mortal. This is the virtue peculiarly proposed to your imitation, after the example of the Queen of Virgins, which should be ever present to you. Implore it through the intercession of the Blessed Virgin, and see what you have to correct on the subject.

Third Point.—Consider the high degree of perfection to which the purity of the Blessed Virgin has elevated her. This virtue renders man like to the Angels—like to God himself; if this be its result in ordinary creatures, in no one was that result ever produced in so high a degree of perfection, as in the Queen of Angels. In giving birth to the Son of God, and still remaining a Virgin, she presents us a bright image of the Godhead, united to His fecundity. Her angelic chastity disposed her to be, not only the Mother, but also the Spouse of Jesus Christ, who loved her more than all created beings; who lavished on her the abundance of spiritual gifts and graces, and appointed her Mother of the elect, who are the children of her adoption. Rejoice at the elevation of the glorious Virgin; return thanks to the adorable Trinity, for the graces bestowed on her as the reward of her purity; desire to imitate this virtue, that you may share in a proportionate degree in its advantages, and implore the mediation of your good Mother for obtaining these graces from her Divine Son.

Aspirations.—"Let my heart be undefiled in thy justifications, that I may not be confounded." (Ps. cxviii. 80.)

Address yourself to the Blessed Virgin. "O most pure Virgin, obtain that I may share in thy purity and thy profound humility."

The Lecture.—24th chapter of the First Part of Platus.

For the Practice, see "Supplement."

SECOND MEDITATION.

At your evening Meditation, read the chapter of the Constitutions on Chastity; observe the high degree of perfection it prescribes, and the motives it presents for faithfully observing your vow. Take a cursory view of the faults you may have to reproach yourself with on this point; humble yourself for them before God; implore His forgiveness, and resolve to avoid in future the faintest shadow of sin.

Examine next, more in detail, the faults into which you are led by attachment to creatures and immortification of the senses. 1st. See if any created object occupies your thoughts, disturbs the peace of your mind, leads you to break any rule, or to commit any other imperfection. 2nd. If you mortify your sight, when the indulgence of it may be dangerous to your soul, for example, by exciting esteem for worldly vanities, or leading to dissipation, and the loss of interior recollection. 3rd. If you mortify your hearing, by refusing to listen to sinful conversation, useless words, uncharitable discourses, worldly news, profane songs, &c., &c., which only serve to distract the mind. Resolve in future to avoid the occasions of all such conversations, if possible; or at least to turn your thoughts to God, and never to lead by your questions to the protraction of an imperfect discourse. 4th. If you indulge yourself by the use of perfumes, either procuring them expressly, or using them too eagerly, when you chance to meet them. If, on the contrary, you submit impatiently to whatever mortifies your sense of smelling. 5th. If you ever infringe the rule which prohibits eating between meals without permission. If you ever trivially exceed the limits of temperance, looking more to sensual gratification than to mere necessity. If you allow your thoughts to be occupied about your corporal food; if you are contented with that which is given you, or if you ever murmur at the want of anything. If you refuse to partake of such things as you may not happen to like. 6th. With regard to mortification of the tongue, examine how you observe the rule of silence, and see if at the times when you are permitted to speak, you refrain from such conversations as you have been already warned against, in the article on the mortification of the sense of hearing. 7th. In fine, consider how you treat your body, if you seek its ease, and study its convenience in the repose allowed it. If you complain of cold, heat, fatigue, &c.,

or permit any such trifling inconvenience to interfere with your duties. Having examined your faults on these various heads, implore pardon for them, and beseech our Divine Lord to purify your soul, with all its faculties, and your body with all its senses, through the merits of the sufferings in which He lived and died. Lastly, briefly revolve in mind the reflections which made most impression on you during the Meditations of this week, and the good resolutions resulting from them, which you will renew in the presence of God, observing particularly the points which require reformation. Write them at your leisure, and beseech the Blessed Virgin to present them to her Divine Son, and to obtain for you fidelity to the inspirations of His grace.

EXERCISES FOR THE WEEK OF OBEDIENCE.

Let your great aim this week be to acquire a perfect renunciation of your will and judgment, that you may learn to submit both unhesitatingly to your Superiors; to accept with indifference all that God ordains for you, and to annihilate your desires and inclinations, that the will of the Almighty may alone exist in and reign over you. Produce frequent interior acts of renunciation of your will; of abandonment to the will of God and your Superiors; of readiness to do and suffer all that is most repugnant to your inclinations, and of ardent desire that the designs of God may be perfectly accomplished in you. Say frequently and fervently, "*Thy kingdom come—Thy will be done.*" In fine, let obedience be the animating motive of even your most trivial actions; let it influence your exterior practices, and lead you to observe perfectly every point of rule. 2nd. Submit your will and judgment, even to your inferiors, when an opportunity occurs of preferring their inclinations to your own, that you may thereby habituate yourself to a more perfect submission. Read the chapter of the Constitutions on Obedience, and the last chapter of the Rule of St. Augustine.

SUNDAY.

FIRST MEDITATION.

On Obedience.

First Point.—In the practice of this virtue is included the third degree of self-renunciation, without which we cannot attain to intimate union with God. Riches are sacrificed by the vow of Poverty; sensual pleasures by that of Chastity; but by Obedience, we renounce ourselves, our will, and judgment. The excellence of this vow surpasses that of the other two, 1st.: because the soul thereby sacrifices her two most noble faculties, her will and understanding, which far exceed in dignity all material objects. 2nd. Because it is from this vow the two others derive their value, being meritorious only inasmuch as they are conformable to the Divine will. Now, the property of obedience is to regulate all our actions by this infallible criterion of sanctity. 3rd. Because by regulating the will, which is the source of life and death, it reforms the whole man, whereas, the other vows effect only a partial reformation. Beg of God to give you grace to love and practise this vow, with all the perfection of which you are capable.

Second Point.—Jesus Christ descended from Heaven to teach us the sublime perfection of the Gospel, and for this end He preached voluntary poverty, chastity, and that self-renunciation which is effected by obedience. "If any man will come after me, let him deny himself, and take up his cross and follow me." (St. Matt. xxi. 24.) If any one mean to attain heaven, after my example, let him renounce his will and judgment, and bearing the cross of the perpetual mortification of his desires and inclinations, let him follow me, by perfect obedience, and submission to my will. This admirable doctrine was reserved for Jesus Christ, who knowing that the perversion of man results from the evil tendency of his will, applied thereto a suitable remedy, in the virtue of obedience, that we might be reformed in the newness of our mind, and prove what is the good, and the acceptable, and the perfect will of God" (Rom. xi. 2), in which consists our sanctification and perfection.

Third Point.— Consider the example our Lord has left us of this virtue. In the first moment of his Incarnation, he offered Himself to His Father, as the Apostle tells us, saying to Him, as David had prophesied: "Sacrifice and oblation Thou wouldst not; . . . Holocaust for sin did not please Thee: Then said I, behold I come: in the head of the book it is written of me: That I should do Thy will: O my God I have desired it, and Thy law in the midst of my heart." (Ps. xxxix. 7, 8, 9.) He then accepted all the pains of His life, and the anguish of His death, in the spirit of perfect obedience to His Father. Until the age of thirty He lived submissive to His Blessed Mother and St. Joseph; and has left us scarcely any account of those years, further than, "that He was subject to them." (St. Luke, ii. 51.) His whole life was but one continued act of submission to His Father's will, which He called his *meat*. (St. John, iv. 34.)

In fine, "He sacrificed His life," as St. Gregory observes, "rather than sacrifice His obedience." Form yourself on this Model; you cannot consider it unreasonable to submit to God, and those who hold His place, after you have seen the Lord of Glory obedient to man. Deplore your past attachment to your own will, and ask the grace to spend the remainder of your life in the practice of perfect obedience.

Aspirations.—Teach me to do Thy will, for Thou art my God. (Ps. cxlii. 10.) Offer yourself to-day without reserve to Jesus Christ, in the holy Communion, and beseech Him to take entire possession of your heart.

The Lecture.—1st, 11th, and 17th chapters of the Treatise on Obedience in Rodriguez.

SECOND MEDITATION.

On the Excellence of Obedience.

First Point.—To comprehend the excellence of obedience, we must be convinced, that by this virtue we subject ourselves, not to the will of man, but to the will of God, whose place man holds in our regard. The words of our Lord are explicit, when having established the Apostles the lawful superiors of the faithful, He said, "he that heareth you, heareth me; and he that despiseth you, despiseth me." (St. Luke, x. 16.) St. Paul assures us, "that there is no power but from God, and he that resisteth the power, resisteth the ordinance of God." (Eph. vi. 5.) Draw from this truth the following conclusions. 1st. Always to see God in your superiors, never allowing your submission to be influenced by their personal qualities, their affection for you, or any such human consideration, which frequently prevents the merit of obedience. As a result of this first resolution, determine to receive their orders with great submission and profound respect, considering the will of God more clearly manifested to you by their means, than if an angel from Heaven declared it. It is of Faith that God governs us by the lawfully established powers, and it is certain that we must obey, where there is no manifest sin.

Second Point.—Having established the maxim, that to submit to superiors is to submit to the will of God, it is easy to infer the second advantage of obedience, which is to elevate the soul to high perfection, consisting in union with God, as our Lord assured the Apostles—" He that hath my commandments, and keepeth them: he it is that loveth me." (St. John, xiv. 21.) And St. John, in his first Epistle, says, that " he that keepeth the word of God is perfected." (1 John, ii. 5.) How can we prove our love for God more effectually than by renouncing our own will to do His? Is it not to this spiritual sacrifice St. Denis alludes, when he says, that Divine love produces ecstacies, transporting the soul it animates, out of herself, into the object of her tenderness, and substituting God's will for hers? Perfect obedience produces this effect, uniting our will to that of God; so that it is no longer we who live and act, but Jesus Christ, who lives and acts in us,—our actions springing from the same source whence His arise—viz. the Divine will. Desire ardently to share in these great advantages, and for this end resolve to animate your acts of obedience, by the motive of love, according to the recommendation of Saint Peter, in his first Epistle: " Purify your souls in the obedience of charity (i. 22), " that you may be among those who are faithful in love" (Wis. iii. 9), and who unconditionally submit to God in all things. Thus will you render the yoke of obedience most sweet and light.

Third Point.—By obedience, we give great glory to God, and in this consists its third excellence. He has Himself delared, that He prefers obedience even to sacrifice, by which man renders Him supreme honour. (1 Kings, xv. 22.) The reason is, that obedience sacrifices to God the most excellent part of His most noble creature, viz. the will and liberty of man; and by thus subjecting to His sovereign dominion the most prized of His works, it glorifies Him more than by the sacrifice of other creatures formed for the use of man. As by obedience we give great glory to God, our liberal Master, in return, bestows peculiar favours on the soul which submits unreservedly to Him by the perfect practice of this virtue. "Thou shalt be called," says He by the Prophet Isaiah, "by a new name, which the mouth of the Lord shall name. And thou shalt be a crown of glory in the hand of the Lord, and a royal diadem in the hand of thy God. Thou shalt no more be called forsaken, but thou shalt be called, my pleasure in her." (Isaiah, lxii. 2, 3, 4.) Such are the glorious privileges of the truly obedient, who observe exactly the orders of their Superiors, and the rules of their Institute. The Almighty looks with complacency on such souls as on the living images of His Son, whom He calls by the same Prophet, "the man of His own will." (Isaiah, xlvi. 11.) Implore grace to practise this meritorious virtue, in imitation of our Lord.

MONDAY.

FIRST MEDITATION.

On the Advantages of Obedience.

First Point.—Obedience derives its first excellence from the union it establishes between the will of man and that of God. Its first great advantage to the soul is, that it enables her to submit to the decrees of God, and walk in the path marked out by His Providence; following this rule we cannot go astray. Obedience is a sure preservative against the dangers of ignorance and error, inseparable companions of all who are led by their own judgment, guiding them into "a way which seemeth just, but the end thereof leads to death." (Proverbs, xiv. 12.) Resolve to enter on the road of obedience, which so securely conducts to God. Renounce your own will and judgment, which are insurmountable obstacles to the practice of this virtue, and if yielded to, infallibly lead to destruction. Beg the grace to abandon yourself totally and unconditionally into the hands of God by the Vow of Obedience.

Second Point.—The second advantage of obedience, says Saint Gregory, "is, that from it proceed all other virtues," which it teaches in perfection. It imparts merit to human actions, substituting the most holy and adorable will of God for the corrupt and vitiated will of man; a sublime motive, which exalts the most common and indifferent actions, and affords an easy means of perpetually amassing treasures for eternity. "How precious," says Saint Jerome, "and how numerous are the advantages of obedience, which includes in itself the perfection of all virtues, and leads us to Jesus Christ by a secure and easy path!" Produce the same affections as at the first point.

Third Point.—Meditate in the spirit of deep gratitude on the advantages of obedience, as enumerated by the Prophet in the twenty-second Psalm, which is descriptive of the happiness of those who abandon themselves to the guidance of God, and may be applied as follows to the Religious soul. "The Lord rules me, and I shall want nothing:" or according to the explanation of Saint Jerom, the Lord is my Shepherd; He will watch over me, as the sheep of His fold; He has led me into the sanctuary of Religion, as into a place of abundant pasture. He has given me free access to the Sacraments, from which flow streams of grace, whereby my spiritual thirst is satiated, and my soul nourished and strengthened. He has drawn me to Himself by the abundance of His favours, and has converted my soul. Then leading me by the paths of justice, He has guided my steps in the way of virtue, for the glory of His name. Though I should walk amidst the darkness of temptation and tribulation, I will fear no evil, for Thou, O Lord, art with me. The corrections of my Superiors, which lead me back to the right road when I am inclined to stray from it, and their exhortations which support my tottering steps and animate my failing courage, are to me an indescribable consolation. Thou hast prepared a table against my enemies, and hast presented me the delicious banquet of Thy holy will, which was the food of Thy Divine Son on earth. In fulfilling Thy adorable will, I experience the unction of Thy grace, and even the chalice of tribulation, which, after the example of Jesus Christ, I desire to drink in obedience to Thy command, is transformed into the inebriating wine of Thy consolations, the reward of adherence to Thy law. My soul is animated with a holy hope, that Thy mercy will follow me all the days of my life, since I have resolved to spend it in the fervent practice of obedience. I firmly trust that it will give me admittance even into Thy glorious temple, that I may dwell there for ever, and praise Thy name eternally. Such is the happy lot of a soul who has subjected herself totally to the light yoke of obedience. Thank our Divine Lord for having called you to Religion, where you may experience the advantages of this meritorious virtue, and implore grace never to swerve from the duties it imposes.

Aspirations.—"I cannot of myself do anything, because I seek not to do my own will, but the will of Him that sent me." (St. John, v. 30.)

Shall not my soul be subject to God, "for from Him is my salvation?" (Ps. lxi. 2.)

The Lecture.—The second and third chapters of the same Treatise of Rodriguez.

For the Practice see "Supplement."

SECOND MEDITATION.

On the Happiness of Obedience.

First Point.—The virtue of obedience is not only productive of the advantages on which you have meditated, but is also a source of happiness even on earth. Nothing is so conformable to man's natural inclination, as to do his own will without opposition or restraint. Now, though the assertion at first appears a contradiction, it may be truly said, that obedience is a sure means of attaining this end. For though the truly obedient perpetually sacrifice their inclinations to the commands of others, yet the will which they have renounced, becomes so closely united with that of God, that they cease to have any will but His. Thus, they rise and retire to rest at the hour most suited to their inclinations, and all things which happen to them are perfectly in accordance with their wishes, because they desire only what God wills, and thereby enter on the road of perfect liberty, wherein nothing opposes or restrains them. "They become as Gods," says Saint Bonaventure, "in the omnipotence of their will." What potentate of earth can say in truth, that he meets no obstacle to the accomplishment of his wishes? This privilege belongs only to those who are perfectly subject to the dominion of God. The liberal Master, to whom they have sacrificed their will, takes pleasure in gratifying their inclinations and condescending to their desires. Can you refuse to exchange your vitiated will, for the holy will of the Most High; or can you prefer the slavery of your own dominion, to the happy liberty of the children of God? The matter is of great importance, and well deserves your serious consideration.

Second Point.—The second advantage of obedience is the peace and tranquillity it invariably diffuses in the heart wherein it has taken deep root. "Peace," according to Saint Augustine, "is nothing more than the tranquillity resulting from perfect order; it is a certain disposition, which assigns to each object its appropriate position." This effect is admirably produced by obedience, which places each individual in the precise situation she is destined by the Almighty to fill, and as this situation is the centre of her repose, nothing can await her in any other but dissatisfaction and anxiety. "Thus saith the Lord thy Redeemer, the holy one of Israel, I am the Lord thy

God, that teach thee profitable things, that govern thee in the way that thou walkest. O that thou hadst hearkened to my commandments, and fulfilled them; thy peace had been as a river, and thy justice as the waves of the sea." (Isaiah, xlviii. 17, 18.) Contrast the misery of those, whose self-will is perpetually thwarted both by God and man, with the calm tranquillity of the perfectly obedient soul; resolve to merit the treasure of peace, by unqualified submission to the Almighty, and to your Superiors, who hold His place in your regard.

Third Point.—God not only bestows on the truly obedient, the happy liberty and calm peace of His children, but also lavishes on them the abundance of His Divine consolations. Simplicity of understanding and submission of will have introduced them to the happy state of spiritual infancy, therefore, the Lord declares by the Prophet, "As one whom the mother caresseth; so will I comfort you—you shall be carried at the breasts, and upon the knees they shall caress you." (Isaiah, lxvi. 13, 12.) The accomplishment of the Divine will is in itself a delicious food, to those who have renounced the direction of themselves; "they shall be delighted in the Lord, and lifted up above the high places of the earth, and fed with the inheritance of Jacob their Father." (Isaiah, lviii. 14.) This inheritance is no other than that of which the Psalmist makes mention, when he says, "O Lord my portion, I have said, I would keep Thy law, I will seek Thy commandments, which are my inheritance, with my whole heart." (Ps. cxviii. 57, 69.) The peace and joy, found in their observance, are beautifully expressed by the same Prophet: "How sweet are Thy words to my palate! more than honey to my mouth." (Ibid. 103.) Such are the temporal rewards attached to the fervent practice of obedience ; resolve to entitle yourself to a share in them, by the perfect renunciation of your will, from which proceed all your pains and disquietudes. Beseech our Divine Lord to grant you this grace through the merits of His submission to the decrees of His eternal Father, and to the will of creatures, for His sake.

TUESDAY.

FIRST MEDITATION.

On the Practice of the Vow of Obedience.

First Point.—The Vow of Obedience consists in the renunciation of self-will, which is thereby resigned, for the love of God, into the hands of Superiors, with the obligation of submitting in future to their commands, provided they involve no manifest sin. This virtue admits of three degrees of perfection : 1st. To obey the orders of Superiors. 2nd. To execute them with conformity of will. 3rd. With submission of judgment. With regard to the first, and lowest degree, we must not only submit, when commanded in virtue of obedience, in which case, a refusal to comply would entail the dreadful guilt of a breach of the Vow, but we should obey all the orders of Superiors, general and particular; even anticipating their wishes, when they have been manifested by any exterior sign, as the Constitutions require. Consider the example our Lord has given us of the first degree of obedience : it was so perfect, so entire, that He was well entitled to exclaim in His last moments on the cross, "*all is consummated ;*" I have completed the work entrusted to me by my Father. Examine how far your conduct has been an imitation of your Divine Model; implore pardon for your past faults against obedience, and determine to practise it in future with generosity and perseverance.

Second Point.—The second degree of obedience consists in not only executing exteriorly the command imposed, but in likewise conforming the will to that of Superiors, labouring constantly for this end to mortify the desires and inclinations of nature, and to destroy self-will, of which, as Saint Climacus says, "obedience is the tomb." Those who have attained the perfection of this grace have but one desire, which is to be totally divested of all desires. They are, according to the excellent comparison of Saint Ignatius, like a lifeless body, which makes no resistance whatever is done with it; being perfectly dead to their own inclinations, the will of God and their Superiors alone sets them in motion. "The obedient man shall speak of victory" (Prov. xxi. 28), says the Wise Man; being guided and influenced, under all circumstances, by the will of God, which nothing can resist, he will perpetually triumph over himself, the flesh, the world, and the devil. We have a perfect example of this absolute submission in our Divine Redeemer, who declared, "that His meat was to do the will of Him who sent Him;" "that He might perfect His work." (St. John, iv. 34.) Having examined in what manner you practise the third degree of obedience, resolve in future to direct your attention and efforts to it, as to the most important point of the spiritual and religious life.

Third Point.—The second degree of perfect obedience is to obey with submission of judgment, and without examining the motives of the command imposed, in all cases where there is no manifest sin; believing with humility that the orders given are just and reasonable; and never listening to the arguments which nature may suggest to the contrary. "Obedience," says St. John Climacus, "is submission without examination or discussion; it is a voluntary death to self; a life which excludes curiosity; a renunciation of worldly prudence; but at the same time the perfection of heavenly wisdom. The third degree of obedience is the most sublime, because it subjects man's noblest faculty of judgment to the dominion of God. It perfects the two other degrees, consummating the sacrifice, and rendering it a holocaust, which consumes the victim without any reserve. The motive of this unqualified obedience should be a firm belief, that God guides and governs us by Superiors; the nature of their commands should have no influence on our submission, for in this case, there would be danger of a failure whenever their orders seem unjust or unreasonable. If we consider the commands of Superiors, as an interpretation of God's orders to us, we shall assuredly acknowledge that His decrees are just and lawful, and as a necessary consequence we shall submit blindly and respectfully to the authorities He has appointed to communicate to us His divine will. "I will lead the blind, said the Lord, into the way which they know not; and into the paths of which they were ignorant," and which they rejoice at being strangers to, that they may be compelled to trust more implicitly to my guidance. "I will make darkness light before them, giving them heavenly wisdom as a substitute for the worldly prudence they have renounced. I will make crooked things straight, and they shall see that I have not forsaken them." (Isaiah, xlii. 16.) It is now at your option either to follow the deceitful light of your own judgment, which will infallibly guide you to destruction; or, by the practice of obedience, to submit to the dominion of God, who will indubitably lead you to eternal happiness. Beseech our Lord to strengthen you to renounce your judgment; resolve firmly to do so at all times, but principally on those occasions, when you feel it most difficult to submit to the yoke of obedience.

Aspirations.—"Speak, Lord, for Thy servant heareth." (1 Kings, iii. 9.)

"Lord, what wilt Thou have me to do?" (Acts, ix. 6.)

"My heart is ready, O God, my heart is ready." (Ps. cvii. 2.)

"I am become as a beast before Thee: and I am always with Thee." (Ps. lxxii. 23.)

The Lecture.—Fourth, sixth, and seventh chapters of the same Treatise in Rodriguez.

For the Practice, see "Supplement."

SECOND MEDITATION.

On the Qualities necessary for the Perfection of Obedience.

First Point.—This Meditation explains more fully the obligations of obedience, and is but a continuation of the preceding. Submission must embrace all the details specified by the Rule, which says—"Their obedience must extend to all things, great and small, easy or difficult, repugnant to their feelings or judgment." The words, "all things," sufficiently proves that obedience must be universal. It must extend, 1st, to all things commanded, whether they be pleasing or disagreeable, conformable or opposed to the will or judgment; whether they lead to our exaltation or humiliation, &c. It must extend, 2ndly, to all persons in authority, whether they be agreeable or repugnant to our natural inclinations, young or old, &c.; nothing can dispense with the obligations of obedience. From this principle of universal obedience, springs a disposition to submit as readily to the subordinate authorities, in what regards their jurisdiction, as to the Superior herself. In fine, it includes obedience at all times, and in all places, depriving the soul which has willingly embraced its salutary restraints, of power to shake off the yoke even for a moment. To consider God alone in Superiors, never looking to their personal qualifications, is, as you have already seen, the most effectual means of practising this universal submission. You will then be indifferent to who is placed over you, and you will find all commands pleasing and easy, because in all you will see only the will of God, which alone you should seek. Accustom yourself to act on these principles; obey generously, never permitting any earthly consideration to influence your submission. Form your obedience on that of your adorable Model, Jesus Christ, who has left you so perfect an example of subjection at all times, in all places, and to all persons.

Second Point.—Obedience, in its practical details, must be exact and entire; it does not admit of omissions, negligence, or imperfection in the execution of the orders imposed. Secondly, it must be so prompt and unhesitating, as, in the words of your Constitutions, to leave the letter unfinished, and the stitch imperfect." Thirdly, it must be joyful and willing, free from repining or discontent. The happiness of accomplishing the will of God, manifested by Superiors, should suffice to fill the heart with fervour and consolation. Sensible satisfaction, which is not always under your control, is not requisite to compliance with this third condition of obedience; it suffices that the will generously overcome the repugnance of the inferior part, and endeavour to place its satisfaction in the fulfilment of the Divine will. The repetition of the beautiful form of prayer taught by our Redeemer, should animate us to the constant practice of obedience. In the petition, "Thy will be done on earth as it is in heaven," we are presented with no less a model of obedience than that rendered to God by the blessed spirits, who, in the words of the Psalmist, "are mighty in strength to execute His word" (Ps. cii. 20), and accomplish His will with so much promptitude, fervour, and charity, as to be compared for this reason to wind and fire, whose effects are so prompt and active. The Religious life is an angelical state, and therefore imposes a peculiar obligation of imitating the heavenly spirits. Implore the grace to do so, by their powerful intercession.

Third Point.—The third point to be considered is the duration of the obligation to obey. It must extend to your whole life, though that were to last a century:—the Vow of Obedience is not made only for the Noviciate; for a few years after the Profession, or for the superiority of any particular individual, but it is made for ever; your submission must have no other limits than those which Jesus Christ put to His. "He," your Model, "was obedient unto death" (Phil. ii. 8), "and being consummated in obedience, He became the cause of eternal salvation to all that obey Him." (Heb. v. 9.) Beg of God to give you the treasure of perseverance, which alone is crowned, and animate yourself to labour in acquiring it, by establishing your obedience on the firm foundation which has now formed the subject of your considerations.

WEDNESDAY.

FIRST MEDITATION.

On the Observance of Rule.

First Point.—The faithful observance of Rule is an important part of obedience; it should be attended to as punctually as the orders of Superiors, because the will of God is equally manifested by both. The first, of many important reasons which might be alleged to prove the necessity of fidelity to your Rules, is, that they are not the invention of mere unaided human wisdom, but an efficacious means of perfection, inspired by God Himself, who guides, by His holy Spirit, the Saintly Founders of all approved Religious Orders. 2nd. The Rules and Constitutions of your Monastery comprise all the perfection required of you, and, if perfectly adhered to, will infallibly sanctify you, as their faithful observance has already sanctified many fervent souls. 3rd. Your Rules will form the subject of your final examination before the awful tribunal of your Almighty judge. 4th. They are the best test of your fidelity and obedience to God, who requires you to observe them for His love, and they furnish you with a continual opportunity of proving the sincerity of your desire to please Him, and your absolute submission to His Divine will. 5. By failing in the observance of your Rules you displease God, you wound your conscience, you grieve your Superiors, you give bad example, you disturb the exact order of your Monastery, and, if you do not entirely destroy the religious spirit, you, at least, prepare the way for relaxation; and, in fine, you deprive yourself of the numberless special graces reserved for those who respect and adhere to the Rules of their state. Serious reflection on these five important considerations must convince you of the necessity of observing your Rules with love and reverence, esteeming them as the channel through which the will of God is made known to you. Receive them today with renewed veneration from the hand of your Divine Lord, and imagine that in presenting you with them, He says, "This is the book of the commandments of God: and the law that is for ever: all they that keep it shall come to life, but they that have forsaken it, to death. Return, and take hold of it, walk in the way by its brightness, in the presence of the light thereof." (Baruch, iv. 1, 2.) How great should be your gratitude to God for having provided you with an infallible means of discerning His will on all occasions; He has not done so to innumerable other souls, who walk in the darkness of their own perverted judgment and corrupt will. Resolve to keep your Rules with inviolable fidelity, and strict exactness, and beg the graces necessary for this end.

Second Point.—The observance of the Rules should be attended with the same conditions as the practice of obedience. It must be accompanied with conformity of will, and submission of judgment; your heart must be so deeply imbued with the spirit of Rule, that that sacred spirit may become, as it were, a substitute for your will and judgment. Your submission to Rule must be exact and universal, it must extend to all times and places, it must be unhesitating and cheerful, it must be formed on the example of our Divine Lord, who said, "I am not come to destroy the law but to fulfil it. For, amen, I say unto you,......one tittle shall not pass of the law till all be fulfilled.' (St. Matt. v. 17, 18.) Make the same declaration with regard to your Rules, and examine how you have observed them hitherto. See if you have kept them in the manner now described, or if, on the contrary, you have adhered to them with repugnance of will and judgment, considering them unreasonable; observing some and violating others, through contempt or dislike of restraint; if, in fine, you have observed them tepidly, without exactness or fervour. After having noticed your most considerable faults in this respect, implore of God, with humility and contrition, to pardon them all.

Third Point.—The means which may most powerfully assist you in the observance of your Rules for the time to come, are, first, a high esteem for them, founded on the considerations presented to your view in the first point, which it would be advisable to reflect on occasionally, particularly when you are inclined to relax. 2nd. A great love for them. Far from considering your Rules as chains which restrain your liberty, and enslave your will, an impression worthy only of tepid, imperfect Religious who have lost the spirit of their vocation, look on them as precious bonds which unite you closely to God,—as a secure path to eternal glory,—as a fruitful source of abundant merit. Let your heart be deeply imbued with the spirit of your Rules, that you may be able to say with your Redeemer, "Thy law, O my God, is in the midst of my heart." (Ps. xxxix. 9.) Love and cherish them ardently, and thereby the difficulty attendant on their observance will vanish, and you will be able to say like the Prophet, "I have run in the way of thy commandments when thou didst enlarge my heart." (Ps.

cxviii. 32). The third means is frequently to read and meditate on them, that you may distinctly comprehend and perfectly reduce them to practice. Consider them as a mirror, wherein you may behold your imperfections, as your holy Father, St. Augustine, recommends; and as a model, according to which your actions, your good works, and, in fine, your whole life should be regulated. Fix a stated time for meditating in this manner on your Rules; resolve to adopt the means which have been suggested to you for this perfect observance, and beg grace to do so.

Aspirations.—"In the head of the book, it is written of me that I should do Thy will: O my God, I have desired it, and Thy law is in the midst of my heart." (Ps. xxxix. 8, 9.) "Thy word is a lamp to my feet, and a light to my paths." (Ibid. xviii. 105.)

The Lecture.—In Rodriguez, 1st, 2nd, 5th, and 6th chapters of the Treatise on the Observance of the Rules.

For the Practice, see "Supplement."

SECOND MEDITATION.

On the Obligation of faithfully discharging the Duties imposed by Obedience.

First Point.—In this Meditation consider the members of the Religious state as a mystic body, of which Jesus Christ is the invisible Head, as He is of the Church in general. Subordinate to His authority, are lawfully constituted Superiors. The members of this mystical body are Religious persons, each of whom has her peculiar office and proper function, tending to the maintenance of the whole. Whence you may conclude, first, that the perfection of a Religious does not depend on the discharge of one duty more than another; on being an eye or a foot to this mysterious body, but in perfectly fulfilling whatever duty may be assigned to her. Secondly, that she must devote herself to the employment marked out out for her, without interfering in any other; for the order and regularity of a Monastery would be as much disturbed by such interference, as the economy of the human system would be were the feet to aim at exercising the functions of the head; or the hands those of the feet, &c. Thirdly, that she should highly esteem the employment assigned her by obedience, considering it as a duty imposed by Jesus Christ Himself, and as a sure means of glorifying God, by the accomplishment of His holy will; of promoting the interest of Religion, and of edifying and serving her neighbour. The serious Meditation of these truths must lead to two important resolutions. First, to be totally indifferent to all employments, neither procuring nor refusing any, but leaving all to the disposal of Superiors, who hold the place of Jesus Christ. Second, to acquit yourself, with the utmost exactness, of those which obedience imposes.

Second Point.—In order perfectly to discharge the duty assigned you by obedience, you must fulfil it in the Spirit of Jesus Christ, of whom you are a member; that is, in the spirit of pure desire to glorify God, and to accomplish His most holy will, for such was the intention by which all the actions of your Divine model were animated. Carefully renounce all imperfect motives, petty interests, desires of the esteem and affection of creatures, and similar earthly views, so unworthy of a Religious soul. Secondly, you must acquit yourself with great exactness and punctuality of all the duties annexed to your charge, considering none as trifling, but discharging all promptly and generously, as the work of the Most High. Thirdly, you must perform your exterior actions with prudence and discretion, avoiding, on the one hand, negligence and indolence; and on the other, precipitation and excessive ardour; the latter dispositions spring from self-love, which desires to succeed at any expense, whereas the soul influenced by the spirit of Jesus Christ discharges her duties serenely and tranquilly, calmly abandoning to God the success of her efforts. Examine what spirit has hitherto guided you in the fulfilment of your duties; you will probably discern many faults, for which implore God's pardon, resolving by His grace to correct all that has been defective hitherto.

Third Point.—The means pointed out to you in the last Meditation, as conducive to the observance of your Rules, may likewise be profitably employed for the perfect discharge of the duties allotted to you by obedience.

These means are, 1st. To esteem your charge as marked out for you by the will of God. 2nd. To love it on this account. 3rd. Occasionally to read the Rules regarding it, examining how you observe them. 4th. In fine, frequently to ask of God, to enable you to acquit yourself thereof with great perfection.

THURSDAY.

FIRST MEDITATION.

The Holy Communion imparts to the Soul a principle of new life, necessary for enabling her to practise perfect Obedience.

First Point.—The corruption of our nature is so great, and the wounds inflicted by the sin of Adam on all the faculties of man, particularly His two noblest powers, the will and understanding, so deep and inveterate, that it became necessary not merely to heal those wounds and rectify that corruption, but totally to regenerate him, making him as it were as a new creature. This end Jesus Christ accomplished by His Incarnation and death; He in a manner re-created the human race in His own person; and by the grace communicated through Baptism and the other Sacraments, He continues to impart His new life to the soul, thus fulfilling the promise, "I will give a new heart, and put a new spirit within you, and I will take away the stony heart out of your flesh, and I will give you a heart of flesh," soft, pliable and unresisting; "and I will put my spirit in the midst of you, and I will cause you to walk in my commandments, and to keep my judgments and do them." (Ezechiel, xxxvi. 26, 27.) Hence you may infer that the divine virtue of obedience, which subjects the will and understanding of man to God, and to creatures who hold the place of God, is not the work of nature, but the fruit of grace. Make an act of Faith in this truth. Secondly, produce acts of Hope, that our Lord will bestow on you the new heart and mind, so necessary for the accomplishment of the Vow of Obedience you are about to pronounce, and earnestly beseech Him to do so.

Second Point.—The most holy Sacrament of the Altar is the principal channel through which this new existence is communicated to us. So close is the union which our Divine Lord therein contracts with the soul, that He imparts to her His heart, His spirit, and His life. "As the living Father hath sent me," He says, "and I live by the Father: so he that eateth me, the same also shall live by me." (St. John, vi. 58.) These words are paraphrased, as follows, by St. Augustine, "I live by my Father, that is, I refer my life to Him, as to one exalted infinitely above me, because by my Incarnation I have humbled myself beneath Him, and in order that the soul should live for me, by referring her being to me, and conforming perfectly to my will, it is necessary that she should participate in my Spirit, by partaking of my flesh. I live for my Father, because I have annihilated myself; man lives for me, because he is infinitely ennobled and exalted." Being thus closely united with Jesus Christ, and vivified by His Spirit, the accomplishment of His will becomes easy and delightful; and the pain and subjection of obedience vanish; according to the words of the Psalmist. "Give bountifully to Thy servant, enliven me: and I shall keep thy words." (Ps. cxviii. 17.) Such is the effect of the holy Communion on those who approach it with great fervour. Sigh for that precious food which is to be the source of so desirable a renewal of life; prepare to receive it with lively faith, unbounded hope, inflamed love, and above all, with an ardent desire to reap from it the fruit it is intended to produce.

Third Point.—As one of the principal effects of the most adorable Sacrament of the Eucharist, as well as one of the chief ends of its institution, is to produce the life of Jesus Christ within us, the desire of participating in that life should form your principal intention in approaching it. "If any one desire life," says St. Augustine, "he not only finds its abundant source in this holy Sacrament, but, likewise, the means of preserving it; let him approach with love and confidence; let him firmly believe the truth of the incomprehensible mystery; let him incorporate himself with Jesus Christ, by a real participation in His sacred flesh, and then he will be vivified by His spirit, because the body of Christ lives but by the spirit of Christ. To be animated by his life, it is necessary to be incorporated with Him, as one of His members; therefore, let your intention in approaching the holy communion be to unite yourself closely to Jesus Christ, that you may be animated by this spirit, and that as the members submit to their head, you may in all things be subject to His holy will, and submissive to the commands of those He has placed over you. Receive our Lord to-day with ardent desire of participating in this divine life. Say, with Saint Augustine, "O life! for which all things live; life, which impartest to me a new principle of existence; life, which art the true source of my being, by which I am strengthened, without which I languish, where art thou? where shall I find Thee, that dying to myself I may live to Thee?"

Aspirations.—"My meat is to do the will of Him that sent me, that I may perfect His work." (St. John, iv. 34.) "Behold, how I loved not only Thy commandments but even Thy counsels, to which I have voluntarily subjected myself; quicken Thou me in Thy mercy, that I may perfectly reduce them to practice." (Ps. cxviii. 159.)

The Lecture.—7th and 8th chapters of the Treatise on Obedience, or the 10th chapter, 1st section, of the first part of the Third Book on the Knowledge and Love of our Lord Jesus Christ," by Saint Jure, treating of the holy communion.

The ardent desire to participate in the divine life of Jesus Christ, with which you should receive him to-day, has been already enlarged on in your meditation.

For the Practice, see " Supplement."

SECOND MEDITATION.

On the Example of Obedience our Lord gives us in the Eucharist.

First Point.—Our Divine Saviour not only imparts to us the spirit of perfect obedience in the holy Communion, but likewise furnishes us with an exterior example of its highest perfection. Not satisfied with living and dying a victim of obedience,—even now though seated on the right hand of His Father as sovereign Monarch of the universe, He has assumed a condition which admits of His still submitting to His own creatures, thereby clearly proving the high value He sets on the virtue of obedience. It is not surprising that man should be subservient to God, but that the Lord of Glory should stoop so low as to obey the voice of man, is a miracle surpassing human comprehension. Implore His forgiveness with confusion and sorrow for having so often refused Him the obedience and docility He justly claims.

Second Point.—Consider the spirit of perfect indifference which accompanies the obedience of our hidden

God and Saviour. 1st. He is indifferent as to places: He remains as willingly in a village as in a city; in a small chapel as in a superb church; though His sacred body were thrown on a dunghill, He would stay there as long as the species lasted; He veils the splendour of His glory equally under a large or a small Host, &c., descending from heaven under all circumstances as soon as the words of consecration are pronounced. 2nd. He obeys with equal indifference all superiors, for, though properly speaking, the sovereign Lord of all creatures can have no superior, nevertheless in this Sacrament He submits to His minister as to His superior, without considering whether he be learned or ignorant, rich or poor, virtuous or vicious, and never failing to obey the sacred words which summon Him from His throne of glory. 3rd. He obeys at all times,—for at whatever hour of the day or night the priest consecrates, He becomes present in the Host. 4th. He is indifferent as to persons, giving Himself indiscriminately to all who approach the Holy Table; to the old and to the young; to both sexes; to poor and rich; illiterate and learned. 5th. He is indifferent as to occupations; He is equally satisfied to remain on the altar a perpetual oblation to His Father, which is a species of contemplative life; or embracing the function of the active life, to enter the hearts of His creatures, to console and strengthen them; He is indifferent whether He be offered as a sacrifice of thanksgiving or of expiation; whether for the consolation of the living or the repose of the deceased; He is indifferent to honour and contempt, and is as willing to be concealed in the tabernacle as to be carried with pomp through cities. Carefully observe these five points of perfect indifference, which should likewise accompany that to which you aspire. See in what you have failed hitherto, and resign your will totally and unreservedly to Jesus Christ, that you may henceforward be indifferent to whatever His providence may dispose for you.

Third Point.—The state to which our Divine Saviour is reduced on the Altar is the effect of His love for His Father and for man; the perfect obedience and indifference of man should then spring from the same principle of love, which can alone overcome his natural repugnance to subjection, and render him pliable and docile to the will of God. A Religious, animated with solid love for Jesus Christ, says, with the spouse in the Canticles: "My soul melted when my beloved spoke." (Cant. v. 6.) At the first intimation of the will of God, she so perfectly renounces her own plans and desires, that like water that has no shape of its own, but is capable of receiving that of any vessel in which it is placed, her soul is ready to assume whatever form is destined for her by her Divine Spouse, and His representatives on earth. Seek the treasure of divine love in the Blessed Sacrament, by frequently receiving Jesus Christ on the Altar, where He dwells as a consuming fire to inflame your affections.

FRIDAY.

FIRST MEDITATION.

On the Example of perfect Obedience which our Divine Lord exhibits in His Passion.

First Point.—Jesus Christ crucified is the perfect model of consummate obedience; from the pulpit of the cross your Divine Master teaches you its sublime lessons; in this sacred book you must seek the treasure of its heavenly precepts. "Jesus Christ humbled himself," says St. Paul, "becoming obedient unto death, even to the death of the cross." (Phil. ii. 8.) Consider the mysteries hidden in these words: "Jesus Christ, the Son of God, who thought it not robbery to be equal with God, humbled himself." The Lord of glory annihilated Himself! To whom did He submit? To His eternal Father,—to Pilate,—to His executioners. To what lengths did He carry His submission? So far as to endure torments, till then unheard of, and, at length, to expire on a cross between two thieves, as a malefactor. Make an act of lively faith in this truth; from this faith will result affections of admiration, astonishment, and confusion, at seeing yourself so far removed from the perfection of the divine Model, whose obedience is proposed to your imitation; affections also of contrition, of desire of amendment, and supplication for the graces necessary for this end.

Second Point.—Consider the qualities of the obedience practised by our Divine Lord and Saviour. 1st. He obeyed with perfect resignation and conformity to the divine will of His Father, as He proved in the garden of Olives, by saying, "Not my will but Thine be done." (St. Luke, xxii. 42.) His divine submission fully verified the prophecy of Isaiah: "The Lord God hath opened my ear, and I do not resist: I have not gone back. I have given my body to the strikers, and my cheeks to them that plucked them: I have not turned away my face from them that rebuked me, and spit upon me." (Isaiah, l. 5, 6.) 2nd. His obedience was accompanied with strict exactitude and punctuality;

He literally and minutely accomplished all the prophecies regarding Him, and, therefore, was well entitled to say, at the end of life: "It is consummated" (St. John, xix. 30); well entitled to commend His spirit into the hands of His Father, whose least orders He had perfectly executed. 3rd. His obedience was animated by an ardent love for His eternal Father, and a pure intention of promoting God's glory; as he manifested when He said to His apostles, before entering the garden, the first scene of His anguish, "That the world may know that I love the Father, and as the Father hath given me commandment, so do I—arise, let us go hence." (St. John, xiv. 31.) This love led Him willingly to renounce all sensible joy and consolation, and to embrace bitterness and affliction; the only ray of comfort, which beamed on His desolate spirit, being that of conformity to the will of God, and even this extended no farther than the superior part of His soul. Thank your Divine Redeemer for having left you so perfect an example of obedience, and with confusion for having derived so little profit from it, implore the grace to act conformably to it in future.

Third Point.—Learn from your Divine Model to obey, under trying and painful circumstances, with conformity of will, with punctual exactness to the least point of duty, and with a pure intention of glorifying God. Prove the solidity of your love by obeying independently of the repugnance arising either from the difficulty of the command imposed, from its opposition to your inclination or judgment, from the interior desolation you happen to experience, or, in fine, from want of natural inclination for the person who exacts your submission; under all these circumstances, obedience is indispensable. Consider Jesus Christ your adorable Model. Could anything be more painful than His ignominious death, with the cruel torments that preceded it? Could anything be more unjust than the condemnation of the *Just One* by His own favoured creatures? How great a trial to submit to barbarous executioners, and to an unjust judge, who owned the innocence of the Victim, on whom he, at the same time, pronounced sentence of death! What interior anguish could exceed that which extorted from Him the sad complaints, "My soul is sorrowful even unto death" (St. Matt. xxvi. 38); "My God, my God, why hast Thou forsaken me?" (Ibid. xxvii. 46.) If we contemplate the crucifix with a lively faith, our repugnances will vanish; we shall be incapable of opposing an argument or an excuse to the claims of obedience, and we shall receive with delight even the most painful and difficult orders of Superiors. It is of incalculable importance frequently to consider Jesus Christ crucified, and attentively to meditate on His divine example, particularly when nature revolts against the subjection of obedience; in Him we shall find abundant strength to persevere courageously. Let us seriously resolve to enter on the road He has traced out for us.

Aspirations.—"My Father, if it be possible let this bitter chalice pass from me: nevertheless, not as I will, but as Thou wilt." (St. Matt. xxvi. 39.) "Father into Thy hands I commend My spirit." (St. Luke, xxii. 46.)

The Lecture.—The 9th and 10th chapters of the same Treatise in Rodriguez, or the 18th chapter on obedience in "Le Livre des Elus," by St. Jure. Make three visits to the Blessed Sacrament to-day; the first in the morning, in honour of the prayer of our Lord in the garden, and of the perfect sacrifice He there made of His whole will. The second after dinner, to honour the obedience by which He submitted to be crucified, and abandoned His spirit into the hands of His Eternal Father. At this visit say the Pater and Ave five times. At your third visit, which is to be made in the evening, in honour of the burial of our Divine Lord, beseech Him to inclose your will and judgment for ever in the sepulchre of obedience, that being dead to yourself you may henceforward live but to Him, according to these words of the Apostle, "you are dead and your life is hidden with Christ in God." (Col. iii. 3.)

SECOND MEDITATION.

Exercises for disposing the Soul for the Practice of Religious Obedience by interior Acts of Oblation and Sacrifice.

Prostrate in spirit at the foot of the Cross, there offer to Jesus Christ the sacrifice of perfect obedience. 1st. Renounce your liberty, choosing a condition wherein you must subject it to the cross of your Saviour; offer Him a sacrifice of the power you still retain to act according to your inclinations, and of the repugnance you may naturally feel to renounce your will, and do it as generously as if you had it in your power to gratify all the desires of your heart. 2nd. Renounce your judgment, attaching it to the foot of the cross, resolving never to listen to what it may suggest in opposition to the orders of Superiors, but always to subject it to theirs. 3rd. Renounce your will and the natural inclination you feel to gratify it, determining to submit, in all things, to the will of those placed over you. 4th. Renounce the comfort you might experience in the exercise of your freedom, and the accomplishment of your wishes; accept, instead of it, the contradiction of your desires, and the constant violence which must be offered to corrupt nature. 5th. Resolve to renounce yourself totally: your pleasures, your interests, and everything in you that opposes the will of God; let your only happiness, in future, be to accomplish that will, and to glorify Him by the perfect sacrifice of your being. In making these acts, consider the particular sacrifices from which you apprehend most pain, that you may generously offer them to God with an ardent love and desire to please Him. Unite this oblation with that which Jesus Christ made of His will to His Heavenly Father, concluding by the expiring words of your Saviour, "Father into Thy hands I commend My spirit;" or by these words of St. Gertrude, "O Divine Jesus! I abandon myself to Thee, that Thy divine will may be accomplished in and by me."

SATURDAY.

FIRST MEDITATION.

On the Example of Obedience displayed in the Life of the Blessed Virgin.

First Point.—The most glorious Virgin, Mother of God, Queen and Model of all virtues, has left us perfect examples of obedience. Conformity to the will of God, which is the soul and spirit of this virtue, was in her most admirable, as appears from her words to the Angel, "Behold the handmaid of the Lord, be it done to me according to Thy word." (St. Luke, i. 38.) As also from her generous submission to the rigorous decree of the Eternal Father against her divine Son, and to the sorrow destined to pierce her own soul. Her resignation was accompanied with profound humility; with total abandonment of herself to God, to whom she committed the disposal of her being, and with peace and tranquillity, calmly abandoning all her concerns to the paternal Providence of her Maker. See whether your conformity to the will of God be accompanied with these three conditions. Resolve to imitate the Blessed Virgin in her practice of this heroic virtue, which will render you a participator in her great dignity of Mother of God, since Christ assures us, that "Whoever does the will of His Father, is His brother, and sister, and mother." (St. Matt. xii. 50.)

Second Point.—From the conformity to the will of God, so strikingly exhibited in the life of the Blessed Virgin, flowed that perfect obedience, which for the love of God she practised towards men. Consider her submission to her parents in her infancy, and to the priests during her abode in the temple. Contemplate her obedience to the emperor Augustus, at whose command she travelled to Bethlehem in the midst of winter, though nine months pregnant. How exactly did she observe the love of Purification, though it was not obligatory for her, and seemed even to derogate from her dignity! How promptly did she flee into Egypt in obedience to St. Joseph, rising by his order at midnight without excuse or murmur, and carrying her Divine Son into a distant land, to remain there as long as God should require! Her submission even extended tothe Apostles, whom as princes of the Church she obeyed with the most perfect submission. In fine, the whole life of our Blessed Mother was one continued example of obedience, which she presents to your imitation; desiring that your conduct should be an exact copy of the model she has left us, as hers was an imitation of the Divine original of all perfection, Jesus Christ.

Third Point.—The only verbal instruction given to man by the Mother of God, was a lesson of obedience. Only seven sayings are recorded of her in the gospel; two of these were addressed to the Angel, two to St. Elizabeth, two to our Lord, and one to the waiters at the marriage of Cana. To them she addressed the comprehensive words, "whatsoever He shall say to you do ye." (St. John, ii. 5.) Engrave on your heart this sublime lesson of your Blessed Mother and Instructress; it is the abridgment of the whole law. To do all that Jesus Christ tells us, is to observe the commandments of God, and the evangelical counsels, to obey His Divine inspirations, to submit to our superiors, to observe our rules. What greater perfection can there be? Reduce this lesson to practice, and you will soon experience in yourself a more wonderful transformation than that of the water into wine at the marriage of Cana; you will be changed into Jesus Christ, and become one with Him, according to the words of St. Paul, "he who is joined to the Lord is one spirit." (1 Cor. vi. 17.) Implore this favour through the intercession of the Blessed Virgin.

Aspirations.—"Behold the handmaid of the Lord, be it done to me according to Thy word." (St. Luke, i. 38.) "Thou hast held me by my right hand; and by Thy will Thou hast conducted me; and with glory Thou hadst received me."

For the Practice, see "Supplement."

SECOND MEDITATION.

First Point.—Read the chapter of the Constitutions on Obedience, and remember that your future conduct must be modelled according to the perfection it requires.

Second Point.—Examine in what points you usually transgress against obedience, and consider, first, whether you execute all the orders, general and particular, given by Superiors. 2nd. Whether you observe the Rule with exactness. 3rd. Whether you obey with conformity of will, submission of judgment, punctuality and fervour. 4th. Whether the motive of your obedience is the glory of God, the accomplishment of His will, or any similar end. Consider also what your duty to Superiors requires; examine whether you evince the respect and esteem you ought to feel in their regard, or whether you have treated them with disrespect or contempt, judged rashly of their actions and intentions, or disapproved of their conduct. 5th. Whether instead of loving them you feel repugnance, or coldness towards them, in consequence of their reprehensions, or from any other cause. 6th. Whether you have failed in exterior respect to your Superiors,—excusing yourself or answering warmly when they find fault with you, or impose any command. 7th. In fine, examine whether the communication of your interior dispositions is accompanied with the candour and confidence the Rule requires, and whether you endeavour to profit of the advice given you. Having examined your most ordinary faults on these points, beg of God to pardon them, through the merits of the perfect obedience practised by His Divine Son, from the first moment of His Incarnation, to the last instant of His life.

Third Point.—Revolve in mind the reflections which most powerfully animated you during the week, to enter on the practice of perfect obedience; recal also the resolutions with which our Lord inspired you; renew them in His presence, and beseech Him, through the prayers of His Blessed Mother, to enable you to accomplish them perfectly. It will be useful to write them at your leisure.

THE FOURTH WEEK OF THE EXERCISES, DEVOTED TO THE MEDITATION AND PRACTICE OF THE VIRTUE OF CHARITY.

The meditations and exercises of this week are intended to lead you to union with God and your neighbour by a sincere and ardent charity; therefore, you should endeavour to perform all your actions in this spirit, desiring that your heart may be perpetually consumed with the pure flames of divine love. Make frequent interior acts of the love of God, esteeming Him above all things created, and loving Him more than all that is dearest to you; rejoicing in His perfections, ardently desiring the increase of His glory; sighing incessantly for the vision of His increated beauty, and resigning yourself into His hands by perfect conformity to His will. Secondly, produce acts of love and esteem for your neighbour, who merits your affection as being the possession and image of God, redeemed by the blood of Christ. Rejoice in His happiness, particularly in His spiritual advantage; desiring its increase, and frequently asking it of God by fervent prayer. Offer yourself to the Almighty to be employed for the salvation of souls, and endeavour to enkindle in your heart a lively zeal for this great work. Renounce sincerely all feeling of resentment, antipathy, or coolness you may experience towards your neighbour, and in order the more perfectly to surmount them, select as the constant objects of your charity, those persons to whom you may feel a repugnance, or from whom you may have received any offence. With regard to your exterior conduct embrace every opportunity of practising charity and meekness, and let your conversation be useful, simple, and prudent. In the course of the week read the chapters of the Constitutions which regard the Institute, likewise that on Charity; also the 13th chapter of the 1st Epistle to the Corinthians, "If I speak with the tongues of men," &c.

SUNDAY.

FIRST MEDITATION.

On the Love of God.

First Point.—The meditations and practices of the preceding weeks inculcate the necessity of detachment from exterior things by poverty, from sensual pleasures by chastity, and from your own will and judgment by obedience; the end of all is only to unite you to God by charity. To excite yourself to His love, consider the many reasons which oblige you to love Him above all things. 1st. He is infinite in perfection. 2nd. He is your Creator on whom you are absolutely dependent. 3rd. He is your Preserver who constantly upholds and protects you. 4th. He is your Benefactor to whom you are indebted for all blessings both of nature and grace.

5th. He is your Redeemer who sacrificed His life to redeem you from sin and eternal death. Direct your affections principally to whichever of these five titles most powerfully excites your love, and endeavour to produce acts of perfect charity. 1st. Select the Lord as the only object of your affections, and in this spirit address to Him the words of David: "Thou art the God of my heart, and the God that is my portion for ever." (Ps. lxxii. 26.) 2nd. Desire that all creatures may know, love, and adore Him, and say with the same Prophet: "Let all the earth adore Thee, O Lord, and sing to Thee." (Ps. lix. 4.) "Let every spirit, human, angelic, and divine, praise and glorify Thee." (Ps. cl. 5, 3.) Regret that you have begun so late to love the eternal source of all perfection; resolve to begin now at least to love Him with all the ardour of which you are capable.

Second Point.—Consider the qualities which should accompany our love for God. 1st. It should be tender and ardent, since its object is our Sovereign Good, who loves us with incredible ardour, and loved us even before we were capable of making Him a return of love. 2nd. It should be active and efficacious, leading us to seek what is most pleasing to His Divine Majesty, and to accomplish His adorable will, without which disposition there can be no real love. 3rd. It must be generous, trampling under foot all worldly considerations; inspiring the contempt of self and the renunciation of our ease and honour, substituting for them the will of God, and His glory. 4th. It must be sovereign, possessing the dominion of the heart, and banishing every affection which does not singly and purely refer to God. Enter seriously into yourself, and examine if your love for God be accompanied by these four qualities; if not, it is only feigned and imaginary. Earnestly beseech our Divine Lord to bestow on you the gift of perfect charity, saying with St. Augustine, " Wound, O Lord, the inmost recesses of my soul with the burning arrows of Thy love; inflame my spirit with the ardours of Thy charity.

Third Point.—Consider the motives for loving God, suggested by the very nature of love itself. 1st. To love God is the noblest occupation which can engage a soul in this world or in the next; it is an exercise which assimilates her to the seraphim, who derive their perfection from the Divine love which consumes them. 2nd. It is the most delightful of all employments, and so transported the saints that they forgot the necessities of the body, and renounced all the pleasures of life to cleave to God as their only treasure. 3rd. It is the most useful and advantageous exercise, since the soul which loves God must infallibly be loved by Him reciprocally, and in His love she finds the combination of every blessing. 4th. It is the most imperative of man's duties, and at the same time the easiest and most secure method of fulfilling his obligations to his Creator; what can be easier than to love such a benefactor? What more reasonable than to devote the whole heart to Him? 5th. Love is the fulfilling of the law; it is the spirit of the gospel, which is a law of love; it is the abridgment of the Rules peculiar to your Order. "Before all things," says St. Augustine—"love God, and then your neighbour." Regret having so late commenced to love, and say with the same Saint, " Too late have I loved Thee, O Beauty ever ancient and ever new! Thou wert present in my heart, whilst I wandered amidst creatures and attached my affections to the beings Thy hands had formed: Woe to the years in which I loved Thee not!" Resolve to spend the remainder of your days in the exercise of Divine love; deeply ponder the remarkable words of St. Augustine, "Any portion of our existence which passes without loving God is lost!" Observe the particular opportunities which God provides you of proving your love for Him by detaching yourself from creatures, by correcting an imperfection, by observing your Rules exactly, and practising the virtues which God particularly requires of you; for true and sincere love is proved only by actions.

Aspirations.—"I will love Thee, O Lord, my stength, my firmament, my refuge, and my deliverer." (Ps. xvii. 2, 3.) "O love, which art ever burning and never extinguished, inflame and consume me with Thy ardours." (St. Augustine).

Receive our Divine Lord to-day in the holy Communion as your Sovereign Good, and the only object of your love.

The Lecture.—In Rodriguez, 13th and 14th chapters of the Treatise on Purity of Intention.

SECOND MEDITATION.

On the Precept of loving God.

First Point.—Although the Almighty possesses all-sufficient happiness in His own essential perfections, and enjoys perfect beatitude in the knowlege and love of Himself, yet, in the excess of His love, He decreed the existence of rational creatures, capable of participating in His felicity. The infinite disproportion between the Majesty of God, and the lowliness of His weak creatures, opposed their aspiring to so high an honour as that of loving the great Creator, but the Almighty has obviated this difficulty and proved the ardour of His desire to possess the heart of man by imposing His love as a strict obligation. "Thou shalt love the Lord thy God with thy whole heart, and with thy whole soul, and with thy whole strength." (Deut. vi. 5.) Endeavour to comprehend the goodness which dictated the command. To allow a being so weak and miserable, to love a God so glorious and perfect, would have been a favour deserving all your gratitude; but, to oblige you to a duty which is the source of innumerable blessings to yourself, is an excess of goodness surpassing human comprehension. "What art Thou to me, O Lord!" said St. Augustine, "and what am I to Thee, that Thou shouldst command me to love Thee, and even threaten me with the effects of Thy anger if I love Thee not? Is it not a sufficient punishment to live without loving Thee?" Return thanks to God for having imposed a precept on you which dignifies your nature, and secures your happiness. Lament that your love for God is so limited, notwithstanding His claims on all its ardours. Beg His assistance that you may henceforward perfectly comply with the precept of His love.

Second Point.—Consider the words of the commandment, "Thou shalt love the Lord thy God with thy whole heart, with thy whole soul, and with thy whole strength." To love God with our whole heart, is to devote to Him all our affections, to love Him more than all things, and to love creatures only with reference to Him. 2nd. As the soul gives life and animation to the body, "to love God with our whole soul," is to consecrate to Him our lives, so that each action they include may be a holocaust consumed for His glory. 3rd. "To love God with our whole mind," is to devote to Him this superior part of the soul as His Temple, and to unite ourselves closely to Him by the exercise of its three noble faculties, the memory, the will, and the understanding. 4th. "To love God with all our powers," is, to direct them all, spiritual and corporal, rational and sensitive, to the service and glory of the Creator. 5th. "To love God with our whole strength," is to love Him ardently and fervently, generously avoiding all that could offend Him; doing everything to please Him; willingly enduring trial and suffering for His love. Consider attentively these characteristics of perfect love, and having examined in what points you fail, implore forgiveness for the past, and resolve to amend.

Third Point.—The Almighty, seeing the coldness and insensibility of the human heart, notwithstanding His imperative command, and the many benefits which should have insured Him its affections, at length sent His only Son from Heaven, "to kindle on earth this Divine fire. (St. Luke, xiii. 49.)

This our Divine Redeemer effected in three ways. 1st. By rendering His Divine attractions visible to our corporal senses, so that our carnal hearts, which find it difficult to love an object purely spiritual, may find in the Incarnate Word one more conformable to their nature. "God assumed human nature," says St. Augustine, "that He might be loved more ardently, and treated more familiarly by man." 2nd. Our Divine Saviour stimulates our love by innumerable proofs of His own ardent charity, the heart which has gained the love of another necessarily finding it difficult to withhold a return of affection. Never was the tender love of God for His creatures more clearly exhibited than in becoming man for their sake.

"By this," says St. John, "hath the charity of God appeared towards us, because God hath sent His only begotten Son into the world that we may live by Him." (1 St. John, iv. 9.) 3rd. He enkindled on earth the divine fire of charity by the example of His own love for His Eternal Father; by His entire accomplishment of the precept of love; by proving to us through life, and in death, the extent to which our love for God should be carried, and the necessity of doing and suffering all things to promote the Divine glory. Offer your grateful thanks to God, for having accommodated Himself to the weakness of our nature, and lavished on us so many blessings through His Incarnation. Consecrate all the affections of your heart to the Incarnate Word, who should be the sole object of your love on earth since He is to be your joy and beatitude in Heaven.

MONDAY.

FIRST MEDITATION.

On the Love of our Neighbour.

First Point.—From the love of God, as from its source, flows the love of our neighbour. "This," said our Divine Redeemer, "is the greatest and first commandment, Thou shalt love the Lord thy God, and the second is like to this; thou shalt love thy neighbour as thyself." (St. Matt. xxii. 39.) These two commandments are like two streams flowing from the same fountain, or like two branches proceeding from the same root. The love of our neighbour proceeding from the love of God as an effect from its cause; it is the mark whereby we may ascertain whether we love God. "If any man say he loveth God, and hateth his brother, he is a liar." (1 St. John, iv. 20.) We cannot really love any one without loving whatever belongs to him, whatever resembles him, or whatever possesses his affections. These three claims on our love are combined in our neighbour. 1st. He belongs to God by the right of creation and redemption. 2nd. He bears the image and likeness of his Creator. 3rd. He is the object of God's most ardent love, as Christ proved by suffering and dying for his redemption. This is a sufficient motive to love your neighbour and so to manifest your love for God. Say to Him with the Prophet, "Thou art my God, for Thou hast no need of my goods." My love for Thee can extend no farther than desires, because Thou canst receive nothing from Thy creatures; but Thou hast made all my desires wonderfully efficacious towards men, whom Thou hast redeemed with Thy blood, that in them I may give Thee the proofs of love which Thou requirest. (Ps. xv. 2, 3.)

Second Point.—Our Lord Jesus Christ presents us Himself with the second motive for loving our neighbour, for, as the incarnate Word is the object, the motive, and the example of the love we owe to God, the same may be said of the charity due to mankind for His sake. 1st. He is the object of our love for our neighbour, because having become man, He desires that we should see Him in all men, whom He considers His brethren. "Whatsoever you do," said He, "to one of these, my least brethren, you do to me." (St. Matt. xxv. 40.) 2nd. His incarnation powerfully induces us to love our neighbour, for, as St. Augustine asks, "Who can hate man, while he beholds his nature in Jesus Christ?" 3rd. He is our model, having left us a perfect example of the love we owe one another, in that which brought Him from Heaven for our salvation, which induced Him to bear our miseries, and to endure unheard of torments to rescue us from destruction, and to open for us the treasures of grace. So great an excess of goodness should not only animate us to love our Divine Lord, who has so much loved us, but should likewise inspire us with affection for our neighbour, since this is the proof He requires of our gratitude for His favours. Resolve to aim at perfect charity to your neighbour, and banish from your heart for ever every feeling of aversion or coolness. Ask of God to enable you to do so.

Third Point.—The express and reiterated command of our Divine Lord is the third motive which obliges us to love our neighbour. It is impossible to consider attentively the words in which the precept was expressed, or the time and place in which it was promulgated, without being affected. The Son of God, on the eve of His death, after the institution of the Blessed Sacrament, the mystery of love, gave to His Apostles His last instructions which He wished to impress peculiarly on their hearts. On that occasion, He said: "I give you a new commandment, that you love one another as I have loved you: by this shall all know that you are My disciples, if you have love for one another." (St. John, xiii. 34, 35.) Weigh these words attentively, and if you have any love for our Saviour they cannot fail to enkindle in your heart an ardent charity towards your neighbour, considering who it is that imposes this command, and the emphatic manner in which He thrice repeats it in the same discourse, calling it His own commandment, and declaring it to be the mark and character by which His disciples may be recognized. Let this motive animate you to love your neighbour, and beg of Jesus Christ to give you the spirit of charity, saying with Saint Augustine, "Give me, O Lord what Thou commandest, and command what Thou pleasest."

Aspirations.—"Who shall separate me from the love which unites me with Jesus Christ, and with my neighbour for His sake? I am sure that neither death, nor life, nor any creature shall be able to separate me from the love of God, which is in Christ Jesus our Lord." (Romans, viii. 35. 39.)

We know that we have passed from death to life, because we love the brethren. He that loveth not abideth in death." (1 Epist. St. John, iii. 14.)

The Lecture.—1st and 2nd Chapters in Rodriguez of the Treatise "on Fraternal Union."

For the Practice, see "Supplement."

SECOND MEDITATION.

On the Practice of Charity towards our Neighbour.

First Point.—The first point to be considered in the exercise of Fraternal Charity, is its motive, which varies according to the different ends we may have in view. 1st. We may love our neighbour because he is united to us by ties of consanguinity; because his natural disposition sympathizes with our own; or because he possesses some peculiar advantage which we particularly prize; all this is but natural love. 2nd. We may love him for his virtue, and for the natural or supernatural qualifications which render him worthy of esteem. This species of love is called friendship, and is a moral virtue, far inferior to real charity, which considers God alone in His creatures, loving them because they belong to God, and have been created for His glory, because their souls bear the impression of His Divine image, because they are dear to His heart, and, finally, because He has expressly commanded us to love them. These are the motives of charity, which being a theological virtue, always tends first to God, though man may be sometimes its secondary object. You will perhaps find on examination that you have but little genuine charity, and that your love for those around you is rather the result of their amiable qualities, or of natural sympathy with their inclinations, than of the pure love of God. A good criterion on this point is to see whether, animated by the spirit of universal charity, you are as ready to serve a person for whom you feel a repugnance, as one to whom you are naturally partial. Purify your affections by substituting supernatural motives for those which have hitherto influenced your feelings, and then " God will abide in you, and His charity will be perfected in your heart." (St. John, iv. 12.) Ask this grace of your Redeemer.

Second Point.—Consider the extent to which perfect fraternal charity should be carried. This our Divine Lord has Himself prescribed ; " Love one another," He says, " as I have loved you." (St. John, xv. 12.) To love our neighbour as Christ has loved us, is then the model of our love; and how did Christ love us? " To the end," as St. John tells us (xiii. 1); to the greatest possible extent, not alone enduring torments but sacrificing even His blood and His life for our salvation the strongest of all proofs of love. 2nd. He loved us to, the end, that is, with a perseverance and a constancy which all our ingratitude and coldness could not diminish. 3rd. " He loved us to the end," by purchasing for us the treasures of grace and glory, and restoring our right to that throne of bliss for which we were created. Such should be our love for our neighbour, and if this appear impracticable, the example of Jesus Christ should smoothen our difficulties, and animate us to aim as nearly as possible at the perfection of charity His life exemplifies. "If God hath so loved us," says St. John, "we ought to love one another." (1 St. John, iv. 11.) How far removed are you from that perfection of charity which would dispose you to sacrifice your life, like Jesus Christ, for your neighbour's salvation, if you will not overcome yourself in a trifle, to avoid giving pain, or if you will not, at the expense of a slight personal inconvenience, perform an act of kindness, &c.? Deplore, in the presence of our Divine Lord, the breaches of charity of which you have been guilty; beseech Him to unite your heart to His, and to communicate to you a portion of the burning love which consumes Him, that you may cheerfully do and suffer all things for the salvation of your neighbour.

Third Point.—Charity is the queen of virtues, therefore it has no sooner taken possession of a soul, than it exercises sovereign sway over all its powers. First, it regulates the understanding, which is permitted to form only the most favourable opinion of our neighbour, and to consider his good qualities alone, and never his defects; avoiding rash judgments, suspicious and contemptuous thoughts. 2ndly. It purifies the heart from envy, jealousy, dislike, coldness, and resentment; substituting for these sinful feelings a cordial and truly Christian charity. 3rdly. It prohibits detraction, murmuring, hasty, petulant words, and all that can injure or annoy our neighbour even in the most trifling degree, inspiring us speak *of* him with charity, and *to* him with gentleness and humility. 4thly. It inspires an efficacious resolution to do good to all men, relieving them in their wants as far as possible, and assisting them at least by prayer. These are the effects which real charity produces in the soul; see if they adorn your's, and resolve to embrace the practice of that active, generous fraternal love which St. John recommends when he says, "My little children, let us not love in word, nor in tongue, but in deed and in truth." (1 Ep. iii. 18.)

TUESDAY.

FIRST MEDITATION.

On Fraternal Union.

First Point.—The holy Spouse in the Canticles says, that having entered into the cellar of his Divine Spouse, "He set in order charity in her." (ii. 4.) This favour God daily bestows on those whom He calls to religion, the mysterious cellar wherein the soul is inebriated in prayer with the love of her heavenly Spouse, whence flows the love of her neighbour. Charity is a divine fire which diffuses its ardour in all directions, but more especially imparts it to objects immediately within the sphere of its genial influence; it consequently obliges a religious soul to direct her charity, first, to those who live with her in the same Community; who tend to the same end; observe the same Rule, and obey the directions of the same Superiors. This charity should be so perfect as to unite the hearts and minds of many in one, according to the rule prescribed by St. Augustine. This holy union is one of the greatest blessings of a religious community, which becomes a faithful representation of heaven, when animated by that peace and concord in which consists one great source of the bliss of the saints. It renders religious houses invincible under every species of adversity, and formidable to the demons as a well ordered phalanx. In fine, it converts a Monastery into a garden of delights, wherein the Son of God Himself delights to dwell, and to lavish His most abundant graces. Contrast the advantages resulting from union and charity with the evils attendant on discord, and resolve, even at the expense of your personal interest, to maintain that general union, and procure its increase. Implore grace to do so.

Second Point.—The high estimation in which the virtue of fraternal union and charity was held by our Divine Redeemer is sufficiently evinced by His recommending it to His disciples at three different intervals in His sermon after the last supper, and asking it for them of His Eternal Father, no less than five times, in the prayer which followed. "Holy Father, keep them in Thy name whom Thou hast given Me: that they may be one, as We also are...... And not for them only do I pray, but for them also who through their word shall believe in Me. That they all may be one as Thou, Father, in Me, and I in Thee: that they also may be one in Us." (St. John, xvii. 11, 20, 21.) These words clearly prove how ardently our Lord desired to see His disciples animated by the spirit of charity, of which He provides them a model in the union existing between Himself and His Father, with whom He forms but one essence, one will, one power and operation. The property of charity, which St. Denis calls "a unitive virtue," is likewise to unite us to our neighbour in heart and affection. The sovereign means of attaining charity for our neighbour is union with God and our

Lord Jesus Christ, as He Himself declares, "I in them, and them in Me: that they may be made perfect in One." (St. John, xvii. 23.) The more intimately we are united to Jesus Christ, the more closely shall we be united with our neighbour; just as lines approach nearer in proportion as they verge to their centre and final term. Desire ardently to attain this precious union with God and your neighbour; renounce all that could weaken and destroy it, and ask of our Lord to impart its plenitude to you.

Third Point.—Consider more particularly the measures to be adopted for the maintenance of union and concord. The first is to divest ourselves as much as possible of all private interest, which looks only to its own honour, advantage, and convenience, substituting instead, a spirit of charity and zeal for the common good, according to the example of St. Paul, who says, "That he pleased men in all things, not seeking that which was profitable to himself but to many, that they may be saved." (1 Cor. x. 33.) Persons living in community are members of the same mystical body, and, as such, should imitate the members of the human body, which all conspire to the general good. The hand does not labour for its individual advantage alone, neither does the foot move only for itself, but each of the members performs its peculiar functions for the utility of the whole system. So it is with charity, which, as the Apostle tells us, "is not ambitious, and seeketh not her own." (1 Cor. xiii. 5.) He moreover assures us, "That if one member suffer anything all the members suffer with it." (Ibid. xii. 26.) If the foot be hurt, the eye is put into requisition to examine the wound, and the hand to relieve it. So should our energies be exerted to console and assist our neighbour under the pressure of spiritual or corporal infirmity. "If one member glory," says the Apostle, "sympathy causes all the members to rejoice with it." (Ibid.) Such should likewise be the effect of charity, which "envieth not." (1 Cor. xiii. 4.) Having considered the union which should exist among the children of God, as also the means of attaining its perfection, resolve to embrace its practice, and to avoid all that could weaken or extinguish the spirit of charity, viz., particular friendships, with their attendant evils; singularity which, unwilling to submit to the common order, requires particular privileges, and interferes in the duties and concerns of others, &c., &c.

Aspirations.—"How good and how pleasant it is for brethren to dwell together in unity." (Ps. cxxxii. 1.)

"Blessed are they that dwell in Thy house, O Lord: they shall praise Thee for ever and ever." (Ps. lxxxiii. 5.)

The Lecture.—Third and fourth chapters of the same Treatise. The evening lecture, second chapter on the End and Institute of the Society of Jesus.

For the Practice, see "Supplement."

SECOND MEDITATION.

On Zeal for the Salvation of Souls.

First Point.—One of the principal effects of charity, and that which may be termed the brightest flame of this heavenly fire, is zeal for the salvation of souls. The natural result of real love is to desire and contribute to the welfare of the object beloved, and, as far as possible, to avert from him all evil; that result is attained so much the more effectually, in proportion as the benefits procured and the misfortunes averted are greater. Such is the effect of zeal which labours to ensure men's eternal glory, and to rescue them from everlasting torments. Ursulines devote themselves to this noble employment by an express vow and public profession to instruct young girls. This Order is thus elevated above others instituted for their sex, because combining action and contemplation, which is the most perfect kind of life, and especially exemplified by our Divine Lord. Their sublime occupation is to watch over the baptismal innocence of the souls confided to them, the preservation of that innocence being a far more precious privilege than is the grace of repentance after sin. Weigh the excellence of your exalted vocation, thank our Lord for it, but, above all, consider the obligation it imposes of leading a holy life.

Third Point.—St. Denis says, "that among all Divine things nothing is so Divine as to co-operate with God in the salvation of souls." This results from the dignity of the soul, which is the masterpiece of the Creator's power, His lively image, the price of the blood of Jesus Christ, the Redeemer's beloved Spouse; therefore the exercise of charity cannot be directed to a more noble object; nor can we better prove our love for God than by assisting an immortal soul which He tenderly cherishes. This good work is most meritorious, for it is a sublime act of charity, that precious virtue which in the sight of God imparts value to every action. Jesus Christ Himself considered the love which His Heavenly Father testified for Him, as the result and reward of the zeal which had prompted Him to assume the nature and miseries of man for the redemption of the human race. "Therefore doth the Father love me, because I lay down my life." (St. John, x. 18.) To a heart penetrated with love for its Redeemer it must be a source of happiness to contribute to His glory, by rendering fruitful the labours and torments He endured for the salvation of souls. This is to secure to Him the inheritance He purchased with so much difficulty, and to render productive the precious blood He shed for our redemption. It is to ornament His diadem with as many pearls, as we gain souls for His glory, for these He considers "His glory and His crown." (Phil. iv. 1.) Excite in your heart an ardent zeal for the salvation of souls from the motive of love of our Divine Redeemer.

Third Point.—Zeal for the salvation of souls should be accompanied with tenderness and love for those objects of our Saviour's special affection. He should be like the great Apostle, who compares himself to a "nurse who cherishes her children." (Thes. ii. 7.) Love sweetens the pains of instruction; because, as St. Augustine says, "the labours of those who love are easy, not insupportable, for love removes difficulty, or changes it into pleasure." 2nd. Zeal must be prudent and discreet, uniting moderation with firmness, so that, as Solomon observes of wisdom, "it may reach from end to end mightily, and at the same time order all things with sweetness." (Wis. viii. 1.) The means employed for leading souls to God should be at once gentle and efficacious. 3rd. Zeal should be accompanied by humility: you should esteem yourself unworthy of so high a function as that of labouring for the good of souls, referring to God the glory of all you do, and humbly accepting the failure of your efforts. In fine, embrace generously the restraint and subjection attendant on the instruction of youth, considering it glorious to imitate Jesus Christ, who for the salvation of souls "debased Himself, taking the form of a servant" (Phil. ii. 7), and declaring "that He was in the midst of His Apostles as the servant of all." (St. Luke, xxii. 27.) Beg of God to give you these three qualifications so necessary to Ursulines.

WEDNESDAY.

FIRST MEDITATION.

On the Union with God necessary for labouring successfully for the Salvation of Souls.

First Point.—Read the second chapter of the Constitutions, and observe the obligation thereby imposed of endeavouring to acquire a high degree of sanctity, and an intimate union with God, that you may perfectly fulfil the end of your vocation. The reasons which oblige you to aim at this exalted perfection are, 1st. because you cannot impart to others what you do not yourself possess; therefore, if you are not inflamed with the love of God you cannot enkindle its Divine ardours in the hearts of others. "Words are of no avail," says St. Bernard, unless the life and actions of the instructor prove that he is animated by the vivifying principle of charity." 2nd. The salvation of souls is a work so great, so absolutely depending on the grace of God, that it is impossible to labour therein with any success unless the heart be intimately united with Jesus Christ. Of this our Divine Lord Himself assured His Apostles, saying, "abide in me, and I in you: as the branch cannot bear fruit of itself, unless it abide in the vine, so neither can you, unless you abide in me." (St. John, xv. 4.) 3rd. The prayers offered to God, in behalf of our neighbour, promote his salvation far more effectually than the most eloquent instructions, for these cannot penetrate the heart, unless God first soften and prepare it. The efficacy of all external exertions for the good of souls depends on the blessing granted to them in prayer. These reasons attentively considered should animate you to aim at intimate union with God, not only with a view to your own perfection but that you may be able to labour profitably for the salvation of souls according to your vocation. Unless you are thus united to God your instructions cannot produce fruit, whatever may be your natural talents for this employment. Beg of God to unite you closely to Himself, and endeavour to render yourself worthy of this favour.

Second Point.—The first step for attaining union with God, is love of prayer and great exactness to spiritual duties. St. Augustine requires that those who are destined to teach others should first learn to pray, and that before the lips pronounce the words of life the heart be raised to God to implore His grace, that it may abundantly impart the treasures with which it overflows. In order then to serve your neighbour without prejudice to your own perfection, you must consider prayer your first and most important duty, looking on all beside as secondary, for in the words of our Divine Lord, "What doth it profit a man if he gain the whole world and lose his own soul?" (St. Matt. xvi. 26.) Jesus Christ, the Divine Model, on whose example every part of our conduct should be formed, commenced His preaching and public labours for the salvation of souls, by a retreat of forty days in the desert, and having devoted the day to instructing, He spent the night in prayer. He frequently withdrew, as the Evangelists remark, from the crowd who pressed around Him, to hear His words of eternal life, and retired apart to pray. (St. Matt. xiv. 13.) Set a high value on prayer and interior recollection, as the principal channel through which will be communicated to you the graces necessary for becoming happily instrumental to the promotion of God's glory. Let your instructions flow from the plenitude of the graces received in communion with God, that like the Psalmist, "you may be worthy to publish the memory of the abundance of the sweetness of the Lord." (Ps. cxliv. 7.)

Third Point.—It is not sufficient that an Ursuline be devoted to prayer, and imbued with the spirit of recollection and solitude. She must moreover combine interior recollection with attention to exterior duties, and learn to [find God amidst the most distracting occupations She must imitate the angels, who never lose the vision of their Creator, though employed in guarding and directing the souls confided to them. She must be like the compass which moves round its circumference without detaching itself from its centre; like the ray of light which illumines the earth without being separated from the globe where it originates; like the stream which fertilizes a large tract of country in its lengthened course, and yet incessantly flows back to the fountain from which it first emanated; thus, must the heart and mind of an Ursuline be inseparably united to God, amidst the exterior functions to which her duty to her neighbour obliges her. To attain this sublime perfection, she must first purify her intentions in instruction, receiving from the hand of Christ Himself this ennobling occupation, and pursuing it solely because this is the proof He requires of her love; for to her, as well as to Saint Peter, He says,

"If thou lovest me, feed my lambs." (St. John, xxi. 15.) Thus will she prove that whether she elevate her mind to God in prayer, or direct her exertions to the service of her neighbour, "It is always the charity of Christ which presseth her." (2 Cor. v. 14.) Secondly, she must consider her Lord and Saviour in each of the little ones confided to her; "Whatever you do to one of my least brethren you do it to me." (St. Matt. xxv. 40.) Thirdly, she must distrust her own weakness, and impress her mind with the conviction of her incapacity to produce fruit in souls; this disposition will oblige her to maintain a constant union of heart and affection with Jesus Christ, and frequently to enter her interior sanctuary, as Moses entered the Tabernacle, to implore the abundance of God's graces. Resolve to unite interior recollection with the discharge of your exterior duties for the time to come. Implore pardon for having hitherto been so much attached to exterior things, and beg of God to give you the interior spirit of a perfect religious.

Aspirations.—"May I abide in Thee, O Lord, and Thou in me, that I may bear much fruit, for without Thee I can do nothing." (St. John, xv. 4, 6.)

May all my energies be devoted, O Lord, to the promotion of Thy glory, and my life be consumed for the salvation of souls.

For the Practice, see "Supplement."

SECOND MEDITATION.

On the Spirit of Mortification requisite in those who instruct others.

First Point.—Mortification is no less necessary than prayer for labouring successfully for the salvation of souls. In the first place, it is impossible to advance in prayer without mortification; moreover the salvation of souls is a grace flowing from the Cross of Jesus Christ, as from its source. As Christ redeemed the world by His passion and death, He has decreed that those who pursue the great work He commenced, shall succeed therein only in proportion as suffering and self-denial render them conformable to Him. His Divine words must be verified in them, as well as in Himself: "Unless the grain of wheat fall into the ground and die, itself remaineth alone. But if it die, it bringeth forth much fruit." (St. John, xii. 24, 25.) The duties of instruction, when perfectly discharged, are extremely laborious, and therefore include the practice of constant restraint and self-renunciation. Our lives must be conformable to our words, unless we mean that bad example should destroy the salutary effects of our precepts, and from this again results the necessity of mortifying in ourselves all that is evil or imperfect. Consider these reasons with attention, and then beg of Jesus Christ crucified to transform you into Himself by mortification, that you may be a worthy instrument for the promotion of His glory by the salvation of souls.

Second Point.—Consider in what particularly consists the mortification necessary for serving your neighbour. It requires first, that in order to govern others with advantage, you subdue your own passions. Secondly, that you renounce your interests, sacrificing to Jesus Christ the love of your ease and convenience which may sometimes conceal themselves, under the specious pretext of the love of spiritual things; thus will you be entitled to say with St. Paul, "I die daily, by the mortification of all my desires and inclinations, that I may have the glory of gaining souls to Jesus Christ." (1 Cor. xv. 31.) Thirdly, that you disengage your heart from earthly things, and evince in your actions and words only indifference and contempt for the honours, wishes, and pleasures which the world prizes. These dispositions will ensure success to your exertions for the good of your pupils, and realize in your regard the words which Christ pronounced of Himself: "When I shall be lifted up from the earth I will draw all things to myself." (St. John, xii. 32.)

Third Point.—To the mortification which retrenches all obstacles to the fruit of your exertions for the salvation of souls, you must add generous patience in supporting the many difficulties attendant on this great work. When St. Paul was chosen for the glorious function, our Lord said of him, "This man is to me a vessel of election to carry my name before the Gentiles and Kings; for I show him how great things he must suffer for my name's sake." (Acts, ix. 15, 16.) The prediction was afterwards literally verified, as we learn from the Apostle, who declares, that, in the exercise of his ministry, he was "persecuted, buffeted, reviled, blasphemed, and made as the rufuse of this world." (1 Cor. iv.) If you desire to participate in the merit of the Apostles' zeal for souls, you must expect to encounter similar trials. See if you have courage to endure them, and remember that this exalted work can be worthily carried on only by those whose generosity of soul elevates them above the weakness of their sex. To be the worthy daughter of the glorious martyr, St. Ursula, you must be ready to suffer all things, even the loss of life, to testify, first, the solidity of your own faith, and secondly, the ardour of your desire to inspire others with practical love for its holy maxims. Beg of

God to grant you invincible patience and courage, through the intercession of this great Saint, and resolve to embrace the trials you may encounter, with a generous spirit, thus gradually to habituate yourself to the practice of perfect patience and forbearance.

THURSDAY.

FIRST MEDITATION.

On the Blessed Sacrament considered as the Bond which unites us with God and our Neighbour.

First Point.—Among other titles which St. Augustine confers on the Blessed Sacrament, he calls it a "symbol of unity and a bond of charity," because it is a Sacrament of union and love, the principal end of which is to unite us to God and our neighbour. For this reason, also, the Church styles it Communion. The union which the holy Eucharist establishes between the soul and God is the closest and most intimate which can be imagined. "He that eateth my flesh, and drinketh my blood," said our Divine Redeemer, "abideth in me, and I in him." (St. John, vi. 57.) What closer union can there be than that of the food which becomes a part of our substance? Yet, such is the union effected by the holy Sacrament, which transforms us into itself, communicating to us its Divine qualities. How admirable is the means adopted by Jesus Christ to unite us to Himself, and through Him to His Eternal Father! Adore His boundless charity and infinite wisdom. Desire ardently to unite yourself to God in this adorable Sacrament, and endeavour to dispose your soul for so great a happiness by the exercise of ardent charity; "for God is charity; and he that abideth in charity, abideth in God, and God in him." (St. John, iv. 16.)

Second Point.—This holy Sacrament unites the soul not only with God but also with her neighbour. The prayer of Jesus Christ, "the glory which Thou hast given me, I have given to them: that they may be one, as we also are one" (St. John, xvii. 22), is understood by the holy Fathers as referring to the union in the Lord which the Eucharist establishes among all Christians. "I have fed them with my deified flesh, that in virtue of that heavenly nourishment, they may be one with us, and one among themselves, imitating the union which subsists between thee and me."

The first effect of this adorable Sacrament is to remove all causes of disunion, such as anger, aversion, and resentment, for they who eat the flesh of the Lamb with due dispositions, become participators in His meekness and mercy. 2nd. It augments grace and charity, which unite us to God, and by a necessary consequence to our neighbour. 3rd. Being united to Jesus Christ by this holy Sacrament, as the branch to the vine, we become capable of producing abundant fruit in souls. "He that abideth in me," said Jesus Christ, "and I in him, the same beareth much fruit." (St. John, xv. 5.) And again, "He that eateth my flesh, and drinketh my blood, abideth in me, and I in him." (Ibid. vi. 57.)

Repeat the same affections as at the First Point, adding the perfect renunciation of every feeling of antipathy or resentment, that you may thus be disposed to receive the abundant fruit of this Sacrament of union and love.

Third Point.—Consider that one of the principal

reasons why our Lord instituted this Sacrament, under the form of bread and wine, in preference to any other description of food, was, that as bread is made of many grains of wheat, and wine of many grapes, all blended into one mass, so the Eucharist might be to us a symbol of the perfect charity which should subsist among Christians. "We being many," says St. Paul, "are one body, all that partake of one bread." (1 Cor. x. 17.) Before wheat becomes bread, and grapes become wine, the former must be ground into flour and the latter trodden in the wine-press, whence we learn that we cannot attain perfect union with God and our neighbour, unless we mortify our passions, and die to our own interests.

Beg this grace of your Redeemer through the love He testifies for us in the Sacrament of the Altar. Receive the holy Communion frequently for this intention, but, above all, never approach it without having first renounced every uncharitable feeling, and reconciled yourself with those towards whom you may have experienced any coolness, persuaded that charity is the principal disposition our Lord requires in you.

Aspirations.—"It is good for me to adhere to my God." (Ps. lxxii. 28.)

"Holy Father, keep us in Thy name, that we may be one, as Thou in Thy Son, and Thy Son in Thee." (St. John, xvii.)

The Lecture.—The 5th and 6th chapters of the Treatise in Rodriguez on Fraternal Union, or the 11th and 12th sections of the 10th chapter of "the Knowledge and Love of Jesus Christ," on Communion.

Receive our Lord to-day in the holy Communion as a consuming fire, whence you may derive that ardent charity which will unite you intimately to God and your neighbour. Say with St. Augustine, "O love! O fire! which ever burnest, and art never extinguished, vouchsafe to inflame me with thy ardours! Would that I were entirely consumed by thy burning flames!" Say, also, with the devout Thomas a Kempis, "I desire, O Lord Jesus, to be inflamed by Thy Divine presence, to be consumed and transformed into Thee, to become one spirit with Thee by the grace of intimate union, and the melting of ardent love."

For the Practice, see "Supplement."

SECOND MEDITATION.

On the Love of Men which Jesus exhibits in the Holy Eucharist.

First Point.—The admirable charity which Jesus Christ had displayed for the human race all through life, He perfected and perpetuated by instituting this sacrament of love. "Having loved His own, who were in the world, He loved them unto the end" (St. John, xiii. 1), and carried the manifestation of that love to the utmost extent. To love another, is to wish him well, and to serve him whenever an opportunity offers. By giving Himself to man in the holy Eucharist, Jesus Christ confers on him the greatest happiness and the highest honour, uniting him closely to God, and rendering him in a manner divine. Secondly. He enriches him with the treasures of His graces and merits, giving him Himself with the abundance of His treasures. Thirdly. He replenishes him with pure joy, and inebriates him with the torrent of His sweetness. Love our Lord Jesus Christ, who has first evinced such tender and ardent love for you. "Nothing," St. Augustine observes, "so powerfully excites the affections, as to find that we are the objects of previous love; the heart which would not be the first to love its God, must indeed be hardened, if it can refuse Him, at least, a return of tenderness." Learn also, from the example of Christ, cordially to love your neighbour, and to do good to all men as far as is in your power.

Second Point.—Love is not only liberal and beneficent, but also compassionate, merciful, and ever ready to succour the miserable and distressed. This our Lord does in the Blessed Sacrament, wherein He exercises the spiritual works of mercy,—visiting His creatures in the excess of His goodness, enlightening the ignorant, giving counsel to the doubtful, and correcting the faults of the weak; for the bread from Heaven is that "bread of understanding" which imparts true wisdom. (Eccles. xv. 3.) He consoles the afflicted in the Sacrament of charity, "whence we may draw waters with joy out of the Saviour's fountains." (Isaiah, xii. 3.) He patiently bears the insults offered Him by unworthy and tepid communicants; He remains on the Altar, as on a throne of mercy, forgiving the sins of His creatures; in fine, He mediates for the living and the dead, intercedes even for those who offend Him, and incessantly offers Himself as a Victim of impetration to obtain for us every grace. Our Divine Lord, likewise, spiritually exercises the seven corporal works of mercy: He feeds the hungry with His sacred flesh; He refreshes the thirsty with His adorable blood; He provides us with a place of rest in His own heart during our weary pilgrimage; He clothes the indigent with the garment of grace; He breaks the chains which captivate the soul in sin; He does not bury the dead, but He gives them life, cancelling their crimes, and entombing their iniquities at the foot of the Cross. Recur to Jesus Christ, present on the Altar, with unbounded confidence in all your miseries, and resolve to imitate Him by charitably assisting your neighbour on all occasions.

Third Point.—Consider the constancy and perseverance of the love of Jesus Christ for us in the Blessed Sacrament; to it may be well applied the words of the Canticles, " Love is strong as death, jealousy is hard as hell; the lamps thereof are lamps of fire and flames; many waters cannot quench charity, neither can the flood drown it." (Cant. viii. 6, 7.) The blasphemies of heretics, and the sacrileges of bad Catholics, have not extinguished its flames, or deterred Jesus Christ from descending on the Altar in obedience to the voice of the priest, to console the few souls devoted to His love. Thus you learn to love your neighbour generously and perseveringly, and not only to pardon the unkindness you may meet from others, but even to love with a peculiar charity those who annoy or injure you. Thus will you accomplish the precept of Christ, " Love your enemies, do good to them that hate you, and pray for them that persecute and calumniate you." (St. Matt. v. 44.) Resolve to do so, and implore grace to this effect.

FRIDAY.

FIRST MEDITATION.

On the perfect Example of Charity, which our Divine Lord presents us on the Cross.

First Point.—The tragic scene of Calvary may be truly called the exhibition of God's most intense love for man. On the mountain of sorrow, the Divine "Sun" of Justice, having reached its meridian splendour, "burneth the earth." (Eccl. xliii. 3.) The adorable Victim of His own tender charity is consumed by its flames on the Altar of the Cross. There He admirably displays His love for His Father, sacrificing life for the reparation of the Divine glory, outraged by the sins of men. Well might He say before His passion, "that the world may know that I love the Father, and obey His commands, arise, let us go hence" (St. John, xiv. 31); and when about to expire, "It is consummated." (Ibid. xix. 30.) I cannot carry my love to a greater excess than I have already done. Contrast your love for God with that of Jesus Christ for His Eternal Father; the result of the comparison must be the acknowledgment that yours is little more than imaginary, since it is not accompanied by that desire to suffer, and that patience under tribulation which are the essential character, and real proof of sincere love. Beg of Jesus Christ to give you a share in His ardent charity, and resolve to co-operate with His grace in labouring to acquire it.

Second Point.—Jesus Christ crucified, not only burns with love for His Father, but is also consumed with love for man, beyond the limited capacity of mortals to conceive. Endeavour, as far as you can, to penetrate its extent, and consider with the Apostle its *breadth*, which embraces all created intelligences; its *length*, which perseveres to the end; its *depth*, which descends to the lowest abyss of humiliation, prompting its Divine Victim to be made "a curse for us" (Galat. iii. 13), and to bear the confusion due to the crimes of the human race; lastly, its *height*, which destines for us no less an elevation than the adoption of the sons of God, and the possession of eternal glory. Admire the infinite charity of Christ, thank Him for the many solid proofs you have received of its ardour and sincerity, and resolve to return Him love for love. The principal lesson you should learn from His Divine example is the love of your neighbour. "In this," says Saint John, "we have known the charity of God, because He hath laid down His life for us, and we ought to lay down our lives for our brethren." (1 Ep. iii. 16.)

Third Point.—The death of Jesus Christ has reunited what was previously divided. Man, who had been separated from God by sin, is reconciled to his Maker by the sacrifice of our Divine Mediator, and those "who were afar off are made nigh by the blood of Christ." (Eph. ii. 13.) Jews and Gentiles have by the same means been united into one Church; hearts torn by hatred and resentment have been restored to peace and charity by the example of the meekness of Jesus Christ, who with His expiring words implored mercy for His persecutors, saying, "Father, forgive them, for they know not what they do." (St. Luke, xxiii. 34.) This astonishing instance of charity must surely induce any one who bears the name of a Christian, and has not quite lost his faith, to renounce every feeling of antipathy or resentment. Deplore, in the presence of Jesus Christ, your past warmth and irritation under the trials you have met in your intercourse with others, and having asked His pardon, resolve never to consider the injury done you until you have first contemplated your Redeemer agonizing on the Cross. If you are faithful to this practice, you will quickly experience the efficacy of the grace of mutual union and concord, purchased for us by the blood of Christ, and every uncharitable feeling will be replaced by sincere and solid love for your neighbour.

Aspirations.—"Love is strong as death," which nothing can resist, "and jealousy is hard as hell," in its ever-enduring perseverance. "Many waters cannot quench charity." (Cant. viii. 6, 7.) "The charity of Christ presseth us to love Him ardently, and all men for His sake." (2 Cor. v. 14.)

The Lecture.—7th, 8th, and 9th chapters of the same Treatise in Rodriguez, or 20th chapter of "Le Livre des Elus," by Père St. Jure.

For the Practice, see "Supplement."

SECOND MEDITATION.

Acts of fervent Charity, tending to Union with God and your Neighbour.

First Point.—Approach in spirit the foot of the Cross, and contemplate its expiring victim, who presents us the most perfect example of charity, and the most powerful motives to love Him ardently and our neighbour for His sake. Make acts, 1st. of ardent love of God, preferring Him before all things, and choosing Him for the only object of your affections. Desire the increase of His glory; offer yourself unreservedly to Him, to accomplish His will, even when it clashes with your own interests, honour, reputation, pleasure, and convenience, or if it should require the sacrifice of your very life. 2nd. Of love for your neighbour, cherishing all men as the images of God, the price of the blood of Christ, particularly those who profess the same faith, and should, therefore, be considered as your brethren, and the adopted children of God. Beg of Him to pour on all His abundant blessings and graces. 3rd. Being associated in community with holy souls, who like you aspire to become perfect spouses of Christ, receive them all into your heart; rejoice at living in their company; bear their faults and weaknesses patiently; participate in their joy, and on all occasions prefer the common good to your own particular advantage. 4th. Banish from your heart whatever could weaken the spirit of sincere charity, as resentment, dislike, envy, contempt, &c. Renounce all particular friendships, embracing instead, a general, sincere love for all creatures. 5th. Accept joyfully your obligation of instructing children, with all the trouble, labour, humiliation, &c. &c. which it includes. Let the view of Jesus Christ crucified for the salvation of men, excite in your heart an ardent zeal to continue the great work He commenced: offer your interests, pleasures, health, and even life, for the salvation of souls. Produce these acts with the most ardent love of which your heart is capable, uniting them to the sacrifice of your Redeemer on the Cross. Say to Him, "O Lord Jesus Christ, who in Thy mercy didst give up Thy life for me, I beseech Thee by Thy sufferings to penetrate my heart with the inflamed arrows of Thy Divine love, and to wound me, like the spouse in the Canticles, with Thy charity."

SATURDAY.

FIRST MEDITATION.

On the Example of Charity which the Most Blessed Virgin's Life presents.

First Point.—One of the most remarkable among the titles conferred by the Holy Scriptures on the Blessed Virgin is that of the "Mother of fair love" (Eccles. xxiv. 24), which she not only claims, on account of having given birth to Jesus Christ, the object of the love of Heaven and earth; but also because her heart was inflamed with the most perfect love for God, of which a creature is capable. She loved God, not only as her Creator and Lord, but with the strong affection of a Mother for her Son. 2nd. She loved Him generously, enduring great afflictions for His sake; consenting that in compliance with the Divine will, a sword of anguish should pierce her soul in the Passion of Christ, and that after the only object of her tenderness had ascended into Heaven, her own life should be prolonged for the benefit of the Church. 3rd. Her love was active and ever-increasing; its actual influence over her was never suspended, so that, like the Spouse in the Canticles, she might truly say, "I sleep, but my heart watcheth." (Cant. v. 2.) In fine, her love having attained the highest degree of intensity of which her mortal capacity was susceptible, and admitting of no further increase, it detached her soul by a last violent effort from her body, and added to her other glorious privileges, that of a holocaust of charity.

Second Point.—With her ardent love of God, the Blessed Virgin combined perfect charity to her neighbour, and lively zeal for the salvation of men. The holy Fathers say, that by her prayers the period of the Incarnation of the Son of God was advanced, so persevering were her supplications to Heaven for the reparation of the human race. But when she had borne the God of charity in her womb, and subsequently witnessed His labours, His sufferings, and His love for man, her zeal and charity attained such ardour that of her may be said in a proportionate degree, what St. Paul says of the eternal Father, that "she spared not even her own Son, but delivered Him up for us all," thereby contributing most efficaciously to our salvation. (Rom. viii. 32.) By her constant prayers, her perfect example, and her instructions, she increased the Church, and confirmed the faithful in their belief, therefore might she say to them with more reason than St. Paul, "you are my little children of whom I am in labour again, until Christ be formed in you." (Gal. iv. 19.) Thank her for her excessive charity; love her and confide in her as your good Mother. Beg of her to obtain for you filial tenderness for herself, and maternal affection for your neighbour, that you may thus imitate her zeal and charity; finally, resolve to do so.

Third Point.—The Blessed Virgin has been appointed by the Almighty the mediatrix between Him and His creatures, consequently she is, next to her Divine Son, the great means of their salvation. "She is," says St. Bernard, "the channel through which the water of grace flows into the garden of our souls, from its eternal source, which is God; for it is the will or God, that we should receive nothing but through her, and that having given Himself to us by her, we should return to Him through the same path." Fervently thank God for having given you so merciful and powful an advocate. Place unbounded confidence in her, and recur to her in all your wants, but particularly when you are employed in instructing others ; earnestly recommend to her the souls committed to your care, and confide much more in her protection than in your own exertions. Beseech her to obtain for all Ursulines the grace to comply perfectly with their exalted vocation.

Aspirations.—" Lord, who shall dwell in Thy tabernacle, or who shall rest in Thy holy hill? He that hath not done evil to his neighbour." (Ps. xiv. 1, 3.)

" The Lord direct our heart in the charity of God." (2 Thes. iii. 5.)

Lecture.—18th, 19th, and 20th chapters of the Treatise on Fraternal Union (Rodriguez.)

For the Practice, see "Supplement."

SECOND MEDITATION.

First Point.—Read the chapter of the Constitutions on Charity ; consider the perfection in which the practice of this virtue is therein inculcated, and the motives suggested for labouring in its acquisition.

Second Point.—Examine the faults you have committed against charity by contempt of your neighbour, suspicions, and rash judgments. 2nd. By jealousy, and envy, grieving at his advantages, whether spiritual or corporal, or rejoicing at his misfortunes. 3rd. By dislike, resentment, or desire of revenge. 4th. By detraction, ridicule, contention, harsh and contemptuous expressions. 5th. By repeating what you may have heard to the prejudice of others, and thereby causing dissensions and division. 6th. By neglecting to assist your neighbour when you could and ought to do so, or by relieving him with reluctance. 7th. Examine also, whether you have discharged your duties in the Institute, with a sincere and zealous desire to promote the glory of God by the advancement of the children. 8th. If you have neglected to instruct your pupils; if you have scandalized them by the immortification of your passions, or your inattention to Rule. Implore pardon for your past faults, and resolve to correct them.

Third Point.—Recal to mind the motives which most forcibly urged you this week to embrace the practice of charity, and to labour zealously for the salvation of souls. Renew your resolutions on these heads, and present them to Jesus Christ, through the hands of His Blessed Mother, beseeching Him to assist you by His efficacious grace to observe them perfectly: write them at your leisure as before. Offer the holy Communion to-morrow, to obtain grace to attend faithfully to the resolutions which God inspired you with during the last four weeks; and beg of Him to imprint on your heart the image of His adorable perfections, that His spirit may reign in you and possess you totally.

SECOND PART

OF THE

EXERCISES PREPARATORY TO PROFESSION.

THE EXERCISES OF THE PASSION.

1. The exercises of the four weeks past were intended for your instruction on the obligation contracted by those who make solemn vows, and on the virtues which Religious are bound to practise ; thus serving as distant preparation for Profession. Now, that the important period draws near, it becomes your duty to prepare your soul with more fervour, and to endeavour to purify your heart by contrition, and adorn your soul with the virtues becoming the destined Spouse of Jesus Christ.

2. The following Exercises are intended to assist you in this undertaking. They are well calculated to produce this double effect, if pursued with fidelity and devotion; therefore they should be commenced with renewed fervour and serious efforts to meditate profoundly on the interior and exterior sufferings of Jesus Christ, and to enter into the true spirit of compunction and penance.

3. You will make the Meditations on the mysteries of the Passion, appointed for each day, unless otherwise directed.

4. You will read two lectures every day, as you have been in the habit of doing for the four preceding weeks, making use of some treatise on the Passion in Grenada, Rodriguez, Moliniere, or any other.

5. Endeavour to accompany the representation of a mystery of the Passion appointed for each day, in the refectory, with the spirit of sincere devotion, dwelling interiorly on all that Jesus Christ suffered for you; and endeavouring to draw from your reflections, corresponding sentiments of contrition and desire to satisfy for your sins.

6. The representation of the mystery of the Passion which you meditate on Sundays and holydays, will be deferred to the following day. Should the time be limited, you may make two devotions on the same day; one at dinner, and the other at supper.

PREPARATORY MEDITATION.

First Point.—The dignity to which that soul aspires, who wishes to unite herself with her God by the vows of religion, is so exalted, so sublime, that properly speaking no preparation on her part can be considered sufficient; therefore, if by this solemn act she becomes so transcendently dignified as to rank as the Spouse of Jesus Christ, the Sovereign Lord of heaven and earth, how fervent should not her preparation be for her happy nuptials; how ardent her desires to attract and secure the love of her heavenly Spouse! The first disposition required then in the soul who aspires so high, is purity, which consists in being exempt from sin, and clothed in the robe of sanctifying grace. This preparatory disposition is signified by the linen robe of pure and dazzling whiteness, given in the Apocalypse (chap. xix.) to the spouse of the Lamb, on the day of her nuptials. But whence does this robe derive its purity, its splendour, if not from the blood of that Lamb, in which it has been washed, according to the words of the same inspired writer, who says, (chap. vii.), that the Saints have whitened their robes in His precious blood. To produce this effect in your soul, is the great object you should keep in view during the exercises you now undertake, as no considerations tend more directly to purify the heart, than serious reflections on the sufferings of Jesus Christ. 1st. Because those reflections naturally excite to sorrow for the sins which caused those sufferings; and 2ndly, because by awaking in your soul holy affections of love, of compassion, of desires, of imitation, &c., you will apply to yourself the merit and fruit of the Passion of Christ. Earnestly implore the Almighty to grant you the grace to enter on these exercises in this spirit.

Second Point.—The spouse of Jesus Christ should not only be clothed in the robe of purity, but, to gain the love of her heavenly bridegroom, she should bear some resemblance to Him, and be moreover adorned with the ornaments of every virtue. Therefore it is, that in the Canticle of Canticles (chap. viii.), Jesus Christ desires His spouse to place Him as a seal on her heart, and on her arm; thereby signifying, that he will have her interiorly and exteriorly bear His image, and exhibit a lively representation of His heavenly virtues. Now it was principally in His sacred passion that the Son of God was pleased to become a seal and a signet to be deeply impressed on all and each of His elect. It was then, that His adorable humanity was lacerated with nails, torn with scourges, crowned with thorns; and that the virtues of the Man God, His humility, His patience, His obedience, His charity, His detachment from all things of earth, shone forth in resplendent perfection. Therefore it is, that the sacred passion of our Lord Jesus Christ which you are about to make the subject of your attentive consideration, should be deeply engraven on your heart; and that the heroic virtues, of which He then gave you the example, should render you interiorly and exteriorly a living image of Jesus Christ crucified.

Have recourse to the Blessed Virgin, to obtain this grace, by her intercession, saying: O holy Mother of God! I beseech thee to implore for me, that the wounds, the sorrows, and the heavenly virtues of thy Son may be deeply imprinted on my heart.

Third Point.—The most efficacious means for deriving from the consideration of Christ's sacred Passion the two important fruits of purity of heart, and imitation of his virtues, is to endeavour that your meditation should produce a third effect, viz., an ardent love for your Divine Redeemer. For this there are two reasons: first, in proportion to your love for God, will be your sorrow for the sins that have offended Him, and your commiseration for the suffering by which those sins were expiated. Consequently, the more ardent your love, the more intense will be your contrition: because, as St. Augustine says, "sorrow springs from love." Secondly, because we shall hereby the more easily attain to a likeness with Christ: for resemblance is either the cause or the consequence of love; it being peculiar to love, either to spring from, or to produce a resemblance with its object. It is love, then, that by melting your heart in its burning furnace, will dispose it, like soft wax, to receive the impression of that divine seal, and at the same time, to exhibit a lively representation of the virtues of Jesus Christ. Endeavour then that each of your meditations should increase this love in your soul. What subject could provide more powerful incentives to love, than the sufferings of your God? Where is the heart, however hardened it may be, which will not melt at the contemplation of a God of infinite majesty, not only enduring such torments to save a weak and guilty creature, but enduring them also with boundless love?

Implore earnestly of our Lord that this divine fire may be enkindled in your soul, while you meditate on His sufferings; and on your part, leave nothing undone to dispose yourself for this grace, by going through these exercises with great fervour, and in the true spirit of interior recollection.

FIRST DAY.

In your meditation of this day, you will consider the sublime lessons given us by our Lord, when He washed His disciples' feet; and dwell principally on two points: First, the profound humility of the Son of God, exhibited for our instruction in this mystery: "I have given you an example," said He, "that as I have done to you, so you do also." Secondly, the absolute necessity of being purified from sin, to be united to Jesus Christ. Weigh well the import of these words: "If I wash thee not, thou shalt have no part with me." (Ibid.)

Aspirations.—Jesus Christ "humbled Himself, becoming obedient unto death, even to the death of the cross." (Philippians, ii.)

Lord, "wash me yet more from my iniquity, and cleanse me from my sin." (Ps. l.)

For the Practice, see "Supplement."

FIRST MEDITATION.

Jesus washes His Apostles' feet. Lord! dost thou wash my feet? (John, xiii.)

First Point.—"Jesus knowing that the Father had given Him all things into His hands, and that He came from God, and goeth to God, He riseth from supper, and layeth aside His garments," and "having taken a towel, girded Himself. After that He putteth water into a basin, and began to wash the feet of His disciples, and to wipe them with the towel wherewith He was girded."

Consider in this Meditation the astonishing and affecting spectacle of the God, at whose word the pillars of the firmament tremble, before whom every knee bows in heaven and on earth, thus bending the knee before His creatures, and washing the feet, not only of His faithful disciples, but those also of the treacherous Judas who He knew was about to betray Him. The admirable humility which impels the Saviour to an action so servile, yet so sublime, is the offspring of charity unparalleled and unconquerable. Knowing as He does that He is the Son of the living God, begotten before the day-star, and sprung from the bosom of the Divinity, to which He was about to return, nevertheless He sinks in proportion to His essential elevation. He knows that His Father has given all things into His hands, even the destiny of the traitor who plots His death, but He loves that traitor, and therefore His power to punish is not greater than His desire to save. His merciful heart melts into tenderness at the view of the self-devoted wretch who thus madly hurries on to his own perdition. He multiplies His mercies to force the brazen barriers, which malice, effrontery and ingratitude had raised against them in the heart of the guilty Apostle. Though Jesus penetrates the designs of Judas, though He reads his inmost soul, He withholds no exterior mark of His favour. His place is allowed him in the midst of the Apostolic College: he shares in the familiar intercourse of the paschal banquet. Jesus unfolds to him, as to the rest, the secrets of His heart, and gives to him, as to the others, the parting lessons of Godlike wisdom and love: but all being vain, He who had come to seek and to save that which was lost, makes a last effort, He sinks at the feet of His perfidious Apostle, He washes them with His own sacred hands, and in that imploring posture, speaking sweetly to his inmost heart, He, as it were, entreats him to accept a pardon. O incomprehensible charity of Jesus! O dreadful obduracy of man! Where will pride, where will revenge hide their heads, to escape the bright light thrown on their deformity by this great example!

Second Point.—When Jesus came to Simon Peter, that fervent Apostle was penetrated with awe at the view of his Lord and Master prostrate at his feet. Long before that time he had publicly acknowledged Him to be the Christ, the Son of the living God, and now that he sees that Being, whose Divinity he recognized, stoop so low, he is confounded in mind, and seized with a holy awe; he even determines never to concur in the degradation of his Master, and in the transports of that zeal and love peculiar to his ardent character and devoted attachment to his Lord, he solemnly exclaims: "Thou shalt never wash my feet!" (John, xiii.) Oh! what would he have said had he been on the mount of Calvary, where the tears, the blood, and the water gushing from the side of Jesus, swept like a tide of mercy over the sins of the world, and provided a fountain ever since open for "the washing of the sinner and the unclean." (Zach. xiii. 1.)

Consider now your own position, and examine your heart. Oh! if the fervent and devoted Peter, the affectionate companion of Jesus, whose heart, more than his person, had, for three years, inseparably adhered to his Divine Master,—if he, the first confessor of His Divinity, the witness of His glories, and the fearless defender of His doctrines, was struck with awe at the view of His humiliation,—what should your feelings be at the near approach of your espousals with the King of Heaven; with Him, to whom "nothing can be added" (Eccl. xiii. 21); yet, who stoops to your nothingness, and desires to unite you to Himself, and to call you His spouse! Be astonished then with Peter, that the God, who "walketh about the poles of heaven" (Job, xxii. 14), should descend, not indeed to wash your feet, but to raise you to a union with Himself. But go farther, and unite with the Apostle in his sovereign dread of separation from Christ, which, appearing to him as the greatest of all evils, induced him not only to accept the overwhelming honour of being served by his God, but impelled him to implore still greater proofs of his Master's love. When assured by Jesus that if he were not washed by him he could have no part with him (St. John, xiii.), Peter's soul expands in ardent desires to have all obstacles removed to the union with his Lord, which he felt necessary to his happiness: "Lord, not only my feet but also my hands and my head." (Ibid.) Ponder these words, penetrate their deep import. Call on Jesus to remove not only all serious obstacles to the union of love He desires to contract with you, but to wash you from every stain of sin, from every shadow of imperfection. Listen to the interior voice, which counsels you on this most solemn occasion to still in your mind the tumult of idle thoughts; to root up from your heart the least fibre of earthly affections; to shake from your feet the dust of deliberate, though apparently trivial imperfections, that thereby you may offer an unblemished victim, well pleasing in the sight of Him "who hates iniquity and loves only justice." Call, with Peter, on Jesus, to wash not only your head, your feet, your hands, but your whole being; and on your part resolve to correspond so faithfully with the graces attached to the exercises you have undertaken, that in the solemn moment of your union with Himself by the vows of religion, you may deserve that your Divine Spouse should whisper to your soul these consoling words: "Thou art clean,—Thou art all fair, and there is no spot in Thee." (Cant. iv.)

Third Point.—The Scripture says, that when Judas had taken the morsel, he left the cenacle. He abandoned his Master, and being by an unworthy communion *strengthened*, as Job expresses it (xv. 25), *against the Almighty*, he promptly becomes the sport of Satan, who begins to sift him as wheat. His feet had just been washed by the sacred hands of Jesus, but he was not cleansed—he had been warned by the awful denunciation that one amongst them was about to fall, but he was not awakened. He had eaten the food of life, but was not strengthened, and drunk the blood of the New Testament, without being refreshed. He departs,—alas! to return no more. Here the Passion of the Son of God may be properly said to have commenced. This was the first wound inflicted on the tender heart of Jesus—a wound deep and agonising in proportion to the black ingratitude of his treacherous, though favoured Apostle.

The feelings of the Man God at this melancholy instance of human depravity were ages before depicted by the prophet, speaking in the person of Jesus Christ, —"If my enemy had reviled me, I would verily have borne with it; and if he that hateth me, had spoken great things against me, I would perhaps have hidden myself from him; but thou, a man of one mind, my guide and my familiar, who didst take sweet meats together with me, in the house of God we walked with consent." (Ps. liv. 13, 14, 15.) Oh! how truly were those predictions accomplished in the wounded heart of the Redeemer, when He sees the treacherous Apostle go to head the ruffian band, with whom he had not only contracted to sell his Master, but engaged to betray Him personally into their hands. Never before was a warning spectacle held up to mankind so well calculated to pierce our hearts and our *flesh with fear*, as the Psalmist expresses it (Ps. cxviii.), and to make us all, whether strong or weak, enlightened or ignorant, holy or sinful, tremble at the judgment of God over the abuse of grace, and at the awful responsibility of those who, having received much, will be rigorously required to make a proportionate return. Ponder well then these impressive truths. The worst, the basest of crimes was committed by an Apostle! He who was called to announce the glory of Jesus, was the first to deliver Him up to the prince of darkness! It follows that the state to which you are called, holy and perfect as it is, will not afford you an infallible security against the tyranny of passion, or the weakness of human nature. Neither will past fidelity, nor present fervour ensure perseverance to the end, for we have no testimony of the unhappy Apostle's having been openly irregular during the three years that he followed his Divine Master with the eleven, preaching the word, announcing the approach of the kingdom of God, and even casting out devils from others in His name. (St. Mark, i. 15.) Still how low he fell! how deeply he sank into irretrievable perdition! How did all this happen? One vile passion seduced his heart: from small beginnings the evil increased, and at length proceeded to such extremities as to become proof against not only the example of the Apostles, but even the eloquence and power of a God! Learn from this, that it is possible you may begin with fervour, and for some time proceed with fidelity—you may join your sisters, as Judas did the eleven, with such exterior regularity, as to merit as little, as he appears to have done, any public reproach; you may, in the discharge of the functions peculiar to your institute, zealously announce by instruction the kingdom of God, and root out from the hearts of your young charge every plant which your Heavenly Father had not planted there; still you may fall an unfortunate victim to one vice unsubdued, or even to the neglect of acquiring one necessary virtue! There is no other security than confidence in God alone, and correspondence with His graces, by endeavouring to extirpate every habitual fault, however trifling it may seem, and generously aspiring to every solid virtue, however much it may cost you.

SECOND MEDITATION.

First Point.—After Jesus had washed His disciples' feet, He sat again in the midst of them;—He gave them the sweet, consoling assurance that they were clean, one only excepted, and asked them a question, for which to that fervent band there would scarcely appear to be any necessity. The Apostles had just received from the divine hand of Jesus, the most precious pledge of His love. He had given them Himself, and made them the first sanctuaries of His sacramental presence. For three years, they had been in His own school, drinking at the fountain of wisdom, folded in the arms of a special protection, and listening to those *words* of life which "are smoother than oil, and the same are darts." (Ps. liv. 22.) Softened by the affecting circumstances of the solemn scene around them,—penetrated with sadness at the mere apprehension of separation from Jesus, and more than ever inflamed with love, they forgot themselves and all things else to centre their affections and desires in the Master they adored, and dreaded to lose. The thoughts of each seemed absorbed in the miracle they witnessed of power, of mercy, of love; and their hearts united in the ardent wish, the firm determination expressed by Peter, to avoid at all hazards the dreaded misfortune of separation from Jesus, and to follow Him resolutely to prison and to death. Still the Saviour says, "know you what I have done to you?" (John, xiii. 12.)

O all-important question! well calculated to awaken the spirit of salutary fear, of earnest vigilance in all those who, like the Apostles, are separated from amongst men, that they may no longer be of this world, which on that very occasion was stamped with the malediction of the Eternal, by being excluded from the prayer of Jesus. Consider this question addressed to you. Imagine you hear Jesus Christ saying to you, as He did to His beloved Apostles, "know ye what I have done to you?" Do you comprehend the priceless value of the gift bestowed on you, in your high and holy vocation? Do you know the height of the dignity to which I am about to raise you? Have you a deep sense of the obligations which such a vocation imposes, and of the extent of the sacrifices, which in consequence will be expected from you? "Oh! if you but knew the gift of God, and who He is" that has deigned to choose you amongst thousands for His spouse, you would sink into the depth of your own nothingness, and exclaim with Job, "My God is higher than heaven, and what shall I do? He is deeper than hell, and can I know Him?" But as He said to His Apostles, "I know whom I have chosen" (John, xiii. 18), so did He know you, and nevertheless, He selected you, though from amongst the weakest things of this world, to elevate you higher than man could aspire. Why did He do this? Look to your past life, which so little entitled you to the immense benefit bestowed on you; consider your present dispositions, which, however fervent, fall immeasurably below what should be expected from you, and in the sincerity of your heart, and in the fulness of your gratitude, you will acknowledge that there is no other reason for this benefit than because He has "loved you with an everlasting love," and, therefore, He has chosen you, taking pity on you." (Jeremiah, xxxi. 3). Earnestly beg of our Lord to speak to your heart, as He did to His Apostles, and to teach you Himself what He has done for you; so that knowing the gift of God you may exert every power of your soul to profit of it.

Second Point.—After awakening the minds of His Apostles to the greatness of the benefit bestowed on them in their exalted destination, the Saviour points out to them the peculiar acts by which He expects they will show their gratitude for all that He has done for them. "I have given you an example," said He, "that as I have done to you, so you do also" (St. John, xiii. 15); and a little later He adds, "I give you a new commandment, that you love one another as I have loved you." (Ibid.) Consider these words as addressed to yourself, and reflect in what manner you are now called on to offer to God a host of praise, a victim of thanksgiving. An example is given to you,—Jesus, the eternal word of God, has descended to wash the feet of His Apostles, you therefore should be ready "to wash one another's feet" (St. John, 14), which in the opinion of sacred writers means that you should embrace, love, and if called on, be ready to spend your life in the exercise of active, menial, and painful duties towards your neighbour. But take care to dwell particularly on the manner in which you are called on to prove that you know what He has done for you, and are determined to make His new commandment the rule of your future life. "Love as I have loved you," says Jesus. When did Jesus love you? Always. How did He love you? Without measure. Why did He love you? For His Father's sake, because you were loved by Him and destined to glorify Him for ever. In this manner, then, He requires you to devote yourself to your neighbour, and particularly to that cherished portion of His elect which His providence may hereafter commit to your care, in the discharge of the duties peculiar to your vocation. You should resolve to love them solely for God, which single disposition will ensure as close a resemblance as it is possible there can be, between your charity for your neighbour, and that with which the heart of your Redeemer burned for you. Your charity will be as His was always, perfectly independent of the vicissitudes accompanying affection merely human: it will be, under all circumstances, no matter how much or how little its objects may personally merit your care and exertion, and surely it will have no measure for its ultimate object will be the Lord and Spouse of our soul, to whom every affection of your head is consecrated. Beg of Jesus to grant you this twofold spirit of ardent charity, without which you may become no better thauan idler in His vineyard, or a hireling in His sheep-fold. Implore that spirit of prayer which is the source of light and sanctity; and that zeal which renders both profitable to the salvation of others. In this holy time of preparation, offer to God your future labours, and pray earnestly for those who may be hereafter committed to your care, tha tin word and work you may edify them; that you may be worthy to mediate for them before the altar of the living God; that you may be their Apostle when you instruct and their successful physician when you correct them. "If you know these things," says Christ, "you shall be blessed if you do them." (St. John, xiii. 17.)

SECOND DAY.

To-day you will meditate on the agony and prayers of Christ in the Garden of Olives, dwelling principally on His extreme sorrow for your sins, that this consideration may inspire you with horror of their deformity and contrition for their guilt.

Aspirations.—"My soul is sorrowful even unto death." (St. Matt. xxvi. 38.)

"My sins are multiplied beyond the sand of sea, and I am not worthy to look up to heaven because of the multitude of my iniquities."

For the Practice, see "Supplement."

FIRST MEDITATION.

On the Prayer of Jesus in the Garden of Olives.

"And He was withdrawn away from them a stone's cast; and kneeling down, He prayed." (St. Luke, xxii. 41.)

First Point.—It was in prayer that Jesus sought strength and comfort amidst the overwhelming desolation which overspread His soul at the commencement of His Passion. Prayer is the element of the Saints; their centre and their refuge; and if they do not always derive sensible consolation from its exercise, it ever proves to them at least a source of heavenly vigor and supernatural courage.

Jesus prayed in the solitude of night, to teach us that the voice of God cannot be distinctly heard by the soul, unless the tumult of worldly cares and distractions has first been silenced. He seeks utter retirement, separating even from His three cherished disciples, because the sacred communications of the soul with God admit neither witnesses nor interruption. Cherish the spirit of interior solitude, and learn that the love of dissipation is totally incompatible with the love of prayer.

Jesus knew that an increase of interior anguish awaited Him in prayer; He knew, too, that ere he terminated His suppliant address to His Eternal Father, His sentence of death would be irrevocably confirmed; yet these considerations were insufficient to deter Him from the holy exercise, which He pursued, not for His own consolation, but to accomplish the will, and promote the glory of His Father.

Are these your dispositions when you pray? Do you approach the throne of God alone, or does the world accompany you there in spirit? Do you seek in prayer only the fulfilment of God's will, and the annihilation of your own? the promotion of God's honour and the destruction of self-love?

O my Saviour, how far am I from these perfect dispositions! How opposed is Thy profound recollection to my dissipation of mind! Thy vigilance to my sloth, Thy zeal to my self-love, which insinuates itself even into my best actions and purest intentions! Mercifully supply, O Divine Redeemer! for my many deficiencies, render me less unworthy of union with thee, and since I am destitute of suitable dispositions for prayer, inspire me Thyself how to petition for them efficaciously.

Second Point.—He fell upon His face, praying, and saying: "My Father, if it be possible, let this chalice pass from me. Nevertheless, not as I will but as Thou wilt." (St. Matt. xxvi. 39.)

Looking on Jesus, your humbled, suppliant God, as your Master and Model, study the sacred and instructive lessons conveyed by His example in the garden, and learn there how to pray. Filled with profound reverence for His eternal Father, Jesus kneels before Him, with extended arms, in the attitude of an humble petitioner for mercy. Laden as He is with the sins of men, and overwhelmed with consequent confusion and shame, He soon exchanges this posture for one more lowly still, and falls prostrate to the very earth. Animated with confidence equal to His humility, He calls on His Father, in accents of tender love and intense agony. Oh! in whose bosom shall the child deposit His sorrow, if not in that of His Father? "Father," He said, "my soul is sad,—it languishes,—it sighs,—it is ready, in its agony, to burst the bonds of mortality. Oh! cast one glance of pity on Thy suffering, innocent Son!" He prays that the destined chalice may pass away, but, at the same time, declares Himself equally prepared for the refusal or the grant of His petition; equally disposed to live or to die. The more His anguish increases, the longer He perseveres in His supplications to heaven, and although He thrice interrupts His prayer, he does so only at the suggestion of charity, which inspires Him to forget Himself, that He may attend to His afflicted followers.

O sweet Jesus! Thou whose example is my refuge, and whose instructions are my treasure, how confounded I feel on comparing my prayer with thine! How lamentable that I should be so distracted, while Thou art wholly absorbed in God! That I should be so cold, while Thou art so ardent! That I should assume a careless attitude, while Thou art prostrate on the cold ground! O heavenly features buried in the dust, may your image be indelibly engraven on the barren clay of my sinful heart! Sacred lips which embrace the earth as a mark of reconciliation with its offending children, speak pardon and mercy to my guilty soul! O Divine Redeemer! deign to animate my prayers with Thine own Spirit, that so they may find acceptance before the throne of the Most High.

Third Point.—"My Father, if this chalice may not pass away, but I must drink it, Thy will be done." (St. Matt. xxvi. 42.)

Jesus prays, and His petition is unheard, yet He complains not of the apparently rigorous dispensation; while I, a miserable, dependent creature, a vile worm of the earth, dare to murmur when my prayers are rejected. O incomprehensible charity of the Son of God! He presents two petitions, one for Himself, the other for us; and as the two are incompatible, He in a manner revokes that involving His own interests, that He may the more securely provide for ours. While there is question of averting the terrible fate from which nature recoils, His desires are imperfect and His prayer conditional,—"if it be possible"—but when our salvation is the point at issue, His will to accomplish it is so absolute and unwavering, that not even the prospect of a violent and ignominious death can shake it. "Not as I will, but as Thou wilt."

Let us learn from this heroic act of submission, that the most sublime prayer is that which severs the will from self, to centre it wholly in the will of the Almighty. Let us also observe that while God hears such petitions as are conformable to the eternal rules of His unerring providence, He rejects those which spring from the unsubdued impulse of an immortified will, thus effectually manifesting the solidity and tenderness of His love. You sometimes seem to yourself to struggle as it were with the goodness of God; you pray, and He does not hear; you attempt to approach, and He repels your advances; you form good resolutions, and you violate them the next moment. It would almost appear as if your heavenly Father delighted to oppose your wishes and disconcert your plans. O divine meekness and mercy, concealed under the aspect of assumed rigour, how clearly dost Thou manifest Thy power, by apparently combating against those, for whom Thou combatest in reality! Sweet Jesus! eradicate from my soul every feeling which displeases Thee. Let but one desire survive on the ruin of all others,—the one, sole, single, earnest wish to do Thy will, and never on any occasion, or for any cause, to swerve from it.

SECOND MEDITATION.

On the Agony of Jesus in the Garden.

"And being in an agony, He prayed the longer." (St. Luke, xxii. 43.)

First Point.—The words of the angelic messenger deputed from Heaven to console the world's Redeemer, while they imparted strength to His suffering soul, communicated no sensible comfort or relief. His humility accepted the one, to teach us distrust of our weakness, but His charity refused the other, to show us that true courage may exist, although betraying no sensible evidence of its influence, and that it is quite possible to adhere firmly to God's service in the absence of every sweet and consoling emotion. Thus does Jesus instruct both the strong and the weak; the one by seeking supernatural support from God, the source of all strength; the other by submitting to the extreme of mental anguish, and admitting no ra yof comfort to dispel the deep darkness. Far from decreasing, His agony gradually redoubles at attaining last a degree of violence immeasurably surpassing that which accompanies the final struggles of ordinary men. Oppressed with fear and sadness, overwhelmed with confusion and desolation, He looks around for some faint beam of hope, some glimpse of comfort; but, alas! on every side He encounters only new sources of affliction. If He raises His eyes to Heaven, He beholds His Father's angry countenance, which fills Him with consternation and terror; if He contemplates His blessed Mother, the anticipation of her approaching bereavement penetrates His heart with grief; if He glances at His cross, the dark vision of ignomony and torture appals His inmost soul; in a word, nothing can comfort, while, on the contrary, all conspires to alarm and afflict Him.

O Jesus, model of the strong! teach me to serve Thee independently of sensible comfort and sweetness. O strength of the weak! assist me to make a holy and profitable use of the consolations Thou hast purchased for me by Thy sorrows.

Second Point.—In His overwhelming sadness, Jesus kneels as a poor criminal, who tremblingly awaits His death sentence, and shrinks from its anticipated horrors. He assumes the most humble and suppliant of attitudes, to disarm the justice of His Father, but seeing that justice to be inexorable, and terrified at the deluge of evils about to burst on Him, His Heart seems rent into two distinct portions, one of which recoils from approaching torture, while the other desires and invokes death with invincible courage and constancy. One trembles at the penalties prepared by God's terrific anger; the other contemplates them reverentially and embraces them voluntarily. One fears pain, the other ardently desires it. The conflict becomes so violent, that Jesus sinks to the earth, convulsed and exhausted; the victim of torments so severe and so multiplied, that but for the exercise of the superhuman power allied to His Divinity, He could not have withstood them.

O Divine Saviour! teach me, I conjure Thee, to subdue myself, and to combat generously and perseveringly for the glory of Thy name and the salvation of my soul. Painful as may be the struggle to resist my passions and surmount my repugnances, it never can equal Thy agony in the garden. Blessed be that mercy which inspired Thee to taste all the bitterness of death, that thus its terrors might be lessened for me. Grant, I beseech Thee, that my life be a perpetual conflict against nature, and my death a glorious victory, to be consummated by a still more perfect triumph in Heaven.

Third Point.—Although oppressed with desolation which no human language can describe, Jesus desisted not from prayer, but on the contrary prolonged it with increasing fervour and earnestness. He thus teaches us an admirable secret replete with divine wisdom, that to conquer our spiritual enemies, we must pray, and that to pray, we must generously overcome the lassitude and discouragement we may experience in that holy exercise. He endures a violent agony, to show us, as St. Chrysostom remarks, that in order to adhere to God, we must courageously trample on all the repugnances of self-will; and He perseveres in prayer, to teach us that we too must pray, if we hope for the strength necessary to subdue those natural repugnances. O my Saviour! assist me to do Thy will at the expense of my own, and to persevere in prayer until my agitation is calmed, my resistance conquered, and my will disposed to suffer all Thou shalt ordain; to submit unconditionally to Thy decrees for life or death; for soul and body; for all I have and am in time and eternity.—Amen.

THIRD DAY.

To-day you will meditate on our Divine Lord's seizure in the garden, considering that Jesus Christ submitted to be bound as a malefactor, in order to atone for that fatal abuse of liberty, which has led to your frequent revolts against God, as He Himself reproaches you by the mouth of His prophet: "Thou hast broken my yoke, thou hast burst my bonds, and thou saidst: I will not serve." (Jer. ii. 20.)

Aspirations.—"The breath of our mouth, Christ the Lord, is taken in our sins." (Lam. iv. 20.)

"Turn to me, O Lord, and deliver my soul: O save me, for Thy mercy's sake." (Ps. vi. 5.)

For the Practice, see "Supplement."

FIRST MEDITATION.

Jesus bound as a Victim.

"Then the band, and the tribune, and the servants of the Jews took Jesus and bound Him." (St. John, xviii. 12.)

First Point.—The liberty of kings is inviolable; amenable only to the universal law which condemns man to dissolution. Why then is the eternal Son of God laden with chains? Is He not the King of all hearts, and the Sovereign of all wills? Yes, most assuredly; nevertheless He is bound, because destined to be immolated as a victim for the salvation of the human race. The law ordained that the victim for sacrifice should be secured, lest its struggles in the compulsory surrender of life should detract from the solemnity of the legal ceremonial. God loves not the reluctant homage of the unwilling heart, but graciously accepts the services of the cheerful giver. Never was a more willing victim pre sented before the eternal throne, than the adorable victim of the new law, Jesus Christ the Saviour of men. He needed no bonds to control His movements, yet He submitted to them, that He might die in the chains of obedience.

O Divine Redeemer! grant I beseech Thee that my obedience, like Thine, may be voluntary and generous, and my will ever subject to that of the Most High. Too happy shall I be in meriting the glorious title of Thy victim! Too blessed in devoting my whole existence to Thy service!

Second Point.—Jesus is bound as a captive of love. He loved me, and delivered Himself for me, and had His heart not first voluntarily assumed the chains of charity, never could His enemies have succeeded in investing Him with the fetters of malefactors. No manacles of their invention could have restrained His freedom, had it been His will to burst them asunder. O charity, how strong are thy bonds, which can reduce the omnipotent God to the condition of a helpless prisoner! Oh! why do you not bind me to Him so irrevocably, that I may have no farther power to separate from Him!

Most amiable Redeemer! when I behold Thee chained as a criminal, I am overwhelmed with astonishment and dismay: yet, when I consider that Thou hast submitted to bonds, only to break the chains of my sins and miseries, gratitude prevails over every other sentiment. But, O Divine Saviour! since Thou hast burst my bonds, why am I still a slave? Or since slavery seems congenial to my inclinations, why at least am I not the captive of Thy love rather than of the world and self? O Almighty Lord! who alone hath power to bind and loose, enslave and free me at one and the same moment. Bind me in Thy chains, and deliver me from those I myself have fashioned. Disengage my heart perfectly from creatures, and attach it firmly and irrevocably to Thy cross!

Third Point.—Jesus is bound as a criminal and a robber. "You are come out," He said, "as it were against a thief, with swords and clubs." (St. Luke, xxii. 52.) O Lord! whose delight is to ravish the hearts of men, when wilt Thou take full possession of mine? When shall I be able to say with the Spouse in the Canticles, that "Thou hast wounded my heart?" (Cant. iv. 9.) Oh! shall I never love Thee as Thou deservest? Since Thou art infinitely amiable, how can it be that I love Thee so little? Am I incapable of loving, or is it that I am blind to Thy attractions and insensible to Thy claims? O my God! my life! my strength! I desire to love Thee with my whole heart, and since Thy enemies treat Thee as a robber, I fervently pray that the imputation may not prove unfounded as regards me, but that Thou mayest appropriate my undivided affections and retain them for ever. Oh! why cannot I become Thy accomplice in the crime with which Thou art charged? Why cannot I forcibly seize on the hearts of all men and lay them captive at Thy feet? How willingly would I endure a thousand deaths for the attainment of this blessed end!

SECOND MEDITATION.

Jesus submitted to be bound of His own free Will.

"They took Jesus and bound Him." (St. John, xviii. 12.)

First Point.—Jesus submitted to wear the bonds of a malefactor, that He might thereby deliver us from the thraldom of sin. He, the independent Monarch of the universe, sacrificed His liberty, that we, His miserable slaves, might be emancipated from Satan's tyranny. He wears bonds of three different kinds, each closely connected; the external bonds imposed by the Jews, the bonds of His own insatiable love, and lastly those of our iniquities. By assuming these three-fold bonds it was, that He rescued us from the dominion of the infernal foe, and restored us to the blessed freedom of the sons of God. "If you seek me," said He to His relentless enemies, "let my disciples go their way in peace." (St. John, xviii. 8.)

O Divine Redeemer, how boundless are my obligations to Thee! Thou hast broken my bonds, Thou hast delivered me from the ignominious servitude of sin; Thou hast called me from captivity to freedom; from darkness to light; from misery to joy of spirit. Oh! may I never consent to resume the fetters from which Thou hast so mercifully, so generously liberated me, at the cost of Thy own great humiliation, and may I devote the whole of my remaining life to praise, bless, serve and love Thee, my most liberal Benefactor!

Second Point.—"The breath of our mouth, Christ the Lord, is taken in our sins." (Lam. iv. 20.) Jesus would be bound, to teach us a salutary dread of that fatal love of liberty whence spring all man's spiritual disorders, and to inspire us with an efficacious determination to live henceforth beneath the shade of His bonds. Fear not the shades of the chains of Christ; it is not deadly nor even dangerous. In His bonds and His cross, on the contrary, are life, security, strength and glory. Jesus first assumed the bonds of His love, and then those of His Passion; but, if we aspire to share His triumph in Heaven, we must first put on the chains of sufferings and then the fetters of love. Let us embrace the cross with our whole hearts, and fervently implore the precious treasure of charity, beseeching Him who deigned for our sakes to become the temporary prisoner of the Jews, that we may be captives of His love for time and eternity.

Third Point.—Jesus was bound, to restrain the hands of Divine justice, and avert the punishment it had decreed for guilty man. Can He not also bind the hands of miserable sinners, and check their fatal facility to outrage and insult Him? Since He compassionated me in my bondage, shall I not sympathize with Him in His? Shall I be so obdurate as to aggravate the weight of His chains, by increasing the already terrific amount of my guilt? O sweet Saviour! who didst restrain Thy justice in order to allow free course to the current of Thy mercy, I conjure Thee to unite me to Thyself by bonds which neither life nor death can ever dissolve!

Jesus was bound to console those among His afflicted servants who groan in chains and languish amidst the horrors of slavery. St. Paul exhorted the Colossians to "be mindful of his bonds" (iv. 18), and St. Chrysostom also counsels the faithful to seek comfort in their tribulations by contemplating the chains of the great Apostle. If the bonds of Christ's servants are so sacred an object of our veneration, love, and pious meditation, what should be our sentiments towards those of Jesus Christ Himself! O how precious are those bonds, and how profitable is it to the soul frequently to contemplate them! Are you oppressed with desolation of spirit? Call to mind the weary night which your Lord and Redeemer spent in bondage. Are you violently assailed by temptation? Bind your will in the chains of Jesus, that it may never revolt against His law or swerve from the path of virtue. Has Providence decreed you a lot of humiliation and dependence? Cast your eyes on Christ laden with chains, and dragged as a helpless prisoner from one tribunal to another. O Lord Jesus! who would not value the honor and happiness of sharing Thy bonds? I esteem them more highly, since Thou hast worn them, than all the diadems of earth, and I deem it a more glorious triumph to bear them in Thy company, than to arrest the progress of the sun, to command the infernal spirits, or to reign sole sovereign of the universe.

FOURTH DAY.

Your meditation of to-day will be on the blow which Jesus Christ received from the servant of the high priest. Contemplating the depths of abjection to which your sins reduced Him, you will endeavour to excite yourself to lively sorrow for all, especially those of pride and impatience.

Aspirations.—"He shall give His cheek to him that striketh Him, He shall be filled with reproaches." (Lam. iii. 30.)

"It is I, I am He that have sinned, I have done

wickedly; let Thy hand, I beseech Thee, be turned against me," and not against Thy innocent Son. (2 Kings, xxiv. 17.)

For the Practice, see "Supplement."

FIRST MEDITATION.

Jesus receives a Blow from the High Priest's Servant.

"When He had said these things, one of the servants standing by gave Jesus a blow, saying: Answereth Thou the high priest so?" (St. John, xviii. 22.)

Oh, how cruel, how humbling, how unjust the insult offered to Jesus by the high priest's servant! Words of innocence and truth flow from those lips whence none but accents of life had ever issued, and one of His own creatures has the barbarity, the criminal courage to strike Him on the face! And for what object? To gratify the hatred of a malignant judge! O spectacle of horror to men and dismay to angels! Ye heavens! veil yourselves in darkness and gloom, and let the earth tremble to its inmost centre! The face of the incarnate God is struck by a hand armed with iron; blood gushes from His eyes, His mouth, His nostrils. The noise of the blow resounds through the room, and as St. Vincent Ferrier assures us, its violence prostrates the Redeemer to the ground. And yet, this most atrocious insult only excites the applause of the judge and the derision of the mob. O insolent menial, who abuse the authority of your masters! O impious masters, who encourage the audacity of your slave! But more base Christians, who outrage the Creator to please the creature! You are awe-stricken at the insolence of the high priest's servant, and yet perhaps you are more guilty in Heaven's sight than he.

Like him you strike Jesus every time you deliberately commit sin, knowing Him, alas! far better than did that unfortunate servant.

Divine Saviour! soften my obdurate heart, I fervently conjure Thee, and grant that I may never be so daring as to offend Thee, or so base as to renounce Thy service from the apprehension of any creature's displeasure.

Second Point.—Consider the patience of Jesus under this most painful insult. "A man," the Scripture says, "is known by his look, and a wise man, when thou meetest him, is known by his countenance." (Ecl. xix. 26.) Contemplate those Divine features, on which Angels gaze in eternal rapture, and which men dare in their brutality to sully and disfigure. The rays of heavenly light which beam from them will discover to you the reasons why Christ endured so great an insult with such marvellous meekness. He bears it, to efface the dark stain of original sin, and to appropriate as His own portion, the confusion which our individual transgressions merited. He bears it, to emancipate the sinner from the slavery of the devil, a blow having been formerly the prescribed signal for the liberation of slaves. He bears it, to give us a strong and striking lesson of patience, and to teach us to forgive injuries, even when circumstances afford facilities for revenge.

Fire fell from Heaven on the rash beings who failed in respect towards the Prophet Elias; bears devoured the heedless children who mocked Eliseus; Core, Dathan and Abiron, who contemned the authority of Moses, were engulphed alive in the yawning earth. How many means of vengeance lay within reach of Him who drew the world from nothing and who views its inhabitants as so many locusts. But instead of exhibiting the might of His terrible vengeance, He preferred displaying a glorious example of that God-like patience which has subdued the world. Learn from your meek and silent Saviour how to suffer insults, and when your patience is put to the test, say in your heart, as St. Christopher observed to his executioners, "I should return your blows were I not a Christian."

O my Saviour! how deplorable a contrast does my conduct present to Thy example! Thou couldst have been avenged, but wouldst not, whereas I on the contrary retain the desire of vengeance, even without the power to carry it into effect. From my heart I now renounce both the will and the power, beseeching thee, O Lord, should I ever be unfaithful to this resolution, to deprive me even of the capability of nurturing vindictive sentiments against my neighbour.

Third Point.—Nothing, says St. Augustine, could be more correct, more gentle, or more just than the reply of the Son of God to His judge. He did not refuse to answer, lest His silence should be construed into an evidence of contempt for the high priest's authority. When struck, He did not turn the other cheek, as He had Himself counselled, but He did far more, abandoning His sacred body to the fury of the executioners, and devoting Himself to death for our salvation.

Ponder His divine words to the servant who dared to raise His impious hand to strike Him, and endeavour to profit of the holy lessons they so strongly convey. He charitably reproves the miscreant for his fault, without harshness, without emotion, without condemning him to well merited punishment, without retaliating insult for insult, His only aim being to save the soul of the wretched being who had added poignancy to His sufferings, and bitterness to His humiliations. From His example we learn to oppose irritated feelings, not by passion, but by calm reason. Fire cannot be extinguished by fire, nor anger subdued by violence. As water checks the devastating progress of the conflagration, so does moderation restrain the outburst of fury. If you employ no other arms against your enemy than those of meekness and forbearance, nothing will so effectually confound him as the very recollection of the injury he has done you. If you seek vengeance, you confirm his ill will, but if you oppose reason to his injustice, you induce him to enter into himself, to recognize his fault, to condemn it, to expiate it by his own remorse, and thus you strike at the root of numberless breaches of charity, which would eventually lead to the eternal ruin of both.

To all sinners, as well as to the high priest's servant, Jesus says, "If I have spoken evil, give testimony of the evil, but if well, why do you strike me?" Why, He asks, do you strike me, by indulging feelings of hatred and resentment? I endured a blow for your sakes, why will you not bear a word for mine? Are you more exalted, more holy, more deserving than I am? Vain, proud, ambitious, vindictive mortal, why do you strike me? To satisfy passion; to gratify the tempter; to hazard your soul's eternal welfare; what have I done to you that you should thus offend and outrage me? Alas! O Lord! what hast Thou not done to prove Thy love for me, and what have I not done to evince my indifference and ingratitude! Henceforth I will live only to give Thee glory, and to suffer for Thy sake a small portion of what Thou hast endured for my salvation.

SECOND MEDITATION.

Jesus accused by false Witnesses.

"And the chief priests and all the council sought for evidence against Jesus, that they might put Him to death, and found none. For many bore false witness against Him, and their evidence were not agreeing: and the high priest rising up in the midst, asked Jesus, saying: Answereth Thou nothing to the things that are laid to Thy charge by these men? But He held His peace and answered nothing." (St. Mark, xiv. 55, 56, 60, 61.)

First Point.—The doctors of the law, and chief priests, it was, who conspired against the Son of God, and so it often happens, that those destined by their peculiar office to lead men to Heaven, are the first to follow the path of perdition; because superior knowledge, when unaccompanied by the fear of God, serves but to injure others and to increase individual accountability. Hating the light, the enemies of Jesus assemble under the shade of obscurity, to concert their measures of iniquity, and perpetrate their deed of darkness. We should never attempt to deliberate on a plan of action, or make any alteration in our habitual sentiments or conduct, while the mind is agitated by uneasiness or obscured by passion, waiting for the hour of restored tranquillity to form new projects or undertake new practices, and under whatever circumstances we hold communion with our own hearts, we should be careful neither to give nor receive counsel against the interests of Jesus and of our own salvation.

The Jews seek false witness against Christ, that they may condemn the Holy of Holies with some appearance at least of formality and justice, because vice is in itself so hideous and hateful, that even its most daring partisans endeavour to hide it under the mantle of virtue. Contemplate the eternal Son of God amidst that iniquitous assembly; the Judge of the living and the dead submitting to the authority of a wicked human judge, that you may one day find mercy at the tribunal of God's dread jûstice. O innocent Lamb! I conjure Thee by Thy humble patience under insult and calumny, to save me from the too just accusations awaiting me at the bar of Almighty justice. May the calumnies Thou endurest prove my justification; may Thy bonds purchase my freedom; may Thy wounds heal my soul, and Thy humiliations ensure me eternal glory!

Second Point.—By their very office, the judges of Jesus Christ were bound in the face of Heaven and earth, to convict and punish false witnesses; yet instead of complying with this their sacred trust, they actually suborned base traitors to the cause of truth to accuse the All-holy God of crime, and heap calumnies on Him, to whom no shadow of evil can approach. How glorious a testimony to the sanctity of Jesus, that the arrows even of calumny fell harmlessly at His feet! The testimony of His wicked accusers proved but a tissue of contradictions, and thus was its falsity manifested to the world. During this tumultuous scene, He maintained profound silence, to show us the inutility of attempting to refute deliberate and premeditated calumny, which silence confounds more effectually than words, and to teach us also the merit and advantage of submitting without a reply to false accusation, committing our defence to the watchful providence of God.

O increated wisdom! shall I listen to the calumnies of

Thy cruel enemies, and still continue to resent the annoyances I encounter from my fellow-creatures? Even though men should accuse me falsely, how well founded are the charges Thou mightest allege against me, were not Thy justice tempered by mercy! But while I acknowledge myself deserving of every indignity, can I cease to wonder that among Thy own creatures should be found accusers against Thee, the God of all sanctity! Can I cease to lament that even Christians repine at the dispensations of Thy Providence, impatiently desiring the blessings Thou hast withheld, coveting riches, talents, and honours; and murmuring at the want of health and other temporal advantages which they would probably possess but to abuse. Permit not, O Lord, that I should fall into this fatal error, or ever bear false testimony against the all-wise arrangements of Thy Providence; but grant, on the contrary, that I may bless Thy holy name at all times, and eternally bear faithful witness to Thy infinite goodness!

Third Point.—Irritated by the silence of Jesus, and still more by the evident futility of the charges alleged against Him, Caiphas burst into a transport of anger very unworthy of a judge, whose external self-possession should but typify the internal calmness of a soul free from passion, and inaccessible to prejudice. This ebullition of indignation was the result of proud resentment at the fancied contempt of his person implied in the silence of Jesus: the fearful punishment he destined for that imaginary insult, recoiled but too surely on himself; descending from his throne in the transport of his rage, he unintentionally sealed his own degradation, and virtually acknowledged his incapacity longer to occupy the position he had disgraced. His anger was a consequence also of his malignant hatred against Jesus, whom he had pre-determined to condemn with utter disregard of truth and justice. He had been anxious to invest the crime with a specious colouring, and unable to succeed in this, he passionately urged the Son of God to declare His identity. It was in fine a secret operation of Almighty power, which compelled him to rise in presence of his Saviour, his Judge and his God, as Valentinian was at a later period constrained by miraculous flames to descend from his throne and render involuntary honour to St. Martin. Oh! what a contradiction to behold a creature of dust and ashes seated on a throne, and the Lord of the universe standing at his feet! The Bishop of Heraclius, St. Potamon, could not restrain his tears at seeing St. Athanasius standing before the Arian council assembled to condemn him, nor could he refrain from expressing his sentiments on the subject to one of the leaders of the faction. "What, Eusebius!" he exclaimed in a transport of holy indignation, "you are seated, while the innocent Athanasius stands awaiting his sentence from your lips! who can bear to witness so great an outrage!"

O Divine Saviour! if it is so afflicting a spectacle to behold a guiltless mortal judged and condemned by his impious fellow-creatures, how sad, how overwhelming to see Thee, the Saint of saints, oppressed and humbled by Thy own creature!

My son, I the Holy of Holies bore that indignity, to show thee that if thou wilt walk in my footsteps, thou must share my humiliations. Prepare then to meet them courageously, for the lips of men are ready now, as in the days of my Passion, to distil their poisonous venom.

FIFTH DAY.

You will meditate to-day on the sufferings of our Divine Lord in the house of Caiphas, on the night of His seizure, considering that He endured those multiplied torments to atone for your sinful gratifications of sense, for which you will excite yourself to lively contrition.

Aspirations.—"I have not turned away my face from them that rebuked me, and spit upon me." (Is. l. 6.)

"Turn away Thy face, O Lord! from my sins, and blot out all my iniquities." (Ps. iv. 11.)

For the Practice, see "Supplement."

FIRST MEDITATION.

Jesus cruelly outraged in the House of Caiphas.

"Then did they spit in His face."(St. Matt. xxvi. 67.) "And the men that held Him, mocked him, and struck Him. And they blindfolded Him, and smote His face. And they asked Him, saying: Prophesy: who is it that struck Thee. And blaspheming, many other things they said against Him." (St. Luke, xxii. 63, 65.)

First Point.—Hitherto the enemies of Jesus had maintained some appearance of formality in their proceedings, thus to cover passion with the appearance of zeal for religion; but having finally determined on His death, and resolved to deliver Him up to the secular power, their fury kept no farther measures. Laying aside even the disguise of feigned justice, they heaped every description of outrage on their suffering victim, and taxed their ingenuity to add new insults to His brimming cup of shame. We are incensed at the lawless tyranny of Christ's persecutors, and loudly demand by what right they dared thus to outrage God's eternal Son. Would it not be more profitable to inquire by what right we ourselves presume to insult Him by our repeated transgressions? Whence do we derive the fatal power to offend Him? Oh! are we entitled thus to usurp authority over our Sovereign Lord and generous Benefactor? Contemplate that adorable countenance which the Jews sully with spittle and disfigure with bruises. It is the same sacred countenance on which the Angels eternally gaze without weariness; the countenance whose very aspect consoled the afflicted; the countenance which Kings and Patriarchs and Gentiles sighed to see. O terrific spectacle; the face of the incarnate God sullied with spittle by the last and lowest of men! O sinful thoughts which obscure the brightness of that glorious image imprinted on my soul, depart from me, for I detest and renounce you! O base calumniators, who destroy the fair fame of a brother! Know you not that he is formed to the likeness even of God Himself? How then dare you distort the features moulded on that Divine Model?

O adorable Saviour, I behold in Thy sacred face, as in a mirror, the hideousness and enormity of my sins. Grant me, I beseech Thee, abundant tears to wash away those sinful stains; grant me a heart of fire to return Thee love for love! When shall I behold Thee face to face, eternally to bless and praise Thy exceeding charity! "Show me, O Lord, Thy face, and I shall be saved." (Ps. lxxix. 8.)

Second Point.—After Caiphas had retired, his soldiers and servants assembled round Jesus to mock and insult Him for the remainder of the night. Who can tell the outrages, who can number the blows they inflicted on Him, inspired as they were by their own unbridled cruelty, as well as by the rage of the demons! An eminent spiritual writer tells us that His Divine face was all covered with wounds and bruises. His forehead was discoloured by a gash over the right eye, and the eye-lids so inflamed that vision was nearly obscured. His cheeks were livid; his lips swollen; the upper one partially torn away; the natural expression of His countenance so altered that He could no longer be recognized. In fine, He seemed "as it were a leper, and one struck by God and afflicted" (Is. liii. 4); and yet, far from presenting a repulsive aspect, His air of Divine majesty and meekness tended rather to inspire admiration and wonder. Oh! how attractive is virtue, even when disfigured by wounds and sprinkled with blood!

Sweet Jesus! how shall I indemnify Thee for Thy sufferings? When shall I suffer for Thee in the same spirit as Thou sufferest for me?

Third Point.—The humiliations of the Son of God on the night of His imprisonment were no less painful than His corporal torments. Prominent among those humiliations was the bandage placed across His eyes, in mockery of His eternal wisdom. St. Chrysostom says, that the glance of heavenly meekness which issued from those dying eyes overcame even His barbarous executioners, who, while captivated by its influence, lost the power to strike, for which reason they covered them with a bandage, that so they might outrage Him at full liberty as an idiot, unconscious whence the insults proceeded. How deplorable the blindness of those unhappy beings, who, by veiling the Redeemer's face, deprived themselves of the most glorious spectacle on earth, and anticipating their final reprobation, condemned themselves never to see Him face to face in His kingdom! How great, too, the folly of sinners, who imagine themselves secure because their iniquities are concealed beneath the veil of darkness, as if He who made the light could not penetrate the deepest obscurity, and draw forth from its shade the deeds of iniquity it shrouds!

Admire and adore the tender mercy of your Lord and Saviour, who submits to be blindfolded, as an evidence that He will for ever close His eyes to your sins, provided you sincerely repent of them, and never again abuse His indulgent mercy.

O most sweet Jesus! though love places a bandage on Thy sacred eyes, I cannot believe that it blinds Thee; and, although I may humbly hope in Thy goodness for pardon of the past, I know I must not presume on Thy future lenity; for Thou art that jealous Spouse who "lookest through the lattices," and seest without being seen. (Cant. ii. 9.) Thine eyes are ever open on the deeds of men, but only the just recognize their influence, and see themselves reflected in Thy sacred countenance as in a bright and burning mirror. Happy he, O Lord! who knows how to open his eyes to his own nothingness, and, at the same time, to close them to dangerous objects, as well as to cover them with the veil of charity through which the errors of a fellow-creature cannot penetrate. Oh! how advantageous to interdict ourselves the sight of objects calculated only to agitate the soul, and excite vindictive feelings in the heart! How profitable, irrevocably to assume the bandage of divine love which hides our iniquities from the Almighty, and conceals our neighbour's frailties from ourselves!

SECOND MEDITATION.

The Conversion of St. Peter.

"And the Lord turning, looked on Peter. And Peter remembered the word of the Lord, as He had said: Before the cock crow, thou shalt deny me thrice. And Peter going out wept bitterly." (St. Luke, xxii. 61, 62.)

First Point.—Jesus had raised St. Peter to the dignity of the Apostleship by a look, and now that he has unhappily deserved to forfeit his claim to that exaltation, Jesus recalls him to it by the same means. It is difficult to contemplate the Apostle's most wonderful conversion without emotions of tenderness and astonishment. While Peter was in the very act of denying his Divine Master, Jesus, fortunately for His fallen disciple, passed from the scene of His mock trial to the dungeon where He was to spend the night. As He traversed the court where Peter stood, He heard his fearful denial, confirmed as it was by oaths and imprecations. Oh! how keen a pang to His all-loving heart! Nevertheless, He pitied His Apostle's weakness, and turning towards him, cast on him one look of ineffable, irresistible meekness. How blessed was Peter in receiving that glance of salvation! How great the charity which imparted to it so miraculous a power! That look was one of preventing mercy; it sought the sinner, even before he had dreamed of repentance, and chased away by its brightness the obscurity which otherwise would never have been dispelled. It was generous,—the Master seeking His servant at the very moment when that servant so basely outraged his Lord and Benefactor. It was charitable,—Jesus forgetting His own sufferings, to minister to the spiritual wants of His erring disciple. It was efficacious,—touching the sinner's heart with deep compunction, and re-animating his drooping courage. It was kind and compassionate,—Christ sparing the criminal the confusion due to his crime, and healing his wound without touching it. After witnessing so wondrous an instance of the goodness of Jesus, who can fear to expose his wounds to the all-merciful, all-powerful Physician.

O sweet Jesus! cast a glance of mercy on all sinners, that like St. Peter, all may be converted to Thee. I offer Thee my heart, and conjure Thee to take pity on it, piercing it not with one glance alone, but with a thousand if needful; for Thy glance is a fiery arrow, which, while it destroys sin, restores life to the sinner.

Second Point.—Jesus desired to leave us an example of true compunction in St. Peter, the Prince of the Church and perfect model of penitents. Contemplate, then, that marvellous miracle of grace, and learn from the consideration of its details to expiate your sins by tears of sincere contrition. The tears of Peter spring from a soul glowing with love for his Divine Master, for his was not an insensible, or even an indifferent heart. No sooner does he recognize his sin, than without the delay of a moment, he weeps for and renounces it. Sin is so horrible a monster, and the invitations of grace so precious a treasure, that he who understands the value of the one, and the deformity of the other, feels he cannot too speedily return to God by repentance. It is the characteristic of the elect to rise promptly after the commission of a fault, and to yield unhesitatingly to the reproaches of conscience.

2nd.—The tears of St. Peter are sincere and heartfelt. So great is his detestation of his crime, that he cannot even endure the sight of the spot which witnessed its commission. In terror, he flies from the occasions which might lead him to relapses. He who refuses to cut away the root, does not really wish that the tree should perish. He who does not strike at the source, aims not at draining the stream; and he who does not avoid dangerous occasions, has no effectual desire to correct vice. "Depart from me, all ye workers of iniquity." (Ps. vi. 9.) I dread your approach as that of the plague-stricken, for experience has taught me that your society is perilous, and that your counsels are fatal. "Depart then from me, and I will weep bitterly." (Is. xxii. 4.)

3rd.—St. Peter's tears are affectionate, springing, not from the apprehension of punishment, but from love for his Divine Master. They are, in fact, but the external manifestation of that tender devotion and lively contrition whose source lies buried in the depths of his heart.

4th.—They are bitter and uncontrollable. The overwhelming anguish of his soul can find no relief in words, and vents itself in tears, which, as St. Augustine observes, speak more eloquently than any human language, and by their silent appeal for Heaven's mercy, effectually appease the anger of God. Blessed tears! exclaims St. Leo, whose virtue, like that of the waters of Baptism, blots out sin, with this advantage, that while the regenerating stream can flow but once, the tears of the Apostle will cease but with life.

O my Saviour! since I have imitated Thy unfaithful follower in his guilt, may I also, through Thy mercy, share in his repentance! May my heart become an ocean of tears, my sorrow embitter all worldly joys, and my sole remaining happiness be to grieve for having offended Thee!

Third Point.—The tears St. Peter shed on quitting the house of Caiphas were but a prelude to those of his future existence. St. Clement, who enjoyed the privilege of familiar intercourse with him, assures us, that at the crowing of the cock, he invariably knelt, to implore the forgiveness of his sin, shedding torrents of tears, which at last impressed their indelible traces on his countenance.

Adore the designs of eternal wisdom in the fall and repentance of this great Saint. God permitted his fall in order to humble his secret pride and presumption; whence St. Augustine infers, that it is sometimes expedient for those whose hearts are the seat of hidden passion to commit a visible crime, that the humiliation thence resulting may open their eyes to iniquities hitherto unnoticed. Again, God permitted the fall of St. Peter, to establish him in humility by the experimental knowledge of his great weakness—as also in holy fear and fervent love—virtues so necessary in the exalted position destined for him as future head of the Church. He permitted it, to inspire him with meekness and mercy towards sinners, and to teach him, as sovereign pastor of the faithful, never to withhold from others the compassionate indulgence he had himself so greatly needed. In fine, he intended that the frailty of the prince of the Apostles should serve as a salutary warning to all Christians, while his repentance should tend to their consolation and encouragement. Who will dare to presume on his own strength, after witnessing the fall of an Apostle? Who will despair of pardon, when he sees the keys of divine mercy confided to a penitent sinner? Let us profit of so glorious an example, and in union with our pastor, enter anew to-day on the career of penance. It is said that he spent the interval between his denial and the resurrection of Jesus Christ, in a subterraneous cavern, weeping over his sin; let us enter it in spirit with him, to listen to his sighs, and mingle our tears with his. "Alas!" he exclaims, in his agonizing remorse, "how could I so basely have denied Him, whom I knew to be the Son of the living God? the generous Master whom I had promised to follow into prison and unto death? the tender Father who so charitably, so considerately warned me of my danger? Oh! how bitter will life be to me, now that I have so ungratefully denied its Author! I have renounced my God! I have forsaken my Saviour! I have denied my Benefactor! Alas! alas! how can I repair so enormous a crime! But let me not sink into despair, and thus immeasurably aggravate my guilt. I know the goodness of my Redeemer; I have fathomed the depths of His exhaustless mercy; I know full well that He never yet desired the death of a sinner. Shall I not then return to His arms without delay? Shall I not fearlessly encounter the human tigers who surround the Just One, and brave that death from which I so lately recoiled, but which I now would welcome as the means of expiating my sin, and the blessed agent in re-uniting me to the source of life. But I dare not trust to my own strength, or aspire to the happiness of laying down this wretched existence with my Saviour. Rather be it my lot to wash away my iniquity in the deluge of my tears. Once I walked on the waves to meet my Saviour, now I will retrace my steps to Him through an ocean of tears; and since all else is lost, I will at least endeavour to retain my claim on His mercy, which all the crimes of the universe cannot exhaust. O Jesus, my Lord and Master! although I have outraged Thy love and wounded Thy heart, still will I trust with unwavering confidence in that ineffable charity which urges Thee to sacrifice Thy life for him who had not courage to acknowledge his connexion with Thee. Oh! let me not be confounded, since I have hoped in Thee; forgive my sins, and every day of my life shall deplore the frailty of a single moment."

SIXTH DAY.

Meditate to-day on the scourging of our Divine Lord, and endeavour to conceive sentiments of lively contrition for your sins, the real cause of Christ's sufferings.

Aspirations.—"He was wounded for our iniquities; he was bruised for our sins." (Is. liii. 5.)

"I am ready for scourges, and my sorrow is continually before me." (Ps. xxxvii. 18.)

For the Practice, see "Supplement."

FIRST MEDITATION.

Jesus stripped of His Garments.

"Then Pilate took Jesus, and scourged Him." (St. John, xix. 1.)

First Point.—The pretorium of Pilate is now transformed into the temporary theatre of Christ's ignomonies, and there angels and men contemplate the incarnate God exposed to the mockery of the very dregs of humanity. O my Saviour! hast Thou not clothed the sun in a vesture of light, and adorned the stars of heaven with their garb of glory? Hast Thou not provided the bird of the air with plumage, the trees with leaves, the fields with verdure, and the garden with flowers? Hast Thou not Thyself given to man the costly silk and purple which ornament his person? Why then art Thou destitute of clothing? Ah! I have but to seek an answer in Thy own boundless charity, which tells me that Thou art thus despoiled of Thy garments, only to restore to me the robe of innocence forfeited by the transgression of our first parents. Oh! may I may never lay aside that precious robe, purchased atso dear a rate!

St. Martin divided his cloak with a mendicant, but Jesus gives us all His garments, reserving none. Jonathan presented David with his sword and his bow, but Christ invests us with Himself, that His merits may screen us against the merited anger of His Father. Carefully cherish the invaluable treasure of grace which He has restored to you, and fly from sin, which alone can deprive you of it. Pray that you may not appear at the table of the Lord in the holy Communion, or at the tribunal of His justice after death, divested of that garb of grace without which the soul is a hateful object in the sight of God and His angels.

Seeond Point.—The present life is a state of warfare, and the Christian is a combatant who struggles, not with visible enemies, but with artful and malicious spirits. He must lay aside the old man with his evil inclinations, lest the wily foe may effect an entrance into his soul, and involve him in his own utter ruin. Jesus desires to stimulate us to the conflict by His example, and to present us, in His external destitution, with a model of that spiritual disengagement to which the Christian soldier should aspire. We are willing enough to put on the new man, if this could be accomplished without renouncing the unruly passions and perverse inclinations of corrupt nature, but the two objects are incompatible. We must put off the garb of the old Adam, before we can assume that of the new; and if, like Joseph, we aspire to victory, like him too we must lay aside the mantle by which the world and the flesh maintain their grasp. But be not alarmed at the anticipated sacrifice of earthly joys and dignities; in renouncing them, you but renounce occasions of sin, and cast off the old man, corrupted by the poison of concupiscence. Return thanks to God who provides you an opportunity of disengaging your heart from sin, by flinging away its incentives, and rejoice, that although condemned through the malice of the serpent to wear its livery, you are now enabled to lay it aside through the grace of Jesus Christ.

Third Point.—Sin is a work of darkness, and cannot bear the light;—so repulsive is its deformity, that men invent numberless pretexts to disguise, if they cannot conceal it. When summoned by the Almighty to come forth and hear His sentence, Adam, instead of humbly confessing his crime and imploring mercy, sought for vain excuses which only aggravated his guilt. Many experience confusion similar to his, when approaching the tribunal of penance, and not having courage to undergo the momentary humiliation of confession, they conceal or disguise their sins, thus adding the crime of sacrilege to their previous responsibility. They entomb themselves in the depths of their guilty consciences, as the Egyptians fled to the caves of the earth for refuge from the darkness that sat on the land; but as a sojourn in their gloomy retreat served but to increase the terror of the latter to frenzy, so is the sinner pursued even to the dark silent depths of his own soul, by the vengeful accents of remorse. Jesus desires to expiate the pusillanimity which shrinks from the avowal of sin, by enduring the last and worst of humiliations. Should not His goodness encourage us to overcome our weakness, and generously manifest our spiritual wounds to the physician empowered to heal them? Alas! we recoil from disclosing our sins to a mortal bound by the most solemn obligations to inviolable secrecy, and we are not ashamed to commit them before God, who will one day publish them to the assembled universe! Draw near to Jesus, and beseech Him with your whole heart to invest you with the royal mantle of charity, which distinguishes the children of light from the sons of darkness. "Put off, O Jesusalem, the garment of thy mourning and affliction: and put on the beauty and honour of that everlasting glory which thou hast from God. God will clothe thee with the double garment of justice, and will set a crown on thy head of everlasting honour." (Baruch, v. 1, 2.)

SECOND MEDITATION.

Jesus fastened to the Pillar.

"Then Pilate took Jesus, and scourged Him." (St. John, xix. 1.)

First Point.—The innocent hands of Jesus are fastened to the pillar! those hands which spangled the dome of Heaven with stars; those hands which healed the sick; which wrought countless miracles; which were so often raised to invoke Heaven's benedictions on the children of earth! those hands are bound to the pillar, as if they had been the hands of a common malefactor! It was not through impotence that the Almighty Word of the Father submitted to this outrage, but as Samson voluntarily presented his hands to the manacles which were to restore peace to his people, so did Jesus freely assume the bonds which were to effect the reconciliation of God with men.

Fear not that the eternal Father will forsake you, while His Son abides in you; fear not either that the Son will first abandon you, for the pillar is an emblem of His constancy, and the cords which fasten Him to it represent the indissoluble bonds of love. On your part, cling closely to Jesus your Lord and Spouse, and never renounce, or even tire of His chains. Faithfully observe your repeated promises of fidelity to His love, looking on them as the precious bonds which attach you to Him. You will find them a source of strength and sweetness, and will one day happily behold the fetters of your servitude transformed into a diadem of everlasting glory.

Second Point.—The Church is the pillar and ground of truth, but it owes its stability to the Spirit of Jesus, who has united Himself to it so intimately, that the power of hell shall not prevail against it. Attach yourself firmly to that pillar, if you desire to avoid error. There you will assuredly find Jesus, and learn from His sacred lips the infallible truths of faith. There will He say to you, "The place whereon you stand is holy ground" (Ex. iii. 5); a land fertile in sanctity and rich in virtue. As long as you abide there, you abide with me, for He who is with the Church must be with me. Remain, then, in that Church, as in a secure haven; beyond its pale, you will not find me, and separated from me, the light of life, you will assuredly be enveloped in darkness and the shades of death.

Jesus, the strength of the infirm, and the support of the strong, is bound to a pillar, to encourage us in our weakness; to animate us in the combat against our enemies; to give us an example of heroic patience, and to merit for us the grace to profit of His lessons. From Him we learn that in order to bear the trials of life in a Christian spirit, we must be bound to the pillar, the strong, steady pillar of patience, which supports the soul in the terrible hour of temptation. His grace attaches us thereto by the bonds of love, which cannot be rent asunder without our own consent. That pillar it was which rendered St. Lucy immovable in the midst of executioners. That pillar it was which imparted resolution to the Stylites; which sustained all the Saints, and still transforms frail mortals into Christian heroes, whom no storm can overthrow, no persecution daunt. Happy the soul, which bound to Jesus by love, and leaning on Him as on a firm pillar, receives with resignation all the afflictions ordained by Providence! She will one day be crowned, not with a wreath of thorns, such as the Son of God selected for Himself, but with a garland of immortal glory, purchased by His sufferings.

Third Point.—When Joseph was about to send back his brethren into their own country, he retained one as a hostage for the rest, saying, "do as I have said, and you shall live, for I fear God. If you be peaceable men, let one of your brethren be bound in prison, and go ye your ways unto your houses." (Gen. xlii. 18, 19.) In this occurrence we have a figure of the mystery now under consideration. We were in this world as exiles from our true country, when the Eternal Father, designing to recall us to our home in Heaven, consented that His only Son should for our sakes be delivered up into the hands of men, and bound to a pillar. This is the sure pledge of our happiness, and solid foundation of our hope. If you aspire to walk steadily in the path to bliss, never lose sight of that pillar. Bind yourself to Jesus, or rather let Him be closely and inseparably entwined around your heart. Say to Him, as Dalila said to Samson, but from a different motive, "Tell me, I beseech thee, wherewith thou mayest be bound." (Judges, xvi. 10.) If you present the petition in sincerity of spirit, He will tell you that the strongest bonds which attach Him to the heart are those of humility, purity, respect for His Sovereign Majesty, and gratitude for His benefits. Submit unconditionally to His law, obey His inspirations, yield to the guidance of His Spirit, and he will voluntarily dwell with you, He will console you, enlighten you, and assuredly conduct you to Heaven, your birthplace and inheritance.

O Almighty and eternal God, the sole support of human frailty! we humbly beseech Thee to compassionate our weakness, and since without Thine aid we cannot endure the numberless trials which assail us, we pray, that leaning on the strength of Thy only Son, as on a firm pillar, we may be ever constant in faith, and immovable in virtue.

SEVENTH DAY.

Meditate to-day on Christ's crowning with thorns, and consider Him treated as a mock king, and subjected to every species of insult, to atone for your pride. Ardently desire to imitate Him in His humiliations, that thus you may recover the crown of glory forfeited by your sins.

Aspirations.—"Go forth, ye daughters of Sion, and see King Solomon in the diadem, wherewith his mother crowned him in the day of his espousals." (Cant. iii. 2.) "The crown is fallen from our head, because we have sinned." (Lam. v. 16.)

For the Practice, see "Supplement."

FIRST MEDITATION.

Jesus Crowned with Thorns.

"And the soldiers platting a crown of thorns, put it upon His head." (St. John, xix. 2.)

First Point.—The crowning with thorns was one of the keenest pangs endured by our loving Saviour. If the wound of a single thorn in the hand or foot produces such severe pain, what must have been the torture of so many thorns forcibly driven into Christ's sacred head, the seat of the most delicate membranes? But as it was the sin of our first parents which covered the earth with thorns, Jesus would suffer all the pain they can inflict, in order to destroy the source whence they originated. Those thorns of ignominy and torture, says Tertullian, are emblematic of sin springing from the barren clay of the heart, and eradicated by virtue of the cross and death of Jesus Christ.

It is written that the purple garment was taken from His sacred shoulders, but no mention is made of the removal of the crown of thorns, for Jesus bore to the last the thorns He had plucked from our path, only to transfer them to His own sacred brow. O Divine Redeemer, so clement towards criminals, so inexorable towards Thyself! how comes it that the malediction which in penalty of our sins condemned the earth to produce thorns and brambles, has fallen back on Thyself? Because, as God alone could destroy sin and save the sinner, to Him alone it belonged to wear a wreath of thorns, the emblem of sin: as thorns wound the body, so does sin wound the soul. Thorns are fit only for fuel, and the sinner merits no better fate than to feed the everlasting flames of hell. But Jesus delights to fertilize those sterile thorns, to render them productive of fruits of repentance, and to transform them into a crown for Himself. It is customary for conquerors to take possession of the arms of the enemy as a trophy of victory; thus Jesus deprives the infernal foe of his arms by destroying the thorns of sin, of which He forms a diadem for His own brow, but a diadem, alas! of pain and ignominy. Oh! how many tears have we cost Him! how many sighs!

Unhappy sinner! each of your deliberate crimes is a thorn which wounds the head and pierces the heart of Christ; nevertheless, His mercy bears with your ingratitude, and even offers you grace to repent, that thus you may weave of the thorns of your sins, a garland of immortal glory. How long will you persevere in grieving His loving heart? Do you not fear that farther resistance to grace may involve you among the reprobate whom He will one day cast into eternal fire?

O my Saviour! destroy in me all that displeases Thee; eradicate from my heart the thorns of sin, consume them in the flames of Thy love, and grant that my soul, watered with Thy precious blood, may become fruitful in good works. Then shall I praise and bless Thee, O innocent Lamb, who takest away the sins of the world! precious Victim who wouldst be crowned with thorns as a sacrifice of expiation for the crimes of the universe!

Second Point.—In our mortal pilgrimage we have to encounter three different kinds of thorns;—the thorns of sin, the thorns of temptation, and those of penance and tribulation. Jesus displayed the power of His Divinity by destroying the first, and He manifested the mercy of His humanity by providing a remedy for the wounds inflicted by the two last; that remedy no other than Himself to assume our infirmities and bear the penalty of our iniquities.

O infinite goodness of Jesus! our mortal existence being but one succession of trials, cares, and anxieties, He took them on Himself, that freed from the perplexity they entail, we might attend with uninterrupted liberty of spirit to His Divine service and our own salvation. In return for such extraordinary charity, shall we not choose Him henceforth as the Monarch and Master of our souls, offering Him our devoted homage, and promising Him our undivided allegiance? O Jesus! crowned with thorns, be Thou the King of my heart, and the absolute Lord of my will! May Thy thorns pierce my obdurate heart, penetrating it with profound sympathy for Thy sorrow, and sincere compunction for my infidelities and ingratitude!

Let us renounce the empty joys of this transitory

world, and select the thorns of Jesus as our portion and inheritance; they will prove a secure refuge in temptation, and a sweet solace amidst the trials of life. Beneath the shade of those thorns, it was, that the Saints sought strength and consolation. There St. Benedict extinguished the fire of concupiscence, and there St. Catherine of Sienna learned to prefer a crown of thorns to one of gold. Godfrey of Bouillon, King of Jerusalem, would not wear a regal diadem in the Holy Land, where Jesus had borne a crown of thorns. For the same reason, St. Elizabeth never prayed before a crucifix without having laid aside her crown, and St. Louis prohibited his children from wearing coronets or flowers on Good Friday. Let us imbibe the sentiments, and imitate the example of the Saints, lest the anger of Christ be enkindled, and His justice involve us in the terrible sentence of the reprobate, "Depart, ye cursed, into eternal fire."

Third Point.—The crowns of earthly potentates produce only thorns, but in the kingdom of God, thorns produce crowns. It is by patience that man acquires dominion over his passions, and it was by patience also that Jesus purchased for him the diadem of eternal happiness which is to reward the victory over nature. Christ would not be adored by the Angels as King of glory, says Tertullian, until He had first suffered on the cross as King of the Jews. If you cannot present Him your head crowned wirh thorns, crown it not at least with flowers. Do not be alarmed by the thorns which encompass your Lord and Master, but plunge through them courageously, that you may deserve to cull the blossom of ever-enduring felicity. Be assured that while their sharp points wound your enemies, they will prove to yourself an invincible shield and strong defence. When peril besets your steps, and temptation presses on your spirit, retire within the shadow of that thorn-crowned head, and you will find it an impenetrable rampart. If you are assailed by vanity, pluck one of the thorns from your Saviour's wreath, and cling to it, as a tower of strength. If you are exposed to the assaults of voluptuousness, recur to the same remedy, and rebellious nature will speedily acknowledge its wondrous efficacy. In fine, turn to Jesus in all your difficulties; seek refuge in His arms, as Elias sought repose under the juniper tree. He will provide you with living bread, whence you will derive strength to attain the Mount of Horeb, and in exchange for a crown of thorns, He will bestow that diadem of unfading glory, which is the object of your holy ambition, and the sole end of your existence.

SECOND MEDITATION.

Jesus scourged at the Pillar.

" Then Pilate took Jesus and scourged Him." (St. John, xix. 1.)

First Point.—Why, O my Saviour! art Thou covered with wounds, and why does blood stream from every part of Thy sacred body? Why art Thou so torn, so bruised, so disfigured, that thou seemest a leper, and one struck by God and afflicted? Why has the tabernacle of the Most High become accessible to torments? Who has given men power over Thy sacred person, and even over Thy life? Ah! Thy love supplies the answer. Thou Thyself, it was, who didst impart to them that terrible power: Thou who didst deliver Thy person,

Thy reputation, Thy very existence into their hands, to show us the excess of Thy sufferings, the incomprehensible extent of Thy charity.

Jesus would be struck, that waters of benediction might flow from His sacred humanity on the sons of men, as the refreshing stream burst from the rock of the desert to allay the thirst of the Israelites. O inhuman executioners! you are more hardened than the rock, but your arms are nerved against one whose tenderness exceeds your obduracy. The echo of your blows proclaims His mercy to the world, and the wounds you inflict are so many precious sources whence flows the healing balm of His charity.

It is not for Himself that Jesus suffers, but for us. He is wounded, to provide a remedy for our infirmities, and He sheds His blood, to wash away the iniquities of the earth. O my soul! adore those sacred wounds, the visible manifestations of the charity of a God. Learn to estimate thy value in His sight, and measuring thy dignity by the amount of thy ransom, shrink with horror from relapsing into sin. O prodigy of mercy! The All-Holy is scourged for the impious! the Innocent for the guilty! the Source of life for base criminals worthy of eternal death!

Second Point.—O ye Heavens, be astonished! Blessed spirits, who recognize in the Victim bound to the pillar the only Son of the Eternal Father, weep and lament! When St. Paul, condemned to the scourge, demanded whether "it was lawful to scourge a Roman" (Acts, xxii. 25), his judges, alarmed at the question, promptly restored him to liberty. And shall the accents of the blood of Jesus produce no impression? Shall the Incarnate Deity be scourged, and no voice be raised to proclaim His innocence? Shall the Holy of Holies fall a prey to the barbarity of sinners, and no one be found to advocate His cause? Ah! if He refrains from asserting His rights, and endures insupportable torments without a complaint, should not His silence touch your heart? Surely if it can resist the sight of His wounds, it must be harder than the rocks. Oh! approach the pillar, and contemplate the wounds of the Lamb, whose only crime is to have assumed the punishment due to you. His flesh is all mangled; His veins opened; His nerves laid bare; His hair torn from His head. He speaks not a word amidst His pangs, but only weeps, and sighs, and shudders. Far from wishing to shorten the period of suffering, His sole desire is to endure yet more, if necessary to ensure your salvation and gain your heart. He even imparts strength to the cruel hands which tear His flesh, and admits no alleviation to His pangs. A few of those terrific blows might have sufficed to deprive Him of life, and He receives a countless number, without exciting in the spectators even an emotion of compassion. Alas! if Jesus has so many enemies, so many persecutors, will He not find at least a few friends to comfort Him, and will you not resolve to rank henceforth among those few? Ah! how will you venture to implore His pity for yourself, if your heart is void of compassion for Him?

Third Point.—With a little reflection, it is easy to discover the cause of the sufferings of Jesus in His scourging. Our sins it was which mangled His flesh, our inherent corruption and deliberate malice which drew the blood from His veins, and reduced His whole body to one vast, deep wound. Consider that bleeding frame, whose tortured existence is prolonged only by miracle. Consider those shoulders, those hands, those arms, that breast all covered with gashes, and looking on them as so many mirrors to reflect the deformity and magnitude of your sins, say can you longer hesitate to detest, to abhor,' to renounce sin for ever!

O my all-merciful Redeemer! although Thou complainest not of the executioners, complain at least of me, the most cruel of them all. It was I who struck Thee, by the almost infinite number of my sinful thoughts, my guilty words, and unworthy actions. O God! how tenderly lenient art Thou in my regard, visiting my iniquities with no greater penalty than trifling sicknesses, slight humiliations, small losses, and transient trials, while I insult Thee by grievous crimes, and afflict Thy heart by my base ingratitude! Oh! how great reason have I to tremble at Thy judgments, if I continue to abuse Thy mercy!

EIGHTH DAY.

To-day you will consider our Divine Lord crowned with thorns, clothed in a purple mantle, holding a reed as a sceptre, and in that condition presented by Pilate to the people; observing, that as man had disfigured by sin the image of God to which he was created, it became necessary that Jesus Christ should be likewise disfigured, to restore the primitive beauty of that image. To recover our original resemblance to God, we must become conformable to Jesus Christ by participating in His sufferings and humiliations; and for this reason the Eternal Father presents Him to us, saying—*Behold the Man* who is to be your model and your guide.

Aspirations.—"I am a worm, and no man: the reproach of men, and the outcast of the people." (Ps. xxi. 7.)

"O Son of the living God! how incomprehensible is Thy humility! how unfathomable Thy mercy! I have sinned, and Thou bearest the penalty due to my iniquities!" (St. Augustine.)

For the Practice, see "Supplement."

FIRST MEDITATION.

Jesus holds a Mock Sceptre.

"And platting a crown of thorns, they put it upon His head, and a reed in His right hand." (St. Matt. xxvii. 29.)

First Point.—The soldiers placed a reed in the hand of Jesus, in derision of His regal dignity, determining to make Him king at least of fools and idiots! O holy and thrice blessed folly! O Sovereign of those saintly souls whom the world reputes fools, what excess of charity prompts Thee to endure the confusion due to that inordinate ambition and insatiable thirst of dignity, which may truly be accounted folly? How strongly that reed exhibits the vanity of earthly sceptres, and the senselessness of those who esteem and covet them! The sceptre of Christ is a sceptre of power, which subdues the arrogance of the proud and crumbles it to dust. It is apparently frail as a reed agitated by the breeze, but it is, in truth, more solid and more lasting than iron, for its dominion is absolute, and its duration eternal. The sceptres of earthly monarchs, on the contrary, while apparently powerful, are in reality weaker than reeds. Though seemingly substantial, the reed is in fact hollow and empty, and bent to the earth by the slightest breath of wind. Such is the vain dignity of earth; such the pomp and grandeur of the world. The lightest breeze agitates; the least opposition disturbs its votaries. In the record of empires overturned, sceptres shattered, crowns laid prostrate, history teaches the great to distrust the smiles of prosperity, while it instructs the humble to place no reliance on reeds so fragile. O Christian, who cling to the support of creatures, instead of placing your hopes in God, to whom do you trust? What infatuation prompts you to presume on your own strength, vainly fancying yourself independent of the aid of the Most High? Ah! too surely do you lean on a hollow reed, which will bend, and break, and in so doing pierce the hand that grasped it.

Second Point.—Nothing can be more frail than man;—he is a faded leaf clinging feebly to the tree over which autumn winds are sweeping; he is a reed without strength or solidity; he is overcome by the slightest temptation, and daunted by the least difficulty. Jesus Christ held a reed, to show you that He is the support of the weak, to whom you should promptly run in all emergencies. By assuming the reed, He at once weakened Satan's empire and strengthened man's weakness. He at the same moment destroyed the power of the enemy, and rendered us invincible against his assaults.

My God! since I am but a weak reed, shield me, I conjure Thee, by Thy power, that nothing may detach me from Thy service. My soul is destitute of charity; it is insensible at prayer; it is devoid of good works, and rich only in useless protestations of fidelity. Oh! take it, I beseech Thee, into Thy hands, and as Thou didst mercifully burden Thyself with its weakness, communicate to it a participation in Thy strength. Then shall I bless Thy name, and exclaim in rapturous joy, "this is the change of the right hand of the Most High." (Ps. lxxvi. 11.) Strengthen me, O my Saviour! and in Thy great mercy do not forsake me.

Third Point.—" What have you come" to the pretorium "to see? A reed shaken with the wind." (St. Luke, vii. 24.) Alas! too truly does your inconstancy resemble the reed which Jesus holds to atone by His own humiliation for your infidelity in His service. As the soldiers took the reed from His hand to strike Him with it on the head, so do you wound Him by your unsteadiness and volatility. You offer to Jesus your will, your judgment, your inclinations, all your faculties, and scarcely has the oblation been presented, when you ungenerously resume it. You form many good resolutions at prayer, but only to violate them when the transient emotion of fervour has passed away. You determine at confession to impose a restraint on your words; to subdue your passions; to discharge the duties of your state with punctuality; and notwithstanding these solemn, deliberate promises, the first temptation overcomes you. Oh! how afflicting to the heart of Jesus is such inconstancy of purpose! Be assured it offends Him more deeply than did the insult of the soldiers who struck His blessed head with the reed. Beg of Him to forgive your ungenerous wavering in His service, and to keep possession of your heart and soul for the time to come. Distrust the transitory impulses of fervour you experience, and never presume on your own strength. Humility will ensure you perseverance, whereas presumption and pride will infallibly occasion your fall, and that at the moment when you imagine yourself most secure.

SECOND MEDITATION.

Pilate interrogates Jesus.

"When Pilate had heard this saying, he feared the more. And he entered into the hall again; and he said to Jesus: Whence art Thou? But Jesus gave him no answer. Pilate therefore saith to Him: Speakest Thou not to me? Knowest Thou not that I have power to crucify Thee, and I have power to release Thee? Jesus answered: Thou shouldst not have any power against me, unless it were given thee from above. Therefore he that hath delivered me to thee, hath the greater sin." (St. John, xix. 8, 11.)

First Point.—Pilate, says St. Augustine, feared at first, in pronouncing sentence against Jesus, to condemn the innocent; but now he fears to condemn the Son of God. He had feared to transgress the law; now he apprehends transgressing against the Author of the law. Pilate only suspects that Jesus may be the Son of God, and yet he trembles at the idea of offending Him; you know well who He is; you understand the extent of His power; you have fathomed the depths of His love, and yet sin has no terrors for you. The report of the Jews fills Pilate with consternation, while the authors of that report are themselves free from alarm. Thus, the souls you instruct are impressed by the maxims of eternal life which you impart; and meantime, you are yourself unmoved by those same sacred lessons.

Pilate's perplexity increases, but his resolution does not keep pace with it;—he fears God, but he fears creatures more. Oh! how many souls can trace their ruin to human respect! Beware, lest you may be among the number.

Pilate fears God;—happy would he have been, if fear had given place to love! Charity would have banished pusillanimous terror from his heart, substituting for it the filial fear which exterminates sin. "Blessed is the man that feareth the Lord" (Ps. cxi. 1); for that salutary fear is at once a shield against sin, and a stimulus to the practice of virtue. It is the production of the Holy Ghost, and as such, can never be incompatible with charity; from which it is, on the contrary, inseparable. Love without fear is of a suspicious character; fear divested of love is unprofitable to the soul.

O Divine Lord! grant me, I beseech Thee, the constant fear and love of Thy holy name, that so I may ever dread to offend Thee, and never grow weary of serving Thee.

Second Point.—Pilate reserved for the conclusion of Christ's trial the question he should have proposed at its commencement. Had he earlier informed himself who Christ was, and whence He came, he would not have dared to proceed against Him. The greater number of our infidelities to God are occasioned by our not knowing Him. This lamentable ignorance Christ Himself deplores in His last solemn prayer on the eve of His Passion: "Just Father, the world hath not known Thee." (St. John, xvii. 25.) Ah! if men knew Him well, they would not have the impious courage to insult Him; they would not be guilty of so much irreverence at prayer; so many breaches of His law; so much negligence in His immediate service.

If you aspire to the spirit of prayer, separate from creatures, and entering into the solitude of your own heart, ask yourself when about to appear in presence of the Godhead, who you are, and whence you come? If you were duly penetrated with the infinite majesty of Him you address, and with your own absolute nothingness, you would not be so cold in heart, so distracted in mind, so languishing in your aspirations after perfection, so inconstant in the observance of your resolutions. O my soul! He whom thou approachest is the source of all created existence; His extent is immensity; His duration, eternity; His height, infinity; His depth, immutability. How profound should be your reverence for Him in whose sight the pillars of Heaven tremble! The angels are not worthy to stand in His sight, and how shall a sinner deserving of hell approach Him!

O abyss of majesty, of wisdom, of power, of all being and all good! who am I that I should presume to speak with Thee! Alas! my unworthiness would condemn me to eternal silence, did not my extreme need of Thy mercy compel me to implore it. O Lord! have compassion on me; disdain not my misery, for although of myself I am nothing and less than nothing, I am nevertheless the work of Thy hands. Thou hast engraven my name with Thy own precious blood on Thy sacred heart; look then on those characters traced by love, and save my soul which has cost Thee so many torments and so many ignominies!

Third Point.—Jesus does not speak to Pilate, because that weak judge had rendered himself unworthy of so great a favour. Convinced of Christ's innocence, he is nevertheless restrained by human respect from fearlessly proclaiming it, although strictly bound, by the very nature of his office, to administer impartial justice. Jesus does not speak, because the words He has already addressed to him have produced no profit. He had told him that His kingdom was not of this world, and that He had come on earth to bear testimony to the truth. To that glimmering of heavenly light, Pilate had wilfully closed his eyes; what then would it avail to unfold the Divine oracles at greater length? He does not speak to him, because his heart is inflated with arrogance, and agitated by ambition, and therefore unfit to hold communion with Him who developes His lessons of eternal wisdom only to the humble and simple.

Why does not Jesus speak to you in prayer? Because you are wise in your own conceit, and an utter stranger to humility. Because your mind is dissipated and distracted. Because you do not follow the light already imparted, or obey the inspirations hitherto bestowed. Because you are unprepared to hear His voice, and undeserving of His favours, in consequence of your unexpiated infidelities.

O sinners, who dread to hear the voice of God, and who abuse of His silence to persevere in sin, what will be your consternation when that same voice reproaches you hereafter with your crimes, and when you can neither reply to the accusation, nor procure the intervention of others in your behalf?

O Lord! I know Thou hast the words of eternal life, but I also know that those same words are arrows of death to the sinner; therefore I earnestly beseech Thee "not to enter into judgment with Thy servant, for in Thy sight no man living shall be justified." (Psalms, cxlii. 2.)

NINTH DAY.

You will meditate to-day on Christ carrying His cross, endeavouring, as in the preceding meditation, to excite yourself to lively contrition for your sins, and an earnest desire to bear the cross generously in company with your Lord and Model.

Aspirations.—"The Lord hath laid on Him the iniquity of us all. He was offered, because it was His own will." (Is. liii. 6, 7.)

"My iniquities are gone over my head, and as a heavy burden are become heavy upon me." (Ps xxxvii. 5.)

For the Practice, see "Supplement."

FIRST MEDITATION.

Jesus condemned to Death.

"Then therefore he delivered Jesus to them to be crucified. And they took Him, and led Him forth." (St. John, xix. 16.)

First Point—Promptly availing of Pilate's extorted permission, the executioners fiercely seized on the meek Lamb of God, who offered no resistance to their will, the same love which had urged Him to descend from Heaven stimulating Him to endure the last effort of human cruelty, to rescue from perdition the souls He so tenderly cherished. Oh! how agonising a spectacle to His holy and loving Mother to see the hapless prisoner abandoned to the power of the brutal populace! How must her tears have flowed when Pilate washed his hands in testimony of his belief in Christ's innocence! How was her soul rent with anguish, as she listened to the appalling imprecation of the Jews, "His blood be upon us, and upon our children!" (St. Matt. xxvii. 25.) How was her heart pierced with sorrow when she beheld her Son, her life, and her treasure snatched from her by the executioners! Sympathise in her griefs, and resolve to indemnify her for her sufferings, by fervently loving and serving her adorable Son.

O my Saviour! I bless and thank Thee with all the ardour of my soul for having delivered me by Thy death from the bondage of Satan, and I earnestly conjure Thee that through the merits of Thy bitter passion my spirit may be received by Angels at its departure from this world, and conducted triumphantly to the realms of everlasting bliss!

Second Point.—"They took off the purple from Him, and put His own garments on Him, and they led Him out to crucify Him." (St. Mark, xv. 20.) At each removal of our Divine Saviour's garments His wounds are re-opened, the remnants of His flesh torn away, and all His corporal pangs redoubled. The object of the executioners in finally replacing His own seamless garment, was that He should be easily identified by the public, and His confusion thus increased; but in a spiritual sense, the circumstance admits another interpretation, replete with instruction for the Christian. We learn from this mystery, that in order to bear the Cross of Jesus worthily and meritoriously, we must divest ourselves like Him of all worldly affections, to assume instead the garb of Divine love and grace, with which God had clothed our first parent. Although Christ suffers that the purple mantle should be removed from His shoulders, He does not lay aside the crown of thorns, thus teaching us that we too must bear a crown of thorns even to the end, if we aspire to imitate Him here, and to share in His diadem of glory hereafter. It is recorded that a lion having been relieved from a thorn which occasioned it great torture, laid aside the ferocity of its nature, and affectionately fawned on the slave who had rendered it so great a service. Will you be more insensible than an irrational animal? Will you steel your heart against the love of your Divine Benefactor, who not only plucked the thorns from your path, but even transferred them to His own? The road to Heaven was once choked up with thorns, which impeded men's progress thither. Now that those thorns have, through God's mercy, been transplanted to the path leading to perdition, how comes it that men so blindly entangle themselves in that road to ruin?

Third Point.—Who can comprehend the sentiments which filled the heart of Jesus when His eyes first rested on the cross—that sacred wood, soon to be sprinkled with His life blood,—that funeral pile, whereon He was shortly to be consumed in the flames of His own boundless love! It was the altar on which He was to be immolated, not as the victim of the Temple, but as a host of propitiation for the crimes of the world. It was the throne of His love; the instrument of His mercies; the trophy of His victories; the object of His inflamed desires; the centre of His heart; the magnet which had attracted Him from heaven; the great term of His mortal mission; what then were His emotions on realizing the end for which He had lived and laboured? How ardent the transports with which He hailed His cross, as it was placed on His bleeding shoulders! Oh! what a triumph to the cross to be exalted to so high, so holy, so honourable a position! O cross, more precious than gold, thou shalt no longer be the instrument of sinners' punishment, but the object of saints' love and angels' veneration. No longer the wood of ignominy, the sterile branch of an accursed root, thou hast become more fertile than the miraculous rod of Aaron. Never was majestic tree more richly laden with foliage, blossoms and fruit;—with leaves to cover the confusion of the old man; with flowers to crown the conquerors of sin; with fruit to satiate all who hunger after justice and happiness. Thou art the saving ark, to protect us from the overwhelming waters of the deluge; thou art the ladder of Jacob, to conduct us to Heaven; thou art the rod of Moses, to divide the billows of the Red Sea; the miraculous wood, to sweeten the bitter waters of Mara, and encourage us to patience under the afflictions of life. O sweet wood, how precious the burden thou sustainest! how bright the light thou reflectest! how wondrous the strength thou impartest to all who contemplate thee with love and compunction!

SECOND MEDITATION.

Jesus carries His Cross.

"And bearing His cross, He went forth to that place which is called Calvary." (St. John, xix. 17.)

First Point.—The great spectacle of Jesus carrying His cross, although a subject of mockery to the impious, says St. Augustine, is in truth a mystery worthy the admiration of men and Angels. Jesus carries the instrument of His own punishment, and in so doing undergoes an extreme humiliation, but at the same time He transforms that ignominious cross into a royal sceptre before which monarchs will one day prostrate, thus achieving a splendid triumph even in the hour of His shame. He advanced in company with two robbers, occupying the last place, as if He had been the greatest criminal of the three. This is no doubt a source of extreme confusion, but as in that abject position He represents the sinner, only for the great and Godlike purpose of destroying sin, the humiliation is converted into a source likewise of unparalleled glory. Humbling as that position may be in the estimation of the proud, it serves, in the eyes of the faithful, only to exalt that meek and merciful Redeemer, who, far from betraying contempt of His two associates, looks on them with compassion and tenderness; who never disdains the sinful, but affectionately bearing them in His heart and mind, desires that they should mutually fix their view on Him, with love and humble hope.

There is no stage of Christ's Passion more calculated to touch our hearts, than that which represents Him bending under the heavy cross, which He assumed with so willing a heart and so generous a spirit. The contemplation of this mystery must necessarily produce three strong emotions;—first, contrition for sin, whence His cross derived its weight; secondly, confusion at our tepidity and negligence in His service, a more exquisite pang to His heart, than were the torments of the cross to His sacred person; thirdly, humiliation at our pusillanimity in avoiding the cross. When St. Peter was fleeing from Rome to escape martyrdom Jesus appeared to him, carrying His cross, and when asked by the Apostle where He was going, answered, "I go to Rome, to be crucified anew." The words produced a deep and lasting impression on St. Peter. Have they wrought the same result in you?

Second Point.—Jesus our good Pastor carries His flock on His shoulders, with His cross, as the bird of Paradise is said to construct on its back the nest destined to receive its young. Our all-loving Father permits us to repose tranquilly in that place of security, while He toils and bends under the weight of His cross and ours. He is not satisfied with assuming the responsibility of our sins, but likewise endures our miseries, performing prodigies of heroism and patience, to animate our courage and revive our hope. Oh! what fortitude must He not exercise, to supply for our weakness! What patience to endure our sinfulness! Christian soul, take courage! Jesus bears you on His shoulders; He is strong enough to carry your cross, and if He requires that you bear it with Him, He will give you grace to do so generously. When He appeared with His cross to St. Ignatius of Loyola, on the road to Rome, He said, "I will be favourable to you at Rome." What Divine unction replenishes the soul whom God mercifully condescends to console by the same cheering promise, amidst her pains and tribulations!

Third Point.—A holy Religious having besought our Lord to make known to him what description of prayer pleased Him most, Christ revealed Himself carrying His cross, as when on the road to Mount Calvary, as if He would have said, "follow Me faithfully; carry your cross after Me; consider the example I have given you, as well as your obligation to imitate it, and you will soon attain the sublimity of contemplation, and the summit of perfection."

Our King and Model walks before us, and it is incumbent on us to pursue His footsteps. There are some who absolutely reject the cross, some who murmur and repine as they reluctantly drag it onward; some who scarcely raise it from the ground, others again who embrace it heroically, and elevate it on high. See among which party you rank, but of this be assured, that all without exception must carry the cross, even those who struggle most violently to fling it away. The Saints bear the cross, the wicked bear one heavier still, and the demons even carry it too, and with it, their hell! Blessed are they who bear it with Jesus! The cross without Jesus crucified is very painful, for it is an unmitigated, and at the same time an unprofitable evil; but with Jesus, it possesses a heavenly unction; it fills the heart with the Spirit of God, and guides the soul to immortal bliss. Bear the cross then with Him; raise it on high like Him; carry it courageously on earth, and it will assuredly conduct you to Heaven.

TENTH DAY.

Meditate to-day on the crucifixion of our Divine Lord, and endeavour to comprehend the enormity of your sins, by which "you crucify again the Son of God" in your heart (Heb. vi.), as the Apostle tells you. Desire to attach yourself to the cross with Him by the religious vows, and to crucify "the old man," by the mortification of all your evil inclinations.

Aspirations.—"They have dug my hands and feet. They have numbered all my bones." (Ps. xxi. 17, 18.)

"What, O Lord! hast Thou done, that Thou shouldst be thus cruelly treated? I, alas! am the cause of Thy sufferings, and for my iniquities Thou endurest a violent death."

For the Practice, see "Supplement."

FIRST MEDITATION.

Jesus is Crucified.

"And crucifying Him, they divided His garments, casting lots upon them, what every man should take. And it was the third hour, and they crucified Him." (St. Mark, xv. 24, 25.)

First Point.—In obedience to the executioners, Jesus extends His sacred person on the cross, presenting His hands and feet to be nailed to the tree of anguish. One executioner seizes the right hand, and binding it to the cross with a rope, pierces it with a large nail, which he drives into the wood with repeated blows of the hammer, while a torrent of blood gushes from the wound. A second executioner seizes the left hand, and drags it so violently to meet the place prepared for it, that he dislocates the arm; then he pierces it also with a nail, forming a second fearful wound, and drawing forth a new stream of blood. Two more drag the feet with equal force, in order to expand the nerves contracted by pain, and tearing them open with another sharp nail, give vent anew to that life-giving blood, which was to wash away the sins of the world. Reflect on the terrific sufferings our Divine Redeemer endured at that awful moment;—His bones dislocated, His nerves rent, His veins torn open, the most sensitive parts of His adorable body gashed with nails. Contemplate Him extended in silence on the wood of the cross; tortured with pain, trembling with cold; raising His languid eyes to Heaven, and offering Himself to His Eternal Father as a victim for the crimes of men. Sympathize with all the affection of your heart in the anguish of the Blessed Virgin, who is a sorrowful witness of this bloody sacrifice. Every blow of the hammer inflicts a wound on her soul, and it is only wonderful that its mournful echo does not deprive her of existence. O obdurate sinner! will not that sound pierce your rebellious spirit and subdue it! Most precious blood, which flowest from the wounds of Jesus, as from the tree of life, flow, I beseech thee, on the wounds of my soul! O sorrowful Mother of my dying Saviour! obtain for me grace to share with thee in the pangs of Jesus!

Second Point.—The executioners having nailed the Son of God to the cross, raised it with ropes, and then let it sink heavily into the place prepared for it in the rock. Oh, what an increase of suffering to Jesus! His adorable body, supported only by His wounded hands and feet, is convulsed at every movement of the cross as it ascends. The arms relax; the gashes of the feet are enlarged; four streams of blood flow from His sacred limbs to purify the earth. By a mysterious dispensation His back is turned to Jerusalem, and His face towards Rome, to mark the reprobation of the Jews, and the election of the Gentiles. The populace distinguish Jesus from the two thieves only by His crown of thorns, by the wounds which cover His whole body, and by the inscription on His cross; and they evince the recognition by shouts, and shrieks, and imprecations, watching with fiendish delight a spectacle calculated to draw tears even from their inhuman hearts. His Blessed Mother, though overwhelmed with anguish, stands with miraculous strength at the foot of the cross, as an object exposed to God's anger and man's barbarity;—she stands, absorbed in the contemplation of her dying Son,—a beauteous sun-flower, ever turned towards the luminary of day. Sinner, raise your eye to your suffering God, and ask yourself how you can testify your sympathy in His anguish. Should He not draw all things to Himself, now that He is raised from the earth? Why would He be thus elevated, if not to disengage our hearts from earth and attract them to Heaven? Call to mind His elevation on the cross, as often as you adore Him during the elevation of the Host at the Holy Sacrifice. See how He bows his Head to give you the kiss of peace; how He extends His arms to embrace you; how His hands are pierced to enrich you with His treasures; His feet nailed, to manifest His desire to remain always with you; His body extended, to give Himself all to you. Devote your heart to Him without reserve, and trusting to His mercy to pardon your past infidelities, resolve with His grace to serve Him fervently in future.

Third Point.—The soldiers having crucified Jesus Christ, took possession of His garments, which they divided into four parts, one for each soldier. His tunic they did not divide, because it was seamless. "They said then, one to another: let us not cut it, but let us cast lots for it, whose it shall be; that the Scripture might be fulfilled, saying, "They have parted my garments among them: and upon my vesture they have cast lots." Oh! how ardently Jesus loves poverty! He had nothing of His own, except a mantle and a seamless robe which His Blessed Mother had woven for Him, and even of those, He would be despoiled before death, to teach us to renounce riches and even conveniences, not only in heart, but in fact, when Providence requires the sacrifice. The garments of Christ, separated into four parts, represent the temporalities of the Church, which extends through the four quarters of the globe. His seamless garment typifies the indivisible unity of faith, the unity of the love subsisting among Christians, and the unity of the head who governs them. Christ is so jealous of the faith, love and obedience we owe the Church, that He can suffer no infringement on them. He is the enemy of schism, which violates obedience, of heresy which attacks faith, and of discord which destroys the union of the faithful. Let us avoid these three rocks, if we desire to rank among His true disciples, and let us not wound the heart of the Church, our Mother, if we profess to claim Him for our Father.

SECOND MEDITATION.

On the Inscription on the Cross.

"Pilate wrote a title also: and he put it upon the cross. And the writing was, Jesus of Nazareth, the King of the Jews. This title therefore many of the Jews did read: because the place where Jesus was crucified, was nigh to the city: and it was written in Hebrew, in Greek, and in Latin. Then the chief priests of the Jews said to Pilate: Write not, the King of the Jews; but that He said, I am the King of the Jews. Pilate answered, What I have written, I have written." (St. John, xix. 19, 22.)

First Point.—Pilate ordered the inscription to be placed on the cross of Jesus, it is true; but God Himself it was, who dictated that inscription. Whatever meaning the Roman governor may have intended to attach to it, in the designs of Providence it proclaims the glory of Christ crucified and the enormous crime of those who nailed Him to the cross. If He is "Jesus," that is the Saviour, why do they put Him to death, who came to restore them to life? If He is "a Nazarite," that is an individual remarkable for innocence and virtue, why do they treat Him as a criminal? If He is "the King of the Jews," how can they, His subjects, condemn their lawful monarch to death? What excuse can they allege for so black a crime? But while you condemn the guilty murderers of the world's Messiah, ask yourself, what excuse you can make when you crucify anew the Holy of Holies, your Saviour, and your Sovereign? "Jesus of Nazareth, King of the Jews." Consider the qualities of Him whom you offend so frequently and so deliberately. As Saviour, His mission is to die for men; as All-Holy, His prerogative is to satisfy for sin; as King, His promise is to open the gates of Heaven for the elect. Oh! what a subject of confusion and contrition that you render so little honour to Him, who in these qualities justly claims all honour!

O Jesus! when the people in the desert desired to make Thee king, Thou didst flee the destined dignity, and now that the title is conferred on Thee in derision, Thou acceptest it with humble meekness. How dear to Thy heart is humility, and how hateful is vanity!

If you desire Jesus for your Sovereign, love contempt and suffering; He has converted ignominy into glory, and affliction into bliss.

Second Point.—Never was an inscription read so universally and so little understood as that on the cross of Jesus. Some read, without comprehending it; others read and understand, without profiting of it. A small number of the elect alone, practically penetrate its meaning, and appreciate its virtue. Endeavour to be of the small but happy number. It was written in the three principal languages, because the triumph of Jesus was to be proclaimed by all nations, and also because His Passion is a source of grace and mercy whence all may draw without distinction. In Him we find a remedy for all evils, for He is Jesus; in Him we find the combination of all virtues, for He is a Nazarite; in Him we find the road to the celestial kingdom, for He is Monarch of the faithful who confess His name, and aspire to eternal union with Him. Enrol yourself under His sacred banner; offer Him your homage; engrave indelibly on your heart the remembrance of His claims to your undivided love, and He will assuredly protect you in life, and receive you in death. He once appeared to St. Edmund under the form of a child, bearing on His forehead the inscription, "Jesus of Nazareth King of the Jews; and exhorted the youthful saint to engrave that sacred name deeply on his heart, and to impress it every night on his forehead, promising him mercy at the moment of dissolution. We read also that a holy religious, who was in the habit of repeating the aspiration, "Jesus of Nazareth, King of the Jews, have mercy on me," received pardon of his sins at the close of life, as a reward for this devotion.

O incarnate Word! it is just that all nations should prostrate at the foot of Thy cross, and acknowledge Thee as their King and Redeemer. Thy infinite Majesty claims claims universal adoration, while the love which fastens Thee to the tree of ignominy furnishes an additional incentive to our grateful homage. Thou hast humbled Thyself to the death of the cross, and therefore the eternal Father has exalted Thee, and given Thee a name which is above all names. I respectfully venerate that adorable name, and desire to engrave it on my heart, together with the inscription of the cross, frequently asking myself, "whose image and inscription is this?" O image of my Saviour, precious title of my Redeemer! invaluable coin which has paid the price of our ransom from hell! Happy the soul, which at the moment of her departure hence is provided with that blessed viaticum! How calm will be her passage from time to eternity!

Third Point.—The Jews, dissatisfied with the inscription, begged of Pilate to alter it, but he refused the petition, perhaps through tenacity of his own authority, perhaps through indignation against the Jews whose importunity had wearied him. In the designs of eternal wisdom, his refusal became subservient to the glory of Jesus and our instruction. We learn, in the first place, inviolably to observe our promises to God; to comply faithfully with our vows, and fulfil our resolutions, knowing that the Almighty will one day exact a strict account of their observance. Secondly, we learn to cling constantly and steadily to the faith of the universal Church, guarding against the wiles of heresy, and to adhere firmly to the holy Scriptures interpreted by the councils and fathers; in a word, to believe all the Church teaches, that simple, unwavering faith being a shield against the errors of hell, and an unfailing support against the weakness of human reason, and the fallacious suggestions of the senses.

Thirdly, we learn to persevere unto death in the service of God, and the pursuit of perfection. To what do all our aspirations tend, if not to the kingdom of everlasting glory? To attain it, we must maintain the struggle to the end. The kingdoms of this world pass away with the present existence, but the kingdom of Heaven dates its commencement only from the life to come.

ELEVENTH DAY.

Meditate to-day on the insults our Divine Lord endured on the cross, and on His infinite charity in praying for His enemies and persecutors. Beseech the eternal Father, through that ineffable love, to grant you mercy and forgive your sins.

Aspirations.—"He hath borne the sins of many, and hath prayed for the transgressors." (Is. liii. 12.)

"Have mercy on me, O God, according to Thy great mercy." (Ps. l. 1.)

For the Practice, see "Supplement."

FIRST MEDITATION.

Jesus prays for His Enemies.

"Father, forgive them, for they know not what they do." (St. Luke, xxiii. 34.)

First Point.—The prayer of Jesus, admirable in all its circumstances, could proceed only from the heart of a God of infinite goodness. It is the prayer of a dying God for those who deprived Him at once of reputation and life. It is a proof of the Divinity of Christ, since only the heart of an Incarnate Deity could conceive, and His lips pronounce a supplication so worthy of Himself. The very first word He uttered on the cross, before He thought of His Blessed Mother, His friends, or Himself, was an appeal to Divine mercy for His enemies. He devotes His primary attention to the concern of most importance, and overlooking His own interests, directs His solicitude first to those who need it most, though they deserve it least. He employs the first moments of His torturing agony on the cross in praying for Judas, His betrayer; for Caiphas, His malignant accuser; for Pilate, His unjust judge; for the Jews who thirsted for His life; for the executioners who imbrued their hands in His blood; for the Scribes and Pharisees who mocked Him, who scoffed at His torments, who denied His miracles, and blasphemed His doctrine. Jesus pleads the cause of His persecutors with the greatest earnestness; "Father," He says, "forgive them, for they know not what they do." Instead of accusing, He excuses them; instead of exaggerating their crime, He palliates it. He seeks mercy, not vengeance, and implores pardon, not justice. Father, forgive them, for they are Thy work, and Thou surely wilt not destroy the masterpiece of Thy own hands. Father, behold Thy Son, and listen to the voice of His blood which invokes Thy clemency for His murderers. I implore forgiveness for them, through Thy own sweet name of Father; through the obedience I have ever shown Thee; through the thorny crown which encircles my head; through the nails which fasten my hands and feet to the cross; Father, forgive them, for I, the object of their malevolence, forgive them, and provided Thou extend to them Thy pardon, I willingly consent to endure torments and death for their sakes.

O noble generosity of Jesus, who seems in a manner to lose sight of His own sufferings while advocating the cause of those who inflict them! It would appear as if His enemies had done Him no injury; He looks on His torments as wounds of love, and is solicitous only for the salvation of those who have pierced His heart. O most amiable Redeemer, truly art Thou the God of love, since the waters of excruciating anguish have been insufficient to extinguish that unbounded charity which embraces all sinners without exception!

Second Point.—What consolation may not the repenting sinner derive from the sweet words, "Father, forgive them, for they know not what they do!" If the Son of God prays for those who crucify Him, what will He not do for the souls who sincerely desire to serve Him? He is the Sovereign High Priest who interposes in favour of the weak and erring;—what then need he fear who is shielded by the prayer of Jesus against the anger of his Judge? The power and mercy of God, the sure foundation of the Christian's hope,—are both admirably displayed in the prayer of Jesus Christ. His lips and eyes are alone at His command, and these He uses in behalf of His tormentors, praying for them by His silent tears, as well as with that omnipotent voice which raised the dead, and put the demon to flight. "Father, forgive them, for they know not what they do!" O charitable Mediator, are they then ignorant that they have extorted the death-sentence of the innocent? Has not the judge who decreed Thy fate publicly pronounced Thee guiltless? Do they not recognize in Thee a prophet, who called forth the dead from their graves, and healed the sick, and exercised dominion over the spirits of evil? If they do not discern in Thee their long-expected Messiah, their blindness is assuredly inexcusable, because voluntary. But although they feel themselves culpable, they do not perhaps know the extent of their guilt, or of the penalty it merits, and on this circumstance it is, that Thou foundest the excuse of their partial ignorance.

Oh! who can lose confidence while possessing so powerful a Mediator? If Jesus Christ pleads for us, who shall accuse? If He justifies, who shall condemn? When, at a later period, says St. Augustine, the Jews recognized their iniquity, with deep compunction they inquired of St. Peter what they should do to expiate it, scarcely daring to hope for the remission of so enormous a crime; but in this they erred, since the Divine Victim of their malice and hatred had Himself implored pardon for them with His last breath, saying "Father, forgive them, for they know not what they do!"

Third Point.—Who can resist the affecting appeal, "Father, forgive them, for they know not what they do!" If you experience reluctance to pardon an injury, consider with deep attention that God-like prayer; ask yourself who it is that offers it; what the nature of the injury He has sustained; what the manner in which He forgives it, and surely the difficulty must vanish. If you imagine that the dignity of your position should exempt you from insults, contemplate the Victim hanging on the cross; compare your rights with His, and then say, if you can seek revenge, while the Son of God forgives. If instead of submitting to an ignominious death for the expiation of your sins, He had resolved to take vengeance for them, where would He now be, and where would you be yourself? You would rank among the reprobate in hell, and His place would never have been between two thieves.

You say the injury done you is very great, and that you cannot so far neglect your own interests as to overlook it. Consider the injury Jesus receives; compare your wrongs with His. His flesh has been torn by the scourge; His head is crowned with thorns; His hands and feet are nailed to the cross; His reputation has been blighted; and nevertheless, forgetting His exterior sufferings and interior pangs, He says, "Father, forgive them, for they know not what they do!"

You say you have been insulted by some perfidious being, unworthy of your clemency or compassion. Listen again to the dying words of the Son of God, and see how far your sentiments are conformable to His. He prays for His enemies, and you wish yours ill; He excuses, and you retaliate; He weeps over their miseries, and you rejoice; He sacrifices His life for their salvation, and you desire their destruction. Is this to be a disciple of Jesus Christ? Is this to imbibe His sentiments, and to enter into the spirit of His dying words?—those words of power, which have triumphed over the obduracy of many a heart;—nay, which touched the heart even of God Himself, arresting for a time the torrent of Almighty anger, which would otherwise have instantly burst on the guilty murderer of the world's Messiah. The prayer of Christ produced so strong an impression on the good thief, as to transform him instantaneously into a penitent and a martyr.

It obtained the conversion of the centurion and many other spectators of the scene of Calvary, who returned striking their breasts, and declaring that Jesus was indeed the Son of God. St. Leo observes that the miraculous conversion of the Jews by St. Peter's first discourse, is also to be traced to the same source; to which may likewise be referred the admirable union of the primitive Christians, who had but one heart and one soul, as well as the heroism of the martyrs, who, like their Divine Model, prayed for their executioners, and returned good for evil.

O adorable Saviour! shall I alone be insensible to Thy claims? Shall Thy words, which softened the hardest hearts, produce no impression on mine? O Redeemer of the world! permit it not, but as Thou hast mercifully forgiven Thine enemies, grant me grace to pardon for Thy sake all who offend me, that so I may deserve to be myself forgiven by Thee. Since it was I who crucified Thee by my sins, may I amply participate in the efficacy of Thy petition for Thy murderers, a favour I implore through the infinite merits of Thy Passion and death.

SECOND MEDITATION.

Conversion of the good Thief.

"Lord, remember me when Thou shalt come into Thy kingdom." (St. Luke, xxiii. 42.)

First Point.—Jesus, dying on the cross, prepared an efficacious remedy for human miseries in His precious blood, and first displayed its miraculous virtue in favour of the good thief. He penetrated his soul with faith so lively, that St. Augustine ventures to say, none like it could be found in Israel, or even in the world. Abraham believed the divine revelation, but it displayed to him the glories of Heaven; Moses believed it, but its accents issued from amidst miraculous flames; Isaiah believed it, but it unfolded to his vision a resplendent throne, surrounded by an innumerable multitude of blessed spirits. The faith of the good thief was far more perfect, for he believed in Jesus Christ hanging in ignominy and torture on the cross. He had not seen a brilliant star, like the wise men; he had not heard the music of the angelic choirs, like the shepherds; he had not beheld the glory of Christ on Mount Thabor, like St. John, nor witnessed His miracles like Magdalen, and yet he confessed His Divinity, and recognized His power, while priests reviled, and Pharisees blasphemed, and Apostles wavered in their faith and fled. How clear-sighted, says St. Bernard, is the virtue of faith, which discovers the Omnipotent, in the form of a feeble infant; the Holy of Holies, on the gibbet of malefactors; the living God, amidst the shades of death! Jesus inspired the good thief with confidence so much the more generous as it seemed unfounded. The holy penitent beheld a human being dying near him, and he hoped that that same being would save him, even after temporal death had exerted its influence over both. He acknowledged himself a sinner, and he trusted for the pardon of his crimes to the generous victim of charity who had interceded for His enemies. He repented almost in the very last extremity, yet he placed unwavering confidence in the God of life and death, convinced that no disease can baffle the skill of an Almighty physician. He had as yet no experience of Christ's mercy, and still he hoped he should not be deceived or disappointed in throwing himself into the arms of the forsaken Sufferer on the cross.

Jesus replenished the heart of the good thief with ardent love for God and his neighbour, the former manifested by loudly proclaiming Christ's innocence, undaunted by the presence of the Scribes and Pharisees; the latter by charitably reproving his companion in guilt and punishment. With the three theological virtues, the holy thief combined profound humility, perfect contempt of the world, disengagement from life, heroic patience, and sincere compunction. Oh! how far removed are we from the sanctity of the good thief? In one day, nay, one hour, he made more progress in perfection than we have done in our whole lives!

Second Point.—Consider the mercy and liberality of Jesus Christ to the penitent thief. He asked but a thought from the Saviour in His kingdom, and, as St. Anselm observes, Jesus offered him that kingdom itself. "Amen, I say to thee, this day thou shalt be with me in Paradise." (St. Luke, xxiii. 43.) Jesus bestowed Heaven on a robber, that is, immeasurable happiness on one who had led a life of iniquity. Who but a God could have imparted so magnificent a present? He granted it promptly, the promise and the gift following almost instantaneously.

"O wonderful favour!" exclaims St. Cyril; Christ has not yet entered the kingdom of Heaven, and it is promised to a malefactor; Moses and the prophets have not been admitted to it, and its gates are opened for a robber. Those who have borne the heat and burden of the day are still excluded, and he who arrived at the eleventh hour is welcomed with delight. Well may St. Paul declare, that "where sin hath abounded grace did more abound." (Rom. v. 20.) How powerfully should this encouraging display of divine mercy stimulate us to return to God, who promises a ready pardon to the repenting sinner.

Jesus bestows the gift disinterestedly: "This day shalt thou be with me in Paradise." He is not jealous of His own happiness; His delight, on the contrary, is to share it with the Saints, whose bliss it is, in like manner, to "receive of His fulness." (St. John, l. 16.) It is a great privilege to be with Jesus in any place, and under any circumstances, for where can we be happy without Him; where unhappy with Him! But to be with Jesus in Paradise is the summit of felicity.

Jesus bestows the gift generously and irrevocably: "Amen, I say to thee, this day thou shalt be with me in Paradise." Do not distrust my power; my cross is the key of heaven's portal, and shall open it for your admittance. Doubt not either of my will to save you, so clearly evinced in my present condition. Fear not your own unworthiness, for I have come on earth to seek sinners and transform them into saints. Apprehend not that my promises shall fail or my love grow cold, for my gifts are irrevocable, and my desire of your happiness enduring as eternity itself.

Most amiable Redeemer! what wilt Thou refuse to those who love Thee, since Thou bestowest Heaven on those who have offended Thee? May I henceforth avail of Thy generosity more amply than I have hitherto done, clothing myself in Thy merits and enriching myself with Thy treasures. Who can complain of spiritual poverty, while permitted, and even invited to supply his wants at the very source and fountain of wealth?

Third Point.—The history of the thief's conversion teaches us, first, that the Master whom we serve is one most kind and generous. He forgets His own torments, to attend to the prayer of a sinner. No sooner have the accents of a fellow-sufferer struck on his ear, than He breaks silence to cheer him with words of consolation; granting him Heaven, in return for an act of repentance. Is it thus that the great ones of the world treat their servants? Alas! the devotion of a whole life is often absolutely unrequited, and the slightest inadvertence punished by irremediable disgrace.

We are taught, secondly, that it is profitable to carry the cross of Jesus Christ. All men must bear the cross here below; the Saints bear it; so do the penitent; so do the reprobate, but each in a different spirit. The Saints carry it with love; the penitent with resignation; the reprobate with impatience and despair. The cross of the Saints increases their merit; that of the penitent expiates their sins; that of the reprobate anticipates their future torments. Choose between the three, and if you cannot aspire to the cross of the innocent, at least embrace voluntarily that of the penitent. Oh! how short is the passage from the cross to Heaven.

We learn, thirdly, the importance of prompt fidelity to grace; had not the good thief availed of that offered him, it never would have been repeated. We are taught, lastly, to combine confidence with fear. Who can refuse to hope, seeing that after a life of sin, the good thief confidently sues for pardon at the hour of death; who can fail to fear, seeing that of two criminals in precisely similar circumstances, one alone is saved! Both have the same Redeemer; for both the ransom of Christ's blood was offered; for both the same example of Divine patience is displayed; to both the grace of repentance is presented—yet one becomes a saint, the other a reprobate! We have then no less reason to tremble than to hope. The only security is to return to God without delay, doing in time what the good thief accomplished in the last extremity, lest his miraculous conversion, by inspiring us with presumption, may prove a remote cause of our reprobation, the ordinary fate of all who forget and neglect God in life.

TWELFTH DAY.

Consider Jesus Christ hanging in agony on the cross, to expiate by His universal sufferings all the crimes of the human race.

Aspirations.—"Surely He hath borne our infirmities, and carried our sorrows: and we have thought Him as it were a leper, and as one struck by God and afflicted." (Is. liii. 4.)

"O mysterious dispensation of Divine mercy! the sinner transgresses, and the innocent is punished! The servant does evil, and his master atones for it! man commits iniquity, and God pays the penalty!"

For the Practice, see "Supplement."

FIRST MEDITATION.

Jesus prays on the Cross, while Darkness overspreads the Earth.

"And when the sixth hour was come, there was darkness over the whole earth until the ninth hour." (St. Mark, xv. 33.)

First Point.—At His birth, Christ illumined the heavens at midnight, but at His death, on the contrary, He veiled the day in the obscurity of night. O Lord

Jesus, the light of the world! what wonder that when Thine eyes are about to close in death, nature should tend once more to the chaos whence it emerged only after darkness had been driven by Thy spirit from the face of the deep? Thou art the splendour of the sun, which shines only by Thy reflected glory; can we wonder that it is eclipsed, when all Thy Divine attributes are in a manner annihilated; Thy wisdom concealed under the folly of the cross; Thy strength under its weakness; Thy glory under its ignominy; Thy innocence under the appearance of guilt; Thy immortality under the shades of death?

On the demise of a parent, his family assumes the garb of mourning, and is it not just that the universe should wear a veil of sadness at the death of its Creator? When God shall come to judge the world, there will be signs in the sun; is it not consistent that there should likewise be signs in the firmament when the world dares to judge its God? In former ages, darkness sat only on the land of Egypt; but now that the whole world participates in the abominations of the Egyptians; now that the earth has been defiled with the crime of Deicide, it is but natural that the obscurity should be universal.

The darkness of infidelity which envelopes all men, including even the Apostles, is still deeper and more appalling. It would seem that the light of faith lives but in the heart of Mary, the only lamp unextinguished on this night of horrors. The superior portion of her soul is resplendent with brightness, but the inferior part is plunged in the gloom of desolation and anguish. Most Holy Mother! obtain for me grace like thee to acknowledge the influence of blind faith and pure love, even when interior tribulation envelopes my soul in obscurity and fills my heart with bitterness. O Jesus, Sun of justice! permit not that my soul be ever deprived of Thy Heavenly light. May Thy Divine Spirit warm and enlighten it, that it may know what Thou requirest, and knowing Thy holy will, faithfully accomplish it.

Second Point.—Jesus wished to impose silence on His enemies while He offered the sacrifice of His life in atonement for their crimes, and for this end He enveloped Mount Calvary in darkness, that alarmed by the prodigy, the Jews might desist from their noisy tumult, and allow Him the tranquillity suitable to the solemnity and importance of the act He was engaged in. He Himself observed silence for three hours, that He might pray with more absorbed attention. By imposing silence on His persecutors, He manifested His irresistible power; by observing silence Himself, He displayed His divine love and patience. Heroic as was that patience, and worthy only of the God who exhibited it, we are nevertheless required to imitate it, as far as our weakness permits. When then you suffer corporal pain, or endure interior trial, or receive an insult from creatures, remember that God requires you to present Him the acceptable sacrifice of your feelings, and that to offer it with the respect due to His Sovereign Majesty you must do so in silence, restraining the complaints and murmurs which anger and pride dictate. Speak to God in those moments of trial, and endeavour as far as possible to conceal your sufferings and your struggles from men. Pray for those who mortify you, and leave it to Providence to impose silence on them at the suitable time. With His grace, you may control your own words and feelings, but power over others He has reserved to Himself, and therefore you should not aim at exercising it.

Third Point.—Jesus had commenced the work of our redemption by a prayer of three hours' continuance, and He consummated it in the same manner. Be assured that you had a great share in this His last prayer on the cross. Contemplate the blood as it streams from His thorn-crowned head and mingles with His tears, and rejoice to think that both eloquently plead your cause with God. "In the days of His flesh," says St. Paul, "He offered up prayers with a loud cry and tears, and was heard for His reverence." (Heb. v. 7.) May we not reasonably conclude that the Mother of Jesus mingled her tears with His, and that she passed those three hours of darkness and silence in uninterrupted prayer, offering to God the sacrifice of her adorable Son, sympathizing in His pangs, resigning herself to the will of Heaven, and imbibing deep draughts from the chalice of gall presented to her. Unite your heart with those of the Son and the Mother, and fervently address yourself to your angel guardian, saying: O my most amiable and faithful protector! obtain that Jesus Christ may apply to my soul the merit of one of the sighs which burst from His heart during His three hours' agony on the cross, thus to calm the terrors and alleviate the pangs of my last hour. Pray also, I conjure thee, that in the awful moment of death, the blessed Mother of Jesus may cast on me one glance of love and compassion, such as she fixed on her dying Son when standing beneath His cross.

SECOND MEDITATION.

Jesus complains of Thirst.

"Jesus knowing that all things were now accomplished, that the Scripture might be fulfilled, said: I thirst. Now there was a vessel set there full of vinegar, and they putting a sponge full of vinegar about hyssop, put it to His mouth." (St. John, xix. 28, 29.)

First Point.—The thirst of Jesus on the cross was among His most severe torments; for as the refreshment of drink is the last, the easiest, and the most necessary means of preserving life, so is the want of it the most insupportable of privations. A burning thirst was the natural result of the dreadful and multiplied sufferings He had endured since the preceding evening, beside which, the loss of blood had parched his whole frame, especially the mouth and throat. "My strength," He says by the royal Prophet, "is dried up like a potsherd, and my tongue hath cleaved to my jaws." (Ps. xxi. 16.) And in another place, "My days are vanished like smoke, and my bones are grown dry like fuel for the fire. I am smitten as grass, and my heart is withered." (Ibid. ci. 4, 5.) Consider the charity of the Son of God in enduring this severe suffering to atone for your sensuality and immortification; to console the poor, whose privations you so seldom endeavour to alleviate, and in fine to deliver you from the eternal thirst which would have been your lot, had He not rescued you from your doom. In the hour of enjoyment, frequently call to mind Jesus Christ crucified and consumed with thirst, and ask yourself whether it is just that while the Master suffers, the servant should revel in comfort and luxury. Cast a thought, secondly, on the poor who languish in destitution more painful than death itself, and ask your own heart whether you deserve to be included on the last day among the objects of your Redeemer's reproach, "I was hungry, and you gave me not to eat: I was thirsty, and you gave me not to drink." (St. Matt. xxv. 42.) Reflect, thirdly, on the rich glutton, who, condemned to everlasting flames, eternally implores one refreshing drop of water, which never will be given to him. Fear to become the companion of his torments hereafter, if you are the imitator of his crimes here.

Second Point.—Jesus complained of thirst, not for the purpose of asking relief, but to create an opportunity of tasting the vinegar, which He knew would be presented to Him, and thus fulfilling the prophecy. He merely states that He thirsts, without requesting refreshment, to teach us to manifest our sufferings and wants with resignation and patience. He speaks of His thirst only in the last extremity, because He is anxious on the one hand to prolong His sufferings, and on the other to show us how gladly He endures privation for our sakes. Finally, He makes it known in one single word, but, an emphatic word, which reveals three great secrets regarding His spiritual thirst, more intense still, and more consuming than that which tormented Him corporally. First, He thirsted to accomplish His Father's will, and for this end, He lived in toil, and died in torture. Secondly, He thirsted to suffer for man's redemption. At the commencement of His Passion, He besought His Father to avert the chalice from Him, and at its close, He declares His desire of greater suffering. Before tasting the bitterness of that chalice, He testified His repugnance to it, and after having drained it, He is disposed to renew the draught. Hence we learn that it is not reprehensible to shrink from tribulation, and pray that it may be averted, provided we are disposed to submit to it patiently when God's will ordains it for us. Thirdly, He thirsted for our salvation and sanctification; our redemption, our perfection, our happiness; and that thirst will never be appeased, for it springs from His insatiable love. His adorable heart pants for the devotion of yours; will you be so ungrateful, so insensible as to refuse it? He thirsts for your love; will you not also thirst for His, saying to Him with the ardour of the royal Prophet, "As the hart panteth after the fountains of waters; so my soul panteth after thee, O God!" (Ps. xl. 1.)

Third Point.—Oh! how revolting the barbarity of the Jews, who refuse a drop of water to their dying God, at the very moment He sheds His blood for them, presenting Him with vinegar and gall, in their heartless desire to aggravate His sufferings. Alas! do you not minister in a similar manner to His necessities in the persons of the poor? Your neglect of their misery, your indifference to their wants, your harsh rejection of their supplications, cause Him more pain than did the vinegar and gall. You increase His spiritual thirst, too, by persevering in sin, and cherishing sentiments unworthy of a Christian. The vinegar typified the souls of the Jews, who had so miserably degenerated from the piety of the ancient patriarchs; is it not also a worthy emblem of your soul, which has degenerated from the virtue of the apostles and primitive Christians? What do you offer to Christ but the vinegar of coldness, indifference, and indevotion? Oh! think of what you do when you offend God. . . . . . You present Him vinegar and gall to drink, in return for shedding His blood, and resigning His life for you. What base, what shameless ingratitude!

THIRTEENTH DAY.

Meditate to-day on the interior anguish and desolation which Jesus Christ endured on the cross, to atone for the insult you offered to God, as often as you forsook Him for His creatures. Of this He complains by the mouth of His prophet: "They have forsaken me, the fountain of living water, and have digged to themselves cisterns, broken cisterns, that can hold no water." (Jer. ii. 13.) Implore grace to return to Him by true and sincere contrition, and to attach yourself irrevocably to His service for the remainder of your life.

Aspirations.—"O God, my God, look upon me: why hast Thou forsaken me?" (Ps. xxi. 1.) "Cast me not away, O Lord, from Thy face, and take not Thy holy Spirit from me." (Ibid. l. 13.)

"O God! behold in Thy Son, a motive for pardoning Thy slave!" (St. Aug.)

For the Practice, see "Supplement."

FIRST MEDITATION.

Jesus complains of being abandoned by His Father.

"About the ninth hour, Jesus cried with a loud voice, saying: Eli, Eli, lamma sabacthani? That is—My God, my God, why hast Thou forsaken me? And some that stood there, and heard, said: This man calleth Elias." (St. Matt. xxvii. 46, 47.)

First Point.—How can the Son of God be forsaken by His Father? Can the union of His soul with God by grace ever be dissolved? No; never were their wills even partially sundered; never did their mutual love decline in ardour; never did Jesus lose a single ray of the beatific light imparted to Him by the clear light of God from the moment of His conception; never can the hypostatic union be weakened, for it is indissoluble. Of what then does Christ complain? Of an abandonment of two different kinds, each of which occasions Him indescribable anguish. Since the commencement of His passion, His soul had been absorbed in an ocean of interior bitterness, and yet His Father had offered no mitigation of His exquisite pangs; no consolation in His intense desolation. Secondly, He was the victim of universal and excruciating exterior torments, and yet was denied even the comparative relief of a momentary respite from suffering. No part of His body is exempt from wounds, and their poignancy is increased by the action of the cold air to which He lies defencelessly exposed. He cannot rest His weary head against the cross, without aggravating its tortures by the increased pressure of the sharp thorns. His enemies rejoice in His agony; His friends afflict Him, some by their absence, others by their presence. His Father permits that He should die in that deplorable condition, and although He prolongs His prayer three hours, He derives no more consolation from it, than if He had been indeed utterly forsaken by the Father He so tenderly loved. So terrible was His desolation that it produced an agony similar to that in the garden, and forced Him to the mournful plaint, "My God, my God, why hast Thou forsaken me!" Thus does the Eternal Father exercise the most rigorous justice against His innocent Son, to chastise the sins not committed by Him, but by you.

Do not be alarmed if in the excess of interior desolation and exterior pain, you are sometimes tempted to think that God has abandoned you, for God thus withdraws His consolations from His greatest Saints, to purify them, and render them worthy of His intimate communications. Sometimes He overwhelms them with internal joy, while He leaves them a prey to exterior crosses. At others He afflicts them with interior trials, but allows them sensible help from external sources. Sometimes, again, He combines pain of mind with corporal suffering, but it is seldom He presents this twofold chalice in unmitigated bitterness. Fear not to drink of it with the Saints, and with the Son of God, who although the best beloved, was the most fearfully forsaken. There are two other ways in which the soul may be abandoned by the Almighty, and which are sovereignly to be dreaded. First when, in punishment of frequent relapses, God abandons sinners to their passions, and permits them to fall into final impenitence. Secondly, when at the close of a life of unrepented iniquity, He abandons them to the fury of demons and the horrors of eternal fire. What a strange inconsistency, that while recoiling from the anticipation of being abandoned like the Saints, we fear not to be for ever forsaken like the reprobate.

O my Saviour! abandon me not, I conjure thee, either to my sinful propensities during life, or to the punishment of their indulgence after death.

My son, fear not that I shall ever relax in tender solicitude for thy interest, for never have I abandoned any one who did not first forsake me.

Second Point.—Jesus Christ endures the sufferings He has voluntarily embraced, with ardent love, invincible patience, perfect confidence, and unbounded submission to the Divine will; it is not then through desire to lay aside the cross that He complains. No sooner are we visited by affliction of any kind, than we complain of its severity, and devise expedients for its alleviation; but the Son of God complains only at the very close of His Passion, thereby proving that His sad lamentation springs from no desire to diminish His pains. Why then does He complain? First, to manifest the excess of His anguish, which by His own permission receives no mitigation from the influence of the hypostatic union, or the light of glory, or the beatific vision. Secondly, He complains, to teach us that it is to God we must apply in the extremity of suffering, and that to Him we may securely confide our miseries, without incurring the guilt of murmuring. Thirdly, He complains, to show us that the source of His sufferings lies not in Himself but in us. Oh! how enormous an evil must sin be, since to atone for it Jesus endures the pang of abandonment by His Father!

I had abandoned Thee, O my God! and thereby merited to be for ever rejected by Thee, but instead of forsaking me, a miserable sinner, Thou forsakest Thine own Son! Oh, how deeply seated must be the disease which required such a remedy! Sweet Jesus! even though Heaven and earth should forsake me for a time, can I complain while I see Thee abandoned for my sins?

Third Point.—Heaven listens to the lament of Jesus with respect; the Blessed Virgin with anguish; the soldiers with scorn, because they know not who He is. They think He invokes Elias, and He is the God of Elias. They fancy His complaint to be an evidence of weakness, whereas it is a manifestation of love. They believe that He wishes to save Himself, and cannot; whereas, on the contrary, He easily could, but will not. How few there are who understand the words of God! how few who truly revere them! how few who really sympathize in His sufferings! If men considered who He is that complains on the cross; if they knew what He endures for them; if they compassionated the tears, the sadness, the bitterness which accompanied the mournful words, "My God, my God, why hast Thou forsaken me?" they could not resist the appeal to their better feelings; though their hearts were of iron, compunction would soften them; though of stone, sympathy would break them; though of bronze, love would dissolve them in tears.

O sweet Jesus! Thou art now forsaken, desolate lonely, and defenceless. It would seem as if Thou hadst no longer a Father, or wert debarred from addressing Him by that title. Ah! who will give water to my head, and sorrow to my heart, to participate in Thy anguish! Eternal God! the powerful protector and only refuge of the orphan, look in Thy mercy on Thy forsaken Son, listen to His sighs; hear His supplications on our behalf. Thou hast abandoned Him for the sake of His wretched slaves. Receive then those slaves for His love. This is the only consolation He looks for before resigning His last breath. Abandon us not to Thy justice, but receive us into the arms of Thy mercy, the only resource remaining to us in our extreme misery!

SECOND MEDITATION.

Jesus commits His Soul into His Father's Hands.

"And Jesus crying with a loud voice, said: Father, into Thy hands I commend my spirit." (St. Luke, xxiii. 46.)

"And bowing His head He gave up the ghost." (St. John, xix. 30.)

First Point.—Jesus cries in a loud voice, to manifest His power, and verify His own assertion, "that no man taketh away His life, but that He layeth it down Himself." (St. John, x. 18.) With the same facility as He assumed strength to cry aloud, could He have assumed the empire over death. Jesus sank into the arms of death, says St. Augustine, as other men resign themselves to repose, just at the moment of His own selection. He laid aside His body, as mortals lay aside their garments. Jesus cried with a loud voice to manifest the violence with which His soul separated from the body, thus dissolving the noblest union ever contracted between the spirit and the flesh. Again, He cried aloud, to summon all nature to contemplate a Man-God dying on the cross by the hands of men, and for their redemption. Hasten then, ye sons of Adam, to behold the solemn spectacle! Listen to the cry of your Redeemer, the tortured victim for your sins, and present Him the tribute of your contrite, loving hearts. In fine, Jesus cries with a loud voice, to intimidate His enemies, and to publish the victory He has achieved over the powers of darkness. It is an opinion that Satan approached the cross, visibly, to assault the Son of God on Calvary, as he had visibly tempted Him in the desert; but he gained only confusion by the attempt. That victorious cry filled him with shame and terror; the death of Christ terminated his tyrannic sway, and he beheld himself chained to the foot of the cross, to serve as a trophy to the conqueror. If he had the insolence to attack your Divine Master, do not expect that he will spare you. Prepare for the combat, and implore the help of the angels who assisted at the death of Christ, not to aid Him, but to celebrate His triumph. Their assistance was needless to Him, but how requisite will it be to you in the most awful and important moment of your life! Endeavour now to merit it, by the fervour of your devotion.

Second Point.—"Father, into Thy hands I commend my spirit." Meditate deeply on these last words of the Son of God, that they may sink into your heart, and form the subject of your daily reflections. He calls God His Father, to testify His confidence, and to show us the necessity of that great virtue in the most terrible and decisive of all our conflicts. How powerful an antidote against the terrors of death is that sweet name of Father! How consoling the thought, that at its departure from this world the soul will return to the bosom of a tender Father, who desires the salvation of all men! Jesus does not commit His wealth to His Father, for He possesses none,—and neither will you take from this world any portion of its perishable riches. He does not commend to Him His reputation, for He has chosen contempt as His portion,—and so should you desire to die in sentiments of profound humility and self-abjection. He does not commend His body to Him, for He has yielded it a prey to suffering and death, and after His example, you should immolate yours, committing your wants to the charity of others, and bearing your infirmities in the spirit of disengagement from this transient life. But Jesus commends His soul to His Father, as the most precious portion of His being: "Father, into Thy hands I commend my spirit;" to Thee alone, can I confide it, for from Thee I have received it. Into Thy hands then I commit it, as Thine own possession, Thine own masterpiece!

Thus does Jesus end His life as He began it, by prayer; not that He needed to recommend to God His soul, which was ever the object of Divine complacency, but that He designed to teach us the necessity of confiding ours to Him. He wished also, to engrave on our deepest hearts the important maxim that we have nothing so valuable as our soul; that all is saved, if that be saved, and all lost, if that perish. Happy he who finds the hands and heart of God open to receive his spirit at the moment of death! But who could presume to hope for such a favour if Jesus had not recommended our souls to His Father in union with His own, those souls which are truly and really His legitimate possession, since he ransomed them by His blood!

Say frequently with your Saviour, both in life and death! "Father, into Thy hands I commend my spirit." Save it from the power of its enemies, snatch it from the jaws of the devouring lion, for Thou knowest that it has been recommended to Thee by Thy dying Son!

Third Point.—In general, it is after death that the head droops; but by a mysterious dispensation, Jesus bowed His before dying. He did so, first, to show that He is the Lord, and that death could have no power over Him without His permission. Secondly, to make manifest the weight of the yoke of sin beneath which He bends. Thirdly, to testify His obedience to His Father, whose will it is His happiness to accomplish in death as in life. Finally, He stoops His head in order to cast a look on the earth, wherein His body is soon to repose, and a farther glance on the prison of limbo into which His soul is about to descend, teaching us frequently to meditate on the last resting-place, destined both for our spiritual and corporal portions. Adopt this subject of reflection, and it will stimulate you to bow your head submissively to all the ordinances of God's holy will. It will render you humble as the publican who dared not raise his eyes to Heaven. It will encourage you to sink beneath all creatures, remembering that you are but dust, and that you will one day return to the clay. How consoling to see the Son of God bend His head, as if to embrace the earth, our final resting-place; to bless it; to reconcile it with Heaven, and to give you the kiss of peace and pardon, before you appear in His presence as your Judge!

O Divine Redeemer! in that dread hour may Thy precious blood plead for me, and Thy sacred Passion interpose between my soul and Thy justice. Sweet Jesus! be to me then truly a Jesus,—a merciful Saviour, and not a terrible Judge! For the sake of all I cost Thee, have pity on me, and receive me among Thy elect, to love and bless Thee for ever. Amen.

THE END.

CPSIA information can be obtained
at www.ICGtesting.com
Printed in the USA
LVHW040429110522
718423LV00002B/393

9 783375 001629